The Sol Empire
Volume 8
Origins

Vic Broquard

The Sol Empire Volume 8 Origins
First Edition
Copyrighted © 2021 by Vic Broquard
ISBN: 978-1-941415-89-4

This is a work of fiction. All characters, organizations, and events portrayed in this novel are products of the author's imagination and are used fictitiously.

Thank you to my colleague, Lisa Walker, for her many useful suggestions and corrections.

Published by:
http://www.Broquard-ebooks.com
Broquard eBooks
1055 Brandy Lake Rd
Woodruff, WI 54568
author@Broquard-eBooks.com

For Morgan and L. Ron Hubbard

Table of Contents

Chapter 1 So It Begins
Chapter 2 The Meeting
Chapter 3 The Boss
Chapter 4 First Days
Chapter 5 Around the World
Chapter 6 Changing Apartments
Chapter 7 Meeting a Neighbor
Chapter 8 Falling in Love
Chapter 9 The DC Trip
Chapter 10 Sorting Things
Chapter 11 Out of Gold
Chapter 12 The Party
Chapter 13 One Too Many
Chapter 14 The Tasks
Chapter 15 Revenge
Chapter 16 A Twist
Chapter 17 Reality Strikes
Chapter 18 Recovery
Chapter 19 Learning
Chapter 20 Interlude
Chapter 21 Trials of Honey Bunny Mounds
Chapter 22 Bebo's Revenge
Chapter 23 Catastrophe
Chapter 24 Conclusions
Chapter 25 Dr. Chandra Hyber
Chapter 26 Major Callahan Takes Action
Chapter 27 Tam's Progress
Chapter 28 Disruptors' Fate
Chapter 29 Aftermath
Chapter 30 Alexa Adriana Soros
Chapter 31 Alexa Adriana Fits In
Chapter 32 Birth of the Two-man Shuttle
Chapter 33 Contempt to Respect

Chapter 34 Longstanding Problems
Chapter 35 The Good and the Bad
Chapter 36 Jihad
Chapter 37 Baby Time
Chapter 38 A New Location and Life
Chapter 39 Validation of My Past Lives

Chapter 1 So It Begins

March 2376
Domes

This lifetime, I'm called Molly Parkinson. My sister Celeste has been helping me erase my recent traumas when I hit some of the most vivid memories I've ever seen. This is what I saw.

Tuesday, May 1, 2035
Chicago

Twenty-six-year-old Tom Durbin ate the last of his oatmeal. He checked his CPD uniform and holster before kissing Kelly and three-year-old son Jason goodbye.

She said, "Don't worry. It's Food Handout Day. We'll have a better breakfast tomorrow."

He grunted. "I swear the world's gone crazy. Wasn't like this when I was Jason's age. Call me."

Just outside their modest house, a construction crew worked on the new Mass Transit Escalator System (MTES), designed to replace all vehicle traffic. The completed downtown section moved tens of thousands. But for now, Tom drove one of the new Chicago Police Department's electric, self-driving patrol cars. His almost empty stomach growled.

He passed shuttered fast-food restaurants. As he parked the car at the station, he spotted Bigsley's food truck parked outside and joined the line.

"Sausage and egg sandwich," he said.

"Twenty-five dollars. Prices rose again today," the man said, handing him one. "Any idea when prices will get real again?"

Tom grumbled and forked over the bills. "Used to be three dollars."

The man chuckled. "Aye. Four when I first started this food truck. I heard next week prices might double again. If I can even get any."

Tom shook his head and headed inside. He had voted for the progressive Dem Socialist, President Betty K. Snowden. He'd taken advantage of the free college education program before joining the Army. Free housing gave his family their current home, though he had to pay some rent because of his salary. Food for all. Plus, Universal Medical Care paid for the birth of Jason.

At ten, Kelly called.

"Hi. We're on the MTES heading home. We got two sacks of food this time. There's a sack of flour. I told Jason there might be enough to make cookies."

"Yeah, Dad. Mom's gonna make chocolate chip cookies."

Tom chuckled. "Well, don't eat them all. Save one for me."

He heard the familiar giggle.

She said, "I can't believe they're charging fifty dollars for a loaf of bread. What's our world coming too?"

"Hand over the sacks," a strange voice interrupted. "Now!"

"No. Mine. Mom's making cookies," Jason said.

"I said hand them over."

He heard Kelly's voice. "No. Leave us—"

A gunshot blasted over the phone, followed by a second one. Silence.

Screams sounded distant.

Kelly whispered, "Stole our food."

"Kelly? Kelly? Jason?" Tom screamed.

2

Trained as a special ops sniper, Tom bolted from his desk, yelling, "Shooting on the MTES! Send Medivac to my location."

His electric car shot out of the lot; his foot slammed the accelerator pedal to the floor. Sirens wailing, the self-driving car ignored his foot while treading the very narrow bit of streets beside the new canopy-covered MTES. He cursed the pathetically slow speed, while his hands gripping the steering wheel turned white. Again, the computer ignored his attempts to control the vehicle. "Safety first" flashed on the dash readout.

Twenty minutes elapsed before he arrived at the scene. Already a Medivac crew covered the two bodies while two police stood by waiting for the detectives to arrive.

"Sir, you can't—"

"That's my wife and son!" he yelled.

The beat cops stepped back, as did the two medical men, who stared down at the pavement.

"Damn! Damn! Someone's gonna pay for this," Tom screamed.

"Sorry, sir," one of the medical men said.

Another police car stopped, and two men in suits stepped out. One said, "Tom, isn't it?"

Tom nodded.

"Is it?

"Yeah," Tom said, turning away as tears lined his cheeks.

"You can't be here. We'll take it from here."

Tom fought to keep his grief from showing and kept his back to the men as he returned to his car. A few blocks away, he stopped and cried before steeling himself. He didn't return to the station for another half-hour.

His boss met him at the door. "Tom. So sorry. Take the week off. We'll catch those bastards."

A steeled anger replaced the signs of grief.

"Like we do the dozens of other murders each day? Have we even solved one of the thousands of murders this year? Fat chance."

"Go home. Make the necessary preparations, Tom. We're all sorry here."

Tom relaxed his clenched fists. He'd managed to not smash the captain's head, but he nearly ripped the door off his car when he climbed back inside. After a moment, he got back out.

"If I'm off-duty for a week, you'll be needing the car. I can walk."

He didn't face his boss and headed to the MTES.

"What's our world coming too?" he muttered as he stepped onto the new transport system. The gas supplies had dried up. The President claimed that was a splendid thing for climate change. Only the wealthy could afford one of these new electric cars.

Half his weekly pay covered their home rent. All utilities were free. When they worked. Rolling blackouts happened with alarming frequency this spring. Even all his wages couldn't pay for one week's groceries. The President's Free Food Program kept millions alive.

He stayed out of the fast lane, ignoring those rushing along. The blue sky punctuated with billowing white puffs reminded him of his many trips to the University of Chicago, where he earned his degree in mathematics. They'd just started construction of the MTES back then. How he'd loved topology. Had he made the wrong decision back then to join the Army instead of getting a doctorate? No, that's when he met Kelly.

His phone rang, jarring him.

"I'm sorry for your loss. But we must make final preparations." The man gave him directions to the West Side

Morgue.

When he arrived, the solemn-faced man allowed him to view their faces. After covering them, he said, "As you know, overpopulation is a monumental problem for everyone. Since 2000, the world's doubled in size. It's mandatory that all deceased are cremated and that their ashes spread on farms as fertilizer. Do you have any farm in mind? Most leave that up to us."

Tom shook his head.

"Very good. I've collected their physical possessions. Her ring and phone are in her purse. With your permission, we'll donate their clothes to Goodwill."

He accepted the bag containing her things and nodded.

"I'll leave you alone. You may say your parting words."

Alone, Jason's words flashed. "Mom's making cookies!"

"It's not fair! Goddamn this world! Kelly, I swear I will hunt down those animals and terminate them! I promise you that much!"

By the time he reached home, his grief flowed.

The next day, he steeled himself for what had to be done. Her clothes reminded him of his loss. Jason's toys scattered about punctuated his loss. He packed up the toys and took them to Goodwill. Next, he cleared out her clothes, taking them there, too.

When he returned home, the only traces of Kelly and Jason that remained were photos on his computer, which he copied onto a backup drive for safety. With almost nothing left to eat, he spent his remaining dollars on six frozen dinners and beer.

Then he unlocked the door to his private workshop. His eyes took in his small arsenal. He touched his sniper rifle, a 300 PRC weapon that he used to hit targets two thousand yards away. Six other rifles of varying calibers lined one wall. Another wall held his collection of semi-automatic weapons and revolvers. His police-issued 9mm paled to these guns.

The stainless steel revolvers gleamed: A Ruger .357 Magnum, several .45 Long Colts cowboy action revolvers, a five-shot 30-30 with scope, and his favorites: a pair of pearl-handled Ruger Bisley-griped .44 Rem Mags. Stopping power. Cases of ammo rested on the floor. His worktable held his reloading equipment. These days, factory ammo cost as much as a loaf of bread.

He strapped a pair of knives to his calves, before fastening his specially-built dual holsters around his waist. He slipped three dozen .44 rounds into the belt, before slipping the pearl-handled .44s into the holsters. He stowed his sniper rifle and a dozen rounds into its carrying case. Stopping power. He'd once killed a charging bear with one of these .44s. The CPD-issued 9mm couldn't kill a fly. Well, Tom knew that wasn't true.

Tom locked the door and deposited the gear on the couch. Then he head back to the police station.

"Just grabbing a few things," he told several who wondered why he wasn't taking the week off.

At his desk, he logged into the city surveillance system, queuing up the location of the murders and the date-time. After trying six different cameras, he found the best images of the three perps. He snapped them on his cell and left.

Instead of going home, he cased the area where the murders occurred. He took the MTES from the Food Distribution Center, following the path Kelly must have used. The overhead canopy kept rain and snow off the riders, blocking sniper shots from the west. Tom chose his firing position well. From the roof of a warehouse, he had a clear line of sight to three blocks of the MTES. Satisfied, he returned home to wait.

The next Food Distribution Day, 8 May, came. Dawn found Tom hidden under a camo net on that rooftop, his 300

PRC trained down on the MTES. His pearl-handled .44s rested in their holsters, just in case.

Patience: a sniper's secret weapon. Tom calculated the first two-dozen prime numbers before using them to map out a topological three-dimensional plane, his favorite pastime. He spotted several women carrying food bags moving along the MTES. Tom readied his rifle, using its scope to scan for the perps. Already, he'd used his radar distance finder, entering the distance into his phone's ballistics calculator app. He had the photos of the perps on his cell before him.

The three men dashed out from a side street. Tom glanced at the cell phone images and then watched the men through the optics. "Turn, turn," he whispered. After snatching two food bags from the women, they faced towards Tom. "Gotcha, you animals!"

Bang. The silencer muffled the sound, and he extracted the round, loading another. Bang. Again, he pulled the bolt back and chambered another round. Bang. Through the scope, he verified none of the three needed a second shot. "I'm getting rusty. That took fifteen seconds. Should've been ten at most. Better practice."

He picked up his brass, stowed his rifle, and headed home. When he entered, he could still detect the flagrance of Kelly. He sighed. "I got the bastards, Kelly. I got them good. Rest in peace."

After stowing his rifle, he headed to the Food Distribution Center for his own free food. They lowered the amount due him by two-thirds. Still, he had something to eat. For now.

As Tom returned, he knew he couldn't be a policeman any longer. Their rules and his conflicted. Based on what he's seen during his time there, he knew they would never have found the three men. Even if they had located them, there wouldn't be any justice. They'd be fined and cautioned not to do it again.

"The world has gone insane," he muttered, collecting his CPD issued items. He dropped them off at the station and quit.

Tom had no idea what he'd do next. Maybe go back to college. That, along with food and housing, were still free.

Chapter 2 The Meeting

Wednesday, May 9, 2035
Chicago

While in the Army, Major Liz Callahan specialized in intelligence gathering. The twenty-eight-year-old now worked for one of the new corporations, Galactic Defense or GD. Here, she continued as their premier Intelligence Officer in Chicago. Her office housed a half-dozen computer systems and monitors. She also flew spy drones when needed.

Everything about Major Callahan spoke of professionalism. Everything from her spotless corporate blue and gold uniform to her matching blue pumps conveyed a "do not mess with me" attitude. She always got results.

This morning, she marched into GD CEO Art Townsend's office. "Boss, got a hot prospect for you."

The middle-aged man pivoted in his chair, looking squarely into her eyes. "Shoot," he said.

A faint smile cracked her lips. "Good one. Precisely why I'm here. This man," she said, bringing up Tom Durbin's image on a giant monitor, "is an ex-army sniper. Renowned for kills a mile away. Worked for the CPD until today. On May Day, three thugs murdered his wife and young son before stealing their free food bags. I became curious when I heard a CPD man's family had been murdered. I dug deeper into Captain Durbin. Had a hunch he'd take action on his own. Outside the CPD. Sent up my drones for the last week. Paid off yesterday. Got some footage to show you. Plug in this drive." She handed him a thumb drive shaped like a tube of lipstick, which she never wore.

"What am I seeing?" Art asked.

"Under the camo netting. That's Captain Durbin and his sniper rifle. Probably a 300 PRC. Haven't gotten word from the CPD about the caliber yet."

"What am I seeing?" he asked again. The video lasted fifteen seconds.

"Put it on auto-repeat. There," she said, "Captain Durbin found the three men who murdered his family and terminated them. One week is all it took him to find them and take them out. Look at the speed, sir. Fifteen seconds by my timing. Three head shots. Took out the backs of their heads. Instant kills. Three. One man. Fifteen seconds. I couldn't do that. Not even close. I estimate he's at least a mile away from the men. I'm a marksman, but not beyond a hundred yards. And he's quit the CPD."

"Ah," a grin formed on Art's face. "Prime recruitment material, eh? I agree. Fifteen seconds. From a mile away. Good lord. We need him on our side. Many things are coming to a head. Make it happen, Major. And well done, by the way."

Major Callahan allowed a fleeting smile. "On it, sir."

"Just Art, Major. Or Mr. Townsend. You're not in the army any longer."

"Aye, sir. Mr. Townsend. I'll bring him in today."

She saluted, pivoted, and left his office. Old habits die slowly, she thought, wishing she hadn't saluted. But she just couldn't bring herself to calling him Art.

Back in her office, she unlocked her cabinet, took out her holster, checked her 9mm, and strapped it around her waist. After smoothing her uniform, she headed out of the skyscraper in downtown Chicago. Liz decided the best way to approach her target was a casual meeting over coffee. She calculated Tom would be at his home, probably in grief or worrying about a job.

As she rode the MTES, she reflected on what she knew

10

about this target. Some men would be grief-stricken over such a loss. All signs suggested Tom had a happy marriage. But he had quit his high-paying job. None of the new galactic corporations supported him. That meant he still dealt with US dollars, which weren't worth the paper on which they were printed. He might be job hunting. She'd checked his bank account. He had very little savings. Wise, since the value of a dollar declined each week.

But with the Dem Socialists Free Food, Free Housing, Free everything policies, he wouldn't have to find a job soon. Unless he took to drink. Some tried to drown their sorrows in booze. Nothing in Captain Durbin's background suggested such an inclination, particularly since he was a sniper. Nerves of steel. His actual activities while in the special ops unit were classified. Liz could have retrieved them, but didn't figure such was needed.

She arrived at his door, noting he lived in the west temp housing zone which Galactic Expansion (GPan) planned to tear down to quintuple the spaceport at New O'Hare. The tiny homes provided needed shelter, unlike the mess on either coast where people still lived in the streets. She'd once had to visit San Francisco. After walking down the streets, she'd tossed her heels away. All manner of disgusting, unsanitary stuff clung to them. Never again, she swore.

Civilization was changing. Liz swore to move with it. She took a deep breath and knocked.

"Er, hello?" Tom said.

She saw a tall, robust man, square-faced, with kindly ashen eyes. Short brown hair. Army cut. He wore a tee shirt and worn-out jeans.

Liz knew what he saw: a young woman, blue eyes, dark hair in a tight bun beneath her blue cap. Her white blouse peeked from beneath her blue with gold trim jacket and matching skirt and pumps. She watched his eyes notice her holstered gun.

"I'm Major Liz Callahan, Intelligence Operations Chief for Galactic Defense. I'd like to talk to you about several things, including a lucrative job offer. Shall we get a coffee?"

"Aye, Sir," Tom saluted, before remembering neither of them was still in the Army.

"Best put on something more formal," Liz said.

He nodded and motioned for her to come in. She took a seat on his couch while he got dressed. He put on a western style snap button shirt and fastened his pair of .44s around his waist.

"Okay, let get that coffee." He noticed her eyeing his revolvers. "I've got stopping power, not like the puny 9mm you carry. No one's gonna mess with us. I give you my word. Where're we going?"

"Starbuck's Downtown."

"Hey, they're a bit pricy. Kind of out of my price range."

Liz chuckled. "You've got a lot to learn. My treat since I want this meeting with you. Besides, they only take the new gold-backed credits. US dollars are worthless there. Pretty much worthless everywhere these days."

As they moved along the MTES, he said, "You're in intelligence?"

"Aye, Captain. My specialty when I was in the Army. When I got out two years ago, I signed on as a Galactic Defense's Intelligence Officer. Now I'm in charge of that department. Love my job. Great pay, too. I'll explain over coffee. By the way, sorry about the murder of your wife and son."

"Yeah. Our world's gone insane."

They rode in silence until entering the fancy Starbucks located on a ground floor of one of the many skyscrapers. She ordered for both. Liz showed Tom how she paid for it. From her purse, she pulled out a strange looking phone and waved it before the register. Both she and the young woman behind the register saw a "payment made" message.

Tom's brows rose. "Two credits? Is that like dollars?"

"Yes, but if you used dollars, it's likely to be a hundred dollars," Liz said.

The young woman chuckled and said, "One hundred six as of this morning. That's why we don't take dollars anymore. Probably be even more by tomorrow."

Lis escorted Tom to a semi-private table.

"How much do you know about what's been happening the last couple years? Here or worldwide?" she asked.

"Not much. Everything seems messed up. Crazy. Nuts. Prices keep going up. Nearly every day. I don't get it. Probably shouldn't have voted for Snowden."

"Kinda figured. Younger generation got brainwashed educations. No chance she and her Dem socialists wouldn't get elected. Free everything. Well, they're paying the price now. Okay. I'll get you up to speed in five minutes."

"Fat chance." Tom chuckled.

Liz allowed him to see a brief smile. "Socialist policies require confiscating other people's money. Wealth redistribution. People like the Waltons, Cooks, Kochs, Buffetts, and many others wanted a way to keep their wealth. Plus, all countries continued to deflate the value of their fiat currency, forcing money lenders into negative interest rates. I have to pay you to borrow money from me. Totally nuts. Massive worldwide economic slowdowns reached the breaking point, with recessions turning into depressions in most all countries.

"Their leaders answered with printing even more fiat money. Massive worldwide inflations began. Money is a means of exchange. Take food, for example. The dollar has lost so much value that farmers no longer accept dollars for payment of their crops and herds. Those who process corn into cereals stopped accepting dollars for their work. Shippers no longer take dollars in return for transporting products.

"The world should have collapsed into a barter dark age, but it didn't. Not likely too. Not everyone is blind. The US, EU, China, and Russia have been working on joint space exploration for decades. Space stations, Moon Base #1, Mars Colony, Ceres Federation, Jupiter Federation, and the Saturn Colonies, for example. All are joint works by these cooperating countries. Yes, I know some of these only have a few people there, but it's the idea that scientists and engineers from all countries can cooperate to make major things happen is the point."

"What's this got to do with the insanity here?" Tom asked.

"These people saw the collapse happening and refused to go along with it. At the same time, the world's wealthiest people also didn't want to lose their wealth. Enter the new Galactic corporations. They are setup outside any country, serving the entire world—er, Sol Empire as we now call it. The wealthy donated their funds to specific Galactic corporations in return for stock in that corporation. Thus, the wealthy avoided having a country confiscate their wealth. The corporations gained the finances to succeed."

"Like your Galactic Defense?" he asked.

"Precisely. There are many of them. Galactic Agriculture, Galactic Transportation, Galactic Medicine, Galactic Manufacturing, Galactic Mining—a big deal for the other colonies, especially the asteroid miners. On it goes.

"With the discovery of the two Earth-like planets—surely you've heard of them."

"Sort of."

"Brussels, Tau Ceti. Pylon, Epsilon Eridani. Their discovery provided the answer to Earth's massive overpopulation—colonization of these new worlds. Still, the corporations needed someone to provide the overall guidance.

14

A company must expand to survive. Shrinking or staying the same dooms them. Thus, Galactic Expansion, or GPan, stepped in to fulfill that role. They provide the long-range goals and targets. What's important about them, one of their people, Karl Oppenstein, just developed the ion engine. With it, ships can travel the ten light years to these worlds in less than a year, making colonization possible. GPan is looking for qualified people to immigrate to these new worlds. I've made the list. One day, I'll be off to Brussels and off this insane world.

"But I digress. When a person accepts a Galactic corporation's sponsorship, it's permanent. Can't be changed. Choose wisely. They guarantee you a decent monthly income. And you must follow their orders, whether you like them. They're serious about this. Disobeying them is a death sentence. Too much is at stake.

"The corporations have their own monetary system based on gold. Their credit, akin to a dollar, has value backed by gold and silver. Around Earth the credit is becoming the universal currency, but only those working for a Galactic corporation has access to the credits."

Tom interrupted. "Are you saying the farmers accept these credits for their crops and so on?"

"That is the only reason there is any food anywhere. Admittedly, it's just catching on. Perhaps in a few years, the Galactic corporations will have total control over Earth and things can become semi-normal again. But I hope to be on Brussels before that."

"Hey, how can there be that much gold in the world? If everyone's on it, I mean."

Liz allowed a brief chuckle. "There isn't, silly. Right now, GD is propping up President Snowden. For each ton of food delivered to her distribution centers, she pays Galactic Transport one ounce of gold."

"You're raiding Fort Knox?" Tom said, his eyes wide open.

Again, Liz allowed a brief chuckle. "One way of looking at it. We're doing this to all other countries. China, Russia, India, for example. All are using their stock pile of gold to prop up their governments. One day, it will run out. Then the fun begins.

"But I digress again. These Galactic credits are electronic. Like the crypto currencies. When a corporation hires you, they'll give you one of these new style cell phones. They're a marvel. Officially, they are called affordable-biometric-voice-activated-actualized-comm-device   or ABVAACD. Everyone just calls them phones. Anyone can make a phone call on them, but all other functions require a biometric match to its owner. That unlocks the advanced features like your credits and bank account. At the Starbucks register, I swiped mine against theirs. Automatically, it debited my account and added the credits to their account. Slick and efficient. You can't overdraw either. I've heard they soon plan to add holographic video transmissions.

"If you get hired by GD, they'll set you up with a bank account, give you one of these phones, and automatically deposit your monthly stipend into your account."

Tom laughed. "Okay, where do I sign up? I've got a math degree, if that matters. Do we choose the corporations or do they choose us?"

"I thought you'd never ask. They do. I've an interview for you set up with GD's CEO Art Townsend. Anytime you're ready."

Tom laughed. "You're pretty sure of yourself, aren't you?"

She allowed a brief smile. "I am their Chief Intelligence Officer. It's my job to know these things. Come on. I'll take you to him. He's a brilliant man to work for."

"How tall is this?" Tom stared up at the skyscraper. "I now get the colors of your uniform." The entrance was painted blue with gold trim.

A security guard nodded to Liz as they entered. She led him to a reception desk, where he received a visitor's pass. Once in the elevator, she said, "One hundred stories. The CEO and other top bosses are on the top two floors. My office is on the ninety-seventh floor."

Tom chuckled. "Is there a thirteenth floor?"

Liz opened her mouth for a moment, but said nothing. "Oh, I get it. A joke. Yes, I'm on floor ninety-seven. Not sure what exactly is on Floor Thirteen. Ah, here we are."

Chapter 3 The Boss

Tom entered a spacious office, again trimmed in gold. Soft blue hues dominated the walls. A bank of monitors positioned to the CEO's left suggested he could view much from this room. CEO Art Townsend swiveled to greet them.

"Major Callahan. Ah, this must be Captain Durbin," he said.

Tom studied the man with a seasoned sharpshooter's eyes. About an inch taller than Tom, Art wore what must be an expensive suit. When he rose to shake hands, Art's well-defined physique hinted at a man who kept fit. He did not seem pretentious.

"First, my condolences on the loss of your wife and son. Perilous times. We at GD are working to end such lawlessness, but I'm not holding my breath. I take it Major Callahan has briefed you on the world situation."

Tom glanced at Liz and said, "Yes. Must say, eye opening. I had no idea. We have you to thank for what food supplies get through?"

"Yes, and much more. Take a seat. Major, stay, too."

After a pause, Art said, "Now, to business. As you know, criminals control Chicago and the country. In fact, one could say most all countries. Our corporations are attempting to create a united Sol Empire, dispensing with these corrupt and failing local countries and their governments that have utterly failed their people. Earth has many critical problems. Only our new Galactic corporations are doing anything about them.

"Why are you here? Simple. Major Callahan has briefed me on your response to those thugs who murdered your family. Fifteen seconds to dispatch three men. And from

18

almost a mile away. Impressive."

"Not really, sir," Tom said. "I'm rusty. Should have been ten seconds. I need practice. I haven't used my skills since leaving special ops. I'll work on my reaction times, sir."

"Heck with the sir. Call me Art. I believe treating my employees as my friends, Captain."

Tom cracked a smile. "Call me Tom. I haven't been a captain since I left the Army."

Liz chuckled. Art grinned.

"Okay, Tom, it is. Though I like Captain Durbin almost as much. Today, GD is hiring security personnel. Men and women like yourself who want to help make the city and world safe from the animals and thugs. Our Intel suggests President Snowden will unleash many more disasters on our land. Plus, petty wars are likely to breakout. Stupid leaders see wars as a way to distract their people from the massive problems facing that country. Misdirection and lies. Lordy, I've had my belly full of them.

"Anyway, don't let me get sidetracked. We could use a person with your skills to help us eliminate the evil men and women who threaten to murder others and destroy our civilization. Major Callahan will identify them for you, and you terminate them before they can kill more people or commit further crimes."

"I like to work alone," Tom said.

"Of course. She'll just identify targets to hit. After that, it's up to you to handle them any way you choose. Try not to accumulate any collateral damage. While the CPD officers are mostly incompetent, they are the good guys. Don't want them hurt. Unless one is corrupt.

"As for pay, you'll find GD is generous. Ten thousand credits per month to start with. After a year and assuming all goes well with your assignments, I'll double it. Since you don't have any way to judge this amount, it's about a hundred times your last monthly pay from the CPD.

"Oh, we'll see you have an official GD security guard uniform to wear when you're not on the hunt. That way, one glance will tell everyone not to bother you. Don't care what you wear while you are doing your hit."

Tom bit his lip. "Mighty generous of you. You want an assassin. I can see terminating the bad guys, but what if I don't think a proposed target is one? Major Callahan said people get killed for disobeying an order."

"Major Callahan is the very best Intelligence Officer in the country. She'll present you with all the known facts. But if you still have reservations about a target, come see me. Let's talk it over. GD is not a dictator. Yes, we are human and can make mistakes. What's at stake here is the very survival of human civilization. Many 'experts' are predicting a planet-wide, dark age. We must avoid that.

"And if you want another incentive, how about an opportunity to immigrate to Brussels or Pylon? She's told you about them, hasn't she? They look like pristine worlds. I'm in line to immigrate to Brussels one day. Do your job and there's a seat for you. Either world. Unless you want to move to one of our local bases."

Tom laughed. "Hardly. Can't see me wearing a spacesuit to survive. No thanks. Do I have to choose which new world to immigrate to now?"

"No. Between us, I'm waiting for the next engineering breakthrough. Both are around ten light years away. Assuming you could travel at the speed of light, that's ten years in a spaceship. Thank heavens for GPan! One of their top people, a Dr. Karl Oppenstein, just invented the ion drive. These new ships cut the travel time to about a year." He chuckled. "I'm holding out for the next breakthrough that gets us there in days. Besides, let the ground crews go first, building the needed infrastructure."

Tom agreed. "Okay. Where do I sign?"

"On the dotted line."

Art whipped out a contract already filled out.

"You figured I'd sign up, eh?" Tom said.

Liz allowed a slight smile. Art laughed.

"Son, Major Callahan and I are keen judges of people. As CEO, I must be. There's none better than she is."

After signing, Art said, "Formally, I'll call you Captain Durbin. You deserve that much as a former special op. When we're alone, just Tom. Unless you have any objections."

"Fine with me, sir."

"Oh, you darn military personnel," Art said, glancing at Liz. "Just Art when we're alone like this. We're friends. At least I'd like us to be. Liz, take him down to Treasury and then to supplies. Get him his new phone. Meanwhile, I'll send them authorization to put his first month's wages into his new account. Report in for work tomorrow. Check in with Major Callahan first thing each morning. You'll have your own small office and computer. Oh, I almost forgot. Will you need any guns? Ammo? That sort of thing?"

Tom chuckled. "Hardly, sir. Art. I reload my ammo. Have to in order to consistently hit at two thousand yards."

"That's well over a mile, isn't it? Amazing, Tom. Impressive."

With that, the meeting ended. During the blur that followed, Tom got photographed for an ID card, fitted for a security guard uniform, one of the new phones which she helped him personalize to his bio metrics, and an office.

"Go home and lay in some groceries. See you in the morning, Captain. Don't worry. We won't have targets for you every day."

"Thanks."

"Oh, one more thing. When you go into food centers, wave your phone about. As soon as someone sees it, they'll usher you into a back storage area where you can load up on almost anything. Our gold-backed credits are accepted everywhere."

An hour later, Tom unlocked his door and carried a backpack stuffed with food items into his home. Later, he examined his phone, discovering Art hadn't lied. His new bank account held most of the ten thousand credits.

For a moment, a pang of grief swept over him.

"Oh, Kelly, I wish you were here to share this good fortune. If I'd only known about this sooner, you and Jason might still be here."

He wiped his eyes and took a long, hot shower. He turned on the Channel Nine news.

"Three MS13 gang members were killed by an unknown person. These vicious men had been stealing food from women and children. A CPD spokesman said these three had murdered Mrs. Durbin and her three-year-old son. Her grieving husband who worked as a CPD officer abruptly left the department. Who can blame him? The CPD can't even protect their own families."

Chapter 4 First Days

Tom donned his new uniform, strapped his pearl-handled revolvers in their holsters around his waist, and checked them before heading off to work. As he navigated the MTES, he marveled at just how well he felt with a full stomach—a nourishing breakfast. If only. If only.

As he approached GD, doubts seeped into his mind. Am I really an assassin? Evil men must be stopped. Am I judge, jury, and executioner? Those three murderers got what they deserved. But what do I know about GD and what they're doing?

The skyscraper appeared far too soon for his mind. No one took any notice of him as he walked inside, though one guard stared at his guns. Tom remembered to first report in to Major Callahan.

He knocked on the doorframe outside her office. She looked up from her myriad monitors.

"Oh, hey. Ready for work, I see."

Tom felt uneasy and shifted his weight from one foot to the other.

"Having second thoughts, eh? Well, that's natural. We're only after the bad guys, Captain. Problem is that President Snowden has erased the entire US judicial system. Someone found the bodies of the Supreme Court justices. All shot with the same 9mm. No one claimed responsibility. The president then abolished all federal courts, claiming the judges lives were in danger. No way to protect them."

"That's what I never understood when I was at the CPD. Who tries these criminals that get arrested?" Tom asked.

"Ultimately, President Snowden and her staff. Stamp

out crime by terminating those arrested. Her words, not mine. But it has reduced the prison populations. GPan has suggested we set up a penal colony on Mercury near the terminator where the temperatures can be best handled. Nothing's come of that idea yet. Maybe in a year or two.

"Yeah, there's only Snowden Justice or ours. If we don't act, anarchy results. So far, between the two systems, that's been kept to a minimum. At least for now. Today, I'm focused on Chicago. Want to make it safer for the normal person who's struggling to survive. I've been tracking the food thefts.

"Governor-Mayor Bebo Ritzker is running a black market, focusing on food. Everyone's desperate for something to eat. He can charge whatever he wants and will get it. From those who can afford it. So, let's tackle this nasty racket first."

Tom said, "Street talk said a Mr. R is behind it. Didn't think that would be the mayor."

"His lackeys handle the details. Hard to pin anything on the slippery weasel. I'm been monitoring the thefts for months. Years ago, there was a massive influx of illegal aliens entering the southern border asking for asylum. Few had any papers, and the government had to give them a judicial hearing on their claims. Problem was, the courts were backlogged over a year. The aliens took that time to fan out across the country. Most never showed up for their hearings.

"Many of the MS13 gang members came in that way. They forced others to join their gangs. At last count, they are the most vicious gang in our country. It's those thugs that are stealing people's food sacks. My guess is they are trading them for other things from the governor-mayor. Unless you have any objections, I want to focus our attention on convincing the thieves to abandon food thefts."

Tom grinned. "I'll back you on this one. We are judge, jury, and executioner."

"Sort of. I'm the judge and jury. You're the executioner.

24

Errors land on me, not you."

"Where do we start?"

"I've been studying all reported thefts," she explained, bringing up a map of Chicago. "The brown circles are the food distribution centers. Six of them. The red dots represent the location of a theft. Sometimes more than one has occurred at the same spot. The diameter of the circle shows theft frequency."

"Wow! You have a handle on this. Nice work."

"It's my job," Liz said.

Tom studied the map for several minutes. "Can I get a copy of this?"

"Why? It's here. You can see it anytime you want."

"Gotta scout out these areas. See how we can best handle those animals. Also, the days when the distributions occur so I can time my actions."

"I'll upload it to your phone."

"It can display this stuff?" Tom's brows rose.

"Yeah, these new phone things are amazing. Makes the cell phones I had as a kid seem pathetic."

Tom spent the day riding the MTES around Chicago, though often he had to walk past construction sites. Signs suggested one day this escalator system would reach St. Louis.

One fact appeared. Most attacks occurred at or near the end of the existing lines, where the people carrying the bags had to transition to walking. The largest circles dotted the western side, though the south side was a close second.

While eating supper, he theorized at least two unique groups carried out the thefts. In his mind, it seemed unlikely one group would travel far from their home zone to steal food bags. He tackled the west side robberies first.

CEO Art Townsend encouraged him to terminate anyone stealing people's food bags. When I was a kid, that would be petty theft, but we depend on these food handouts just to survive. How times have changed.

That reminded him of how many days he'd left for work with an empty stomach. Yeah, I told Kelly I was full. I wanted her and Jason to have enough. Damn, I never asked her if she did. I should have talked more with her. Though he'd disposed of her clothes and possessions, he still felt Kelly's presence in the house.

During the week, he found six ideal locations for his sniper nest. On Monday, he set up his first position. Before long, two men tried to rob an older woman. They knocked her down, grabbed her food bag, and turned to flee. The first one dropped to the ground, the back of his skull gone. The other turned to see what happened to his pal and then slumped to the ground, dropping the stolen bag. The woman rose, waited a moment, snatched her food bag, and ran off. Tom changed his nest and watched as the CPD arrived and had the bodies removed.

By the end of the week, Channel Nine news headlined the results. "West Side Vigilante slays those who try to steal food bags. Noticeable drop in thefts, noted an anonymous source within the CPD. In other news, President Snowden ordered the Treasury to print more dollars to offset the doubling of the cost of a loaf of bread. She promises we'll be seeing larger paychecks next month."

The following week, Tom focused on the south side thefts. Then he returned to the west side, randomly alternating between locations. He didn't want to be predicable to the thieves.

At last, no thieves appeared during the first weeks of June. While boredom set in, Tom believed he had given security to those in desperate need of the food handouts.

Chapter 5 Around the World

Many claimed June was the start of World War III. Perhaps it seemed so. North Korea starved by sanctions for years finally broke. They launched a nuke attack on Seoul, following it up with a ground assault.

Because the main-stream media had lied so often to viewers, viewers abandoned those stations. Loss of ads followed soon after. Today, they've long since shut down. Thus, much of the world didn't learn of the attack for days, as the news spread via local outlets.

CEO Art Townsend explained that the new Galactic Entertainment or GEnt would be up by the end of summer. The corporation planned to show movies, news, and old TV shows worldwide.

Mid-June, when Tom reported in to Major Callahan, she said, "Incredible. North Korea just declared war on South Korea. Looks like they've nuked Seoul. I'm monitoring nearby stations. Have a seat. This takes precedence."

They watched for hours. The devastation shown via drone cameras sickened them.

Tom said, "Don't we have to defend South Korea? A treaty or something?"

"Yeah, but Congress must authorize it. As far as I can tell, they're arguing. Many don't want to get involved. GD has sat coverage coming online now. Look at that!"

A giant radioactive dust cloud carried by winds drifted over the peninsula jutting into the Yellow Sea.

She said, "I'd hate to be under that cloud!"

"Wonder if the Chinese will respond?"

Liz said, "Don't be silly, Tom. I'm sure Art and many

other GD CEOs are discussing the situation now."

Around noon, CEO Art Townsend made a public address to everyone inside the building.

"May I have your attention? North Korea nuked Seoul and invaded South Korea this morning. Fallout has drifted over several Chinese towns on their peninsula. They expect many long-term casualties. GD Peking and GD Vladivostok have launched a devastating counterattack, using conventional weapons. Two hundred thousand troops from each GD area have invaded North Korea. Their goal is the total annihilation of that regime. We expect such within a week. They've convinced GD Seoul to focus on recovery and salvage operations and not to counterattack. While the US has a treaty with Seoul, Congress is debating what to do. We expect they'll do nothing. That is all."

The next day, Major Callahan grabbed Tom when he arrived. She said, "Come on. More breaking news."

This time, they had overhead satellite images to go along with the foreign newscasts. Pakistan fired a nuke into the disputed Kashmir territory. India fired back, obliterating Islamabad. They watched tiny soldiers and machines on the move towards each other in Kashmir. No doubt a bloody battle soon.

If that wasn't bad enough, Iran made its power move, launching many missiles at Israel, including two with nuclear warheads. Most were intercepted, but the Israelis launched a massive counterattack, their armored fighting vehicles and soldiers sweeping through Gaza first before plowing through southern Iraq, heading towards Iran. The Iranian ground forces flooded into eastern and northern Iraq. Many headed towards Syria, too. Not to be intimidated, Turkey declared a National State of Emergency, mobilizing its armed forces.

She said, "We need a translator to tell us what the Turkish news station is saying."

By late afternoon, they also witnessed a massive buildup of Ukrainian forces close to the Russian border to the east and towards the Crimea in the south. Tom headed home that night having wagered this was the start of another World War. Liz wasn't so sure and countered his bet.

Tom arrived to work an hour early, eager to learn what had happened. From Major Callahan's smile, he suspected he had lost the wager.

"Well, new situation today. GD people in Pakistan have tkilled their political leaders along with the top generals involved in the attack on Kashmir. Because of intense GD pressure, India has agreed to a cease-fire. The Ukrainians adopted a wait and see approach. Saudi forces have swept into southern Iraq, attacking the Iranian forces on their flank. Turkish and Russian forces have moved south to meet the Iranian army there. No world war. Yet," she said.

"We're on alert here. Art said to expect an announcement from GD Moscow."

"Okay, Major, I admit had no idea just how much influence Galactic Defense offices have worldwide."

"Silly boy," she said with a snicker. "Every GD office has their own security forces now. Did you think you were the only sniper? Well, I admit you're damn good. Perhaps the best of them all. Yeah, our Pakistan offices eliminated the war makers, ending the conflict. And GD India joined the cease-fire."

"Amazing. For the first time, I have hope for the world."

"I admit," she said, "I fretted a lot yesterday. Ah, GD Moscow's online. That's Boris Borodinsky himself. He's the head of the Sol Empire-wide GD. He's Art's boss. Super-big shot."

We watched the feed. He spoke in what Tom presumed was Russian. Several translators responded, but we only heard the English person.

"This message is for the leaders of Iran. We give you twenty-four hours to pull all your forces out of Iraq and other countries. To that end, the Israelis, Turks, Saudis, and Russian forces are returning to their homelands as I speak. If you do not pull back your forces, Iran will cease to exist. That is all."

"Short and to the point," Liz said.

"What does he mean cease to exist?" Tom asked.

Liz shrugged her shoulders. "I can't predict that. Russia has a huge stockpile of nukes. But would they use them?"

Art joined us. "I just got word that GD Tokyo is sending as many bio-radiation suits to Seoul as they can spare. Asking us to do the same. You two, see what we can scrounge up around Chicago. I doubt you'll find many, but my God, they need every suit. Millions to rescue."

"On it, sir. Er, Art," Liz said. "Come on, Tom. I know where we might find some suits."

They traipsed around Chicago all day. The spaceport at New O'Hare provided two suits. Another three came from private pharmaceutical companies. Tom hoped five suits would help the rescue teams. It didn't seem like much to him. But then he realized the other GD corporations were searching their cities, too.

That's when it dawned on Tom that there must be hundreds of GD offices in the US alone! And many wealthy men and women who refused to let the Dem Socialists take away their fortunes. Likely so, in most other countries. Had to be, since the original core put a base on the moon and started small colonies on planets as far out as Saturn.

"Might be a chance," Tom muttered.

"What's that?" Liz asked.

Tom's cheeks felt hot. He said, "It hit me. These corporations—we might have a chance of preventing a dark age."

"Of course, silly man. That's the whole point of the

Galactic corporations. We're not about to let the dopes of Earth destroy everything. Not until we get migrated to Pylon and Brussels. After that, they can nuke everything as far as I'm concerned."

The next day, Tom watched Major Callahan's video feeds, wondering what Iran would do. Liz assured him that the Iranians would retreat.

"Hate to interrupt your video watching, but we've got a top priority job to do," CEO Art Townsend said.

Both Liz and Tom jerked and turned to see their boss.

"Springfield GD asking for help. Seems a rogue sniper is killing off our State congressmen and women. A dozen dead thus far. Assassinated. Also they've killed Springfield GD's top enforcer. They're desperate for help."

"Who's killing them? On orders from the Governor-Mayor Bebo Ritzker I'll bet," Major Callahan said. "Don't trust that man. He's got the entire criminal underground of Chicago on his payroll."

"CEO Ashford doesn't know who's behind it or why or even the identity of the shooter. I'm sending Captain Durbin down there. Major, you're to go with him. Find this assassin and terminate him by any means. Make it fast. Those Congressmen and women are all that's holding Governor-Mayor Bebo Ritzker back."

"Aye, sir. Er, Art," Liz said. "How do we get there? Is there enough jet fuel for a plane?"

"Fuel's a nightmare. The refineries shut down long ago. Everyone's hoarding what they have. Springfield GD has promised to refill our jet. I've gotten GPan's CEO Eric Paddock to agree. Head out to New O'Hare. He'll have a jet waiting. Damn costly trip, but we have to keep Bebo in check a little longer. We can't take on the entire Chicago mob just yet. Get moving, you two."

An hour later, Tom joined Liz at the spaceport entrance.

He'd never been to this super-secure place that sprawled over what once had been a huge commercial airport.

"Wow. Everything's jammed in," Tom said.

Liz chuckled. "Take it you've never been here recently."

"I was when I was in sixth grade. Field trip. It's grown."

"Yes, I heard the CEOs talking about building a major expansion, but they have to confiscate the whole western side of Chicago to do it. Bet it happens one day. You got everything?"

"Yes, my baby's in my backpack. .44's at my side. Plenty of ammo, too."

Liz allowed herself a brief smile. "Ready for a small war then. I brought along ten clips for my 9mm. Hope I don't have to use them. Mind you, I can shoot. But I'd rather not."

"You've never killed anyone?"

"Actually, I killed two men who were robbing a store close to my old apartment. I interrupted them. They'd killed the owner, Mr. Chin, an Asian-American in his sixties. It's just I've a fear of getting shot. Damn it. I want nothing to interfere with my chance to immigrate to Brussels. Nothing! Phil and I have plans."

"Who's Phil?"

"None of your business. This way."

Liz has a boyfriend, Tom thought. Wonder who he is? What's her type? Ah, well, she's not mine.

They found the jet waiting for them. The purple jet had gold trim and the GPan logo plastered on its side and tail. The small plane could carry six passengers and cargo.

A middle-aged woman wearing a purple suit trimmed in gold poked her head out of the cockpit door.

"I'm Flight Captain Jenkins. You two must be really important. This is the first flight I've had in six months. Fuel is more valuable than gold. Paddock has gotten Springfield to fill us up. We're actually getting fuel out of this trip. Anyway, settle in. Be there in under an hour."

With that, she shut the door. Soon engine whines dominated conversation. Tom settled down, wondering what they'd find in Springfield. He'd never been there.

Six security guards met them at the airport and ushered them into the city proper. From the GD CEO's fiftieth floor office, the city sprawled before them. Nothing like Chicago, Tom thought.

"The congress people are holed up there. In the capitol building," he said.

"Are those dead people?" Major Callahan said, pointing the sidewalks leading to different doors.

"Yes. We tried to sneak food and water into those being held captive. Ah, my rescue crews are retrieving the fallen now."

They watched as guards in heavy armor and carrying deflective shields shuffled towards one of the downed men. In slow motion, they retrieved the man, though signaling he was dead.

"Heavy body armor and shields," the CEO said. "Like to see the assassins harm them. Going to use them to get food and water into the building. Oh, shit!"

All spotted a man's face peering out a window, watching the security men removing another wounded man. Crack! Even from inside the building, they heard the rifle shot, but first they saw the glass shatter and the man falling.

"Ah, 30-06. Shooter is old school," Tom said. "No silencer or muzzle brake. Probably a five hundred foot shot. From the angle, the shooter must be over there somewhere. Couldn't see the entrance shot too well, though."

"You got all that? I just heard a boom," the CEO said. "Well, there's four of them, one on each side. They've killed six Congressmen and ten others coming to their aid."

"Can I get access to your roof? I'll need another roof on

the opposite side of the Capital Building. Major, can we get live sat views of this area? Spot the shooter's positions?"

"That's why I brought my drones, Captain. To the roof," she said.

Her pack doesn't contain clothes. I keep underestimating her.

On the rooftop, Tom picked a spot near on edge where he could look down on the general area the last shot originated. Liz sat down in the center of the flat roof, opened her pack, and prepared her drones. She hooked up her video feed system.

"This'll be tricky. Dinky monitors. Maybe I can get them to give me a decent monitor."

Tom ignored her and began his search. He trained his scope on various rooftops. Knowing a sniper was out there, he knew what to look for. If the sniper fired again, Tom knew he'd have the assassin spotted in seconds. He just hoped those trapped inside took the hint and didn't make themselves another target. Give me time.

The faint whir of drones lifting off behind him caused Tom to smile. Eyes. That's what's needed. And patience.

A flash of sunlight caught his attention. Tom moved his scope towards it. "Bingo. Got one sniper located. Two o'clock, Major. Watch the quadrant at nine o'clock. Going to take this one out."

Tom used his distance radar machine for an exact measurement. Eight hundred six yards. His mathematical mind solved the ballistics for the shot. He dialed in the changes on the scope. He could only guess at the wind speed, only a very light breeze. Only now did he slide the bolt back and ram a 300PRC cartridge into the chamber. He exhaled. Then inhaled and held his breath. Ever so slowly his finger pushed on the trigger.

"You sure that wasn't a misfire?" Liz said. "Hardly any

noise."

"Muzzle break and silencer. Exit one sniper. Now, did the others see or hear that? You finding anything over there?"

"Maybe." She directed his attention to an unusual pile of boxes on an apartment roof.

"Yep. You found him. Now go find us a new location on the opposite side of the Capitol Building."

Liz flew her drones back, landed them, and unhooked everything. Bang. Another shot brought a smile to her face.

"Get him?" she asked.

"Yeah. Head shot. I go in for them. Harder to hit, but guaranteed to take the perp out. Too risky to take a torso shot. Doesn't always kill them, unless you hit the heart. I don't like taking second shots."

Three hours later, the duo took out the last sniper. This time, her drones spotted both sniper locations for Tom. They packed their gear and headed for the stairs of the building.

As they rode the elevator down, Tom took out one of his pearl-handled .44's.

"Liz, get your gun out. Company awaits us when we leave. I spotted six rushing towards the building as we stored our gear. Guard our rear."

"Shit! Shit! Shit! Okay. Hold on a minute. Let me get my spare clips ready."

He heard her deep sigh.

Sure enough, when they walked out of the abandoned department store, six dark-skinned men carrying semi-automatics rushed towards them.

"There they are. Kill 'em," one yelled.

Tom almost laughed as they began firing. All held their guns out with one hand, the gun's side parallel to the ground. No possibility to even aim. They shot wildly. Windows shattered behind the two.

Tom dropped to his knees, cocking the revolver.

Holding it in two hands, he fired at the closest man. Liz watched the man's head jerk backwards before brain matter splatted out behind him. The body dropped.

Bang. Tom fired again. Then again. Two more attackers dropped.

"Oh, shit!" screamed one man. "Out'o here."

The three remaining men turned and raced away as fast as they could. Tom fired two more times, as Liz shot off four rounds, dropping one of the fleeing men. Since the man still wiggled, she fired a kill shot.

"Well," Tom said, "that went well. Local thugs. Didn't even know how to shoot a gun."

Liz allowed herself a brief smile. "Does look impressive—gun held out and sideways. But you can't hit anything that way."

When they returned to GD, the CEO begged them to stay and work for him. He offered to double their salaries. Both refused.

"Damn, that was fast," their pilot said when they walked up to the plane. She glanced at her watch. "Five hours. And I thought I was gonna have a delightful time seeing the nightlife of Springfield. Ah well, don't suppose you two are interested in spending an evening at a fetish nightclub."

She brought a smile to their faces.

"Hardly," Liz said.

"Okay. We're not dressed for it either. Home before dark. Fasten your seatbelts."

Liz said, "I bet you say that to all your passengers. The seatbelt thing, I mean."

Tom noticed a slight flush on Liz's face. Again, he wondered what the Major's type was.

Chapter 6 Changing Apartments

"What happened?" Tom asked when he reported to Major Callahan the next morning.

"Iran didn't back down. Didn't think they would. The world sanctions left them no choice but to attack others to get their supplies."

"So..."

"We'll find out today. Time's more than up. Trouble is, communications are down in that area. Nothing out of Iraq, Syria, or Iran. Jordan reports loud explosions. That's about it."

"Never a dull day. Any chance I can take some time off now? I need to move. Everything about the house reminds me of Kelly and Jason. What's weird is it's become hard to remember what they looked like."

"They say time heals. Nothing going on today. Yeah, take the day off. You need to move on. Find someone new."

Fat chance. "Thanks. I've got to get out of the house ASAP."

"Try Uptown area. MTES is completed up there to downtown proper. Tad expensive, but not like what it used to be. When I was in grade school, a loft there cost a fortune. These days, with our Galactic credits, you should be able to find something good for a reasonable amount. Just don't offer payment in dollars."

"What're those?" Tom teased. *Months ago, I had to make every dollar count. And today? Wow.*

Tom meandered around most of the day, checking out various apartments. Late afternoon, he found one on West Leland Avenue close to Montrose Beach. The Lake and the nearby open space appealed to him. Plus, New O'Hare lay due west a few miles. As a GD security guard, he had access to the spaceport and planned to watch ships landing and taking off when he wasn't working. New to this Galactic credits as money, Tom didn't know if five hundred credits per month was expensive or not. But he could easily afford it. He signed the papers and received the keys to #2 on the main floor.

His door lay opposite that of #1. The two renters shared the same primary entrance, along with those in the units above them. However, those people had to walk to the end of the hall and take the stairs or elevators. The easy access appealed to him, though the backdoor also sold him.

He checked in late that afternoon. "I found an apartment," he said.

Major Callahan helped him update their records.

"Good timing," she said. "With the weekend coming up, you've time to get moved in."

Tom chuckled. "Anything on the Iranians?"

"Still quite the unexplained blackout on communications. Sat images aren't helpful. The Israelis have gone berserk. They're wiping out their enemies in Gaza and other southern areas and have invaded Lebanon, attacking terrorists there. Strangely, they are staying away from Iraq. Over a hundred thousand killed in Tel Aviv. I bet more will die from radiation illnesses. Not a pretty picture. Same with Seoul. Need any help moving?"

"Glad we're not at war. No, I don't have much stuff to move. I can take the MTES all the way. See you Monday."

"What about your guns?" she said. "You can't go carrying those around the city. Why don't you sign a corporation electric car out for the weekend?"

"Didn't know we could do that."

Liz shook her head. "Men. Come on. I'll show you how."

The paint job was the only difference between the GD car and his CPD car. Blue with gold accents. Like the other one, a computer controlled the driving. Tom suspected that could be overridden, but he didn't know how. Besides, the computer drove safely.

But the tiny car couldn't carry much. On Saturday morning, he took his clothes on the first trip. Guns filled up the second trip. Ammo, the third. Reloading equipment, the fourth. His books, mostly math ones, took two trips. Then came kitchen stuff, taking three trips. His food supplies brought up the next-to-last trip.

With little remaining, Tom spent Sunday morning cleaning up the house before making a last trip. That done, he handed in the keys and dropped the car off at GD headquarters in their underground parking lot. He took the MTES north to his new apartment.

He spent the rest of Sunday arranging things and setting up his reloading equipment and kitchen. A long, soaking shower ended the day.

Monday morning, Tom reported to Major Callahan, who seemed in a pleasant mood. She smiled more.

"Ah, hey. News from the Mideast. Russia obliterated the Iranian army and most of their cities. Much of Iraq is radioactive, as is the western half of Iran. GD Moscow refused to say how many nukes they dropped, but it must have been many dozens. China made quick work of the North Korean army and now controls that country. They're in talks with Seoul about having them take over the north, uniting them once more. Probably that'll be the outcome. I doubt China wants to mess with the impoverished North Korea."

"Glad we're not involved," Tom said. "Things are bad enough over here."

Both laughed.

She said, "One day, they'll be much worse, buster. Just heard President Snowden has ordered the printing of another four trillion dollars, giving everyone a free pay boost. Lot a good that'll do. Prices will just go up again as the fiat dollar get worth even less."

"I admit I didn't take economics in school," Tom said, "but anyone can see you can't keep printing money. It's only as good as others will accept it in exchange."

"Precisely. If we don't intervene, the dark age will center on bartering as a means of exchange. What can I get for an old pair of shoes? A loaf of bread?"

"Have the billionaires of the world traded their wealth for Galactic credits?"

She nodded. "Many millionaires, too. Anyone with any sense has. A few wise people built up stashes of gold and silver. No matter what happens, they'll be all right."

"Real estate any good? Like owning a couple apartment buildings?" Tom asked, since apartments were on his mind.

"Those who took in dollar-paying tenants are losing their shirts. The few who took in Galactic credit payers will do well. I'd say only about one in ten real estate holders did the right thing. Some of the biggest losers have been the oil and gas companies, along with major automobile manufacturers. Those who retooled to make the tiny self-driving electric cars can't make enough of them. All others and their employees depend on the President's free-everything program.

"You found one of the smarter landlords who only accepts Galactic credits. Nice going, Captain."

Tom laughed. "Not so fast. The four units above us on the first floor are vacant. I bet it's hard to find Galactic credit paying tenants."

"Mark my words, Captain, that will change. Soon, I hope. I want to move to Brussels and out of this trash dump. Hey, stick around. The Starburst is returning from Brussels this afternoon. We'll get a briefing from them. Art has asked me to attend and told me to bring anyone I choose. Want to hear what this new world is like?"

"Sure! Thanks! I hope it's a good as everyone wants it to be."

That afternoon, the three walked a block to the GPan skyscraper. They joined hundreds of other CEOs and personnel, packing the small auditorium. The room tingled with from excitement of those present.

"Hello. I'm Commander Jackson of the Starburst exploration spaceship. As you know, we just returned from Brussels, Tau Ceti. During the flight back, I prepared this presentation for you. I'll preface the show by saying Brussels exceeds our wildest expectations!

"It has two continents, both thousands of miles across. We spent most of our time surveying North Continent, because the South Continent lies smack across the equator and is hot. North Continent is much like temperate America, perfect in every way. Watch."

The video presentation began with drone footage slowing zooming in on this new world of forests and grasslands. Herds of animals wandered, unfazed by the approach of the drone. His voice said, "No primates of any kind, anywhere. These are akin to cattle, according to our biologist. These vast northern plains are perfect for massive farming enterprises."

Later, the drone flew over hills that gave way to a mountain range. "We named these the Southern Range. Our geologists have already discovered large deposits of gold, silver, copper, tin, and iron. Heck, you name it, and we found it."

"Building materials galore. While wood is prevalent, we're recommending homes be made from stone. No shortage of that.

"Days are thirty hours long. The planet's axis isn't tilted. There's only one season. Rain is plentiful. From evidence gathered, three crops can be grown and harvested each year, which is twenty days longer than Earth's."

As the video rolled along, the excitement grew.

"So, here's paradise if ever there was one." The Commander ended his prepared remarks. "Let's hope Pylon is as perfect as Brussels."

After wild applause, he took questions. Many focused on just how soon immigration could begin.

A Chinese man took the stage. Lis whispered, "That's CEO Wang Chan head of the Sol Empire-wide GPan. Top man over us all."

"Meeting be broadcast around world, translated when needed. Travel time one year make most trips long. Remember, Brussels no town, cities, utilities, or facilities. Immigration, not soon. First groups prepare housing, utilities, crops. What most needed is faster ships to make moving happen sooner. First group hardy pioneers must be. Will send them off next month. None this be possible except for Karl Oppenstein's invention of ion engine. Applaud him, please. GPan CEOs, send list of first pioneer candidates to me by next week. That is all."

He stepped down, and the flood of questions continued. Night had fallen when the three headed back to GD. Art hopped and skipped along.

Art said, "This is the greatest news ever! All we're doing is actually worth it. Paradise awaits us. We just have to keep this crazy world going until the base crews get initial facilities up and running. Liz, I had always hoped for this day, but the news. It's much better than anything I'd ever hoped to hear. I'm giddy!"

"What's the criteria GPan uses to decide who gets to go and who can't?" Tom asked.

Art said, "The best and brightest. The able and the skilled. Since we're making a whole new civilization, we need people from all trades and skills. But they must be healthy and fit. Like he said, there's nothing there but wilderness. No towns, no hospitals, no schools, no stores, no farms. We will have to set up everything from scratch. I won't kid you. Life will be harsh and challenging for the first arrivals. Hardy pioneer types at first. Once a basic civilization is established, I suspect they might relax the harsher physical requirements. Each person chosen must be able to pull their own weight. Figuratively, I mean.

"Don't worry, Tom. You are a prime candidate, but not for the initial settlers. Neither is Liz. Both are you are likely to be on the second tier of immigrants, once the base is established. Give it five years, maybe. Just guessing. A round trip to either planet takes two years. It'll be slow going. Main thing is, it's paradise. For that, I can wait a few years."

"Phil and I are waiting, too. We want to be in that second group," Liz said.

The way she said it, Tom thought she was reminding him of a former promise made.

"I'm in no rush," Tom said.

Chapter 7 Meeting a Neighbor

Monday, August 6, 2035

As Tom finished dressing for work, a scuffing noise in the hallway caught his attention. Curious, he opened his door.

"Wow!" he said.

The door to #1 was open. A twenty-something woman sat on her butt, pushing a box of food supplies down the hall, presumably left inside their door. She had long, lustrous black hair that touched the floor. She scooted up a bit and used her legs to push the box another foot towards the open door.

"Hello, neighbor. Oh! Want some help?"

At first, his attention was on her beautiful face and striking bosom before seeing her arms were missing. Hence, his exclamation.

"I can manage, but I suppose it wouldn't hurt to have you carry my food box inside for me today. You're the new renter, right?"

"Er, yeah. Tom. Tom Durbin."

The attractive woman made it to her feet using unusual motions. Tom wanted to give her a hand up, but stood there unsure how to do it.

"Jenna Sweet. Ah, a GD man. I figured that might be the case. Landlord only takes Galactic credits. You have to be one of us. I'm with GPan. Hate purple, though."

He picked up the box and followed her inside her apartment, which he surmised was a mirror image of his place.

"Put it on the table for me. I'm independent, but carrying things is always challenging. Thanks for the help."

"You're welcome. Sorry if I'm staring. It's—"

"You never met an armless person before?" Her tone hinted at sarcasm.

"Er, not that. Well, that's also true. No, you're beautiful. Gorgeous, in fact. Your hair shines."

"Well, you are different. Yeah, you're staring. Most people do. When they meet or see me. I hate the staring, but I do see their point of view. I'm different from everyone else. Okay, handicapped. I hate that word."

"Differently challenged?" Tom suggested with a grin.

That brought a smile to her charming face. Her blue eyes gazed at his. "Precisely. I do everything I need to do, but with my feet. And yes, I'm vain about my hair. But not gorgeous, though. Do you need your glasses?"

Tom chuckled. "Touché. Your face seems familiar to me. Like I've seen you somewhere before. But I can't place it."

She sighed, and her shoulders slumped. "Probably my Mom. She was Miss Universe in 2024. Her face got plastered all over the world."

"Yeah! That's it. You look much like her."

"Not really. She has arms and is normal. I don't and aren't."

"Well, neighbor Jenna Sweet, I'm glad to have met you. Kind of wondered who lived here. No one's in the other apartments above us. It's only you and me."

"Was only me. I suppose I can get used to having a neighbor. In case you're wondering, I rent the four apartments above us. I don't want to hear thumping and bumping noises at night. But I agreed to let the landlord rent out #2. Please don't go making noises when you're here or I'll have you kicked out."

"A door mouse."

"Huh?" she said.

"I'll be quiet. Holler whenever you need carrying done. And sorry if I keep staring. Can I buy you a coffee when I get back tonight? To make up for staring?"

She bit her lip for a moment. Tom got the impression she was deciding something.

"Well, I've been rather rude to you. Only if you let me buy you a cup. Tea, not coffee. Hope you like tea."

"Okay. Say around six?"

"Sure. I'll pick the place. Bye and thanks."

Tom couldn't get her image out of his mind as he rode to work. He must have looked different somehow.

Liz said, "What's up with you?"

His face felt warm. "Met my neighbor. Works for GPan. No wonder the upper four apartments are empty. This woman has rented them, too. Doesn't want to hear noises above her apartment."

"Strange. What's her name?"

"Jenna Sweet. Looks like her mother. Miss Universe of 2024. I should have remembered that face, but she had to tell me."

"She's a looker. Wait, she works for GPan? I wonder what she does?"

"I'll ask her when I see her."

Monday seemed to go on forever for Tom, who kept glancing at clocks. Boring. Nothing happening. At last, he headed home for supper. At six o'clock, he stood before her door and knocked.

And there she stood, but not like he expected. She stood on one foot. Her shoe was off her other foot, which she lowered to the waiting shoe. She'd used a foot to open the door. Jenna wore a pullover top and shorts. No socks. A belt held her phone and a small purse. Keys dangled from a chain around her neck. She stepped outside, took off the shoe again, reached up, and used her foot to close the door. Jenna used the key to lock it. Now, he saw why her keys were on such a long chain. Perfect for her reach.

46

Tom still wore his security guard uniform, sans guns. He tried not to stare too much. Her well-defined legs suggested exercise, as did her figure.

"Where are we going?"

"The Amp Tea Gardens. These people need our Galactic credits to survive. You'll see. It's on the main floor of what once was a church—whatever those were. Near here. They have the best choices of tea I've ever found. And they make mouth-watering muffins. I've begged them for the recipe, but no luck. Trade secret. Ah well, baking is challenging for me. This way."

They walked several blocks before Tom spotted what once was a church. A simple sign hung over a side door. Amp Tea Garden.

"So, I checked my contacts at GPan. Apparently, you are valuable to GD. They didn't say what you did, though. Looks to me like a security guard. Here we are. Promise me you won't stare. They don't like it either."

The odor of fresh breads mingled with fragrant teas captured his attention as he opened the door for them. Inside was an old-fashioned cash register. A middle-aged woman greeted them.

"Welcome to the Tea Gardens. Ah, Jenna. Good to see you again. And who's this?"

Tom stared. How could he not? She had hooks instead of hands.

"Tom Durbin. My neighbor. Works for GD. Table for two. Oh, Tom, this is the owner, Irene Clemens. Don't shake hands with her or you'll regret it."

Irene chuckled and caused her hooks to open and shut a couple times, mimicking a shark's bite.

She said, "Phillis, table for two."

Another young woman, Tom guessed a little older than Jenna, stepped forward. She wore a simple day dress with low pockets. Tom stare. She too had no arms, at least none he could see.

"This way. Jenna, good to see you again."

She winked at Jenna, but Tom had no idea what that implied.

"Phillis Underwood is our waiter. Oh, we get the secluded table tonight."

She'd led them deep into the room where the only light came from a candle in the center of the table. After the two sat, she asked, "What'll you have?"

She sat down, kicked off a shoe, retrieved a pen and pad from one pocket.

Tom observed her and said, "Ah, right-footed."

Phillis looked up. An enormous grin formed. "Good one. That's a good one. Gotta remember that, Jenna."

"I'll have Earl Grey. Tom, try their Assam. It's incredible. Oh, and bring us two, no three, of the baker's muffins. Guess that makes me right-footed, too. Do we know any lefties, Phillis?"

After jotting the order, she said, "Nope. Doesn't mean she's not out there some place."

Tom watched her stow the pad and pen before donning her shoe. She, too, made awkward motions to rise. He realized the motions allowed her to keep her balance. Interesting, he thought.

Tom looked around. Only two other customers were present, all sipping tea. One also read a book, while the other typed on a laptop.

"Please don't stare at our server when she comes. She's a recent amputee. Had a bad industrial accident. Lost all her left arm and part of her left leg. I think she's adapting well, but she's self-conscious. Ah, here comes Patsy Wells with our treats."

The teen carried a tray in her right hand. A wooden

pegleg formed the lower part of her left leg.

"Jenna, right? Good to see you again."

"Hi, Patsy. This is my neighbor, Tom Durbin."

"Pleased to meet you."

To his surprise, she held out her hand to shake before stumping back towards the front.

"Can't she get a prosthetic leg or something?" Tom asked.

Jenna sighed. "She could have back when I was a little girl. Things were different then. Her accident happened early this year. No one has the money to pay for such things. Lordy, if one used dollars, it'd cost a million dollars. I checked. I offered to pay for one with my Galactic credits, but like the women here, and me too, we don't want charity. Or sympathy, either. Just respect.

"Same with Irene. She used her accident settlement money to set up this teashop to make a living. No one will hire her. Good move. She's also helping the bakers and even the night cleaner survive. One baker hasn't got a left arm, while the other hasn't got a right arm. Together, they make a whole and can bake. I don't know the cleaner's name. She's called Stumpy Brentwood. Lost both legs at the knees. Wears padded booties and stumps along. She keeps the floor spotless."

"Now I get the name of this place. I had no idea people were in such difficulties."

He watched as Jenna used her foot to lift the teacup, though she had to lean over to reach it. She pealed back the paper around the muffin.

Tom sipped his tea. "Hey, this has quite the punch."

"Try the muffin, silly. It's superb."

"Can't eat just one," he muttered through a full mouth.

Jenna smiled. "That's why I ordered more."

"Thanks. Did you have an accident? Or should I mind my own business?"

She chuckled. "Born this way. Somehow, the body forgot to grow arms. That's what I always said in grade school."

"You do almost everything?"

"Of course. Don't you? Sorry. I'm being rude. You're naturally curious. I get stared at everywhere but in here."

"Did the kids make fun of you in school?"

She paused a moment. Her face flushed. "Well, yes. But not because of no arms. It's these monsters." Her right foot pointed to her bosom.

"Jenna's growing boobs instead of arms. God, did that ever embarrass me. Every day until high school. But I realized the girls were jealous of my budding endowment, while they had to wear pasties in their bras to attract boys' attention. Me, attention was the last thing I wanted."

"I can understand that. High school went better for you?"

"Yeah, but then I moved to Chicago to go to the university here. Had a scholarship. That's before everyone gets a free education. Got two degrees. Math and physics. How about you?"

"Dad runs, er ran, a hardware store. He closed it two years ago. Economy collapsed and took his store with it. He and Mom depend on the free-everything of President Snowden, like many are. I was too until recently. Anyway, I went to CU too. Got my degree in math. Loved topology, but joined the army. I've no idea why I did that. Became a special op sniper. Got married while I was in the service, and we had a son. Worked for the CPD when I got out. This June, while Kelly and Jason were walking home carrying our free food bags, three thugs jumped them. Jason was three, and they shot him for resisting. Both died before I got there. Don't worry. I tracked those three down and eliminated them—MS13 gang members the Soc Dems allowed into our country.

50

"That's why I got this apartment. Everything about the home reminded me of that terrible day. At least I don't have nightmares anymore."

"Say, I remember hearing about that on the Channel Nine news. Sorry. Must have been an enormous loss."

"Thanks. GD discovered what I did and offered me a job. I'm their paid assassin. It feels like I've already sold my soul to GD. Now what do I do?"

"Do good things, Tom."

"Thus far, I've only killed evil, wicked men out to harm others or our world. I'm not about to harm a good guy. I'd rather let them murder me for not obeying such an order."

"Cool. Say, we need more tea."

"And more muffins. Phillis," Tom said.

After Patsy brought them another round, Tom asked, "You said you moved here to go to college. Where are you from?"

"Arizona. A small town near Flagstaff. Mom and Dad run a dude ranch. They've capitalized on her fame as Miss Universe, though she looks much older now. I send Galactic credits home to help them out. No one visits the dude ranch these days. They're also dependent on all the free stuff."

"Are you planning to return home now?"

"Do I look like someone who wants to work on a dude ranch? Or haven't I said I have a hard time carrying things?" She grinned, suggesting she was playing with him.

Tom took it that way.

He said, "Oh, I can see you now, Jenna, astride a tall horse leading the pack of visitors. Wait. Could you even ride a horse?" His face felt fiery again.

"Of course, silly. I grew up there. I need help with the saddle and bridle. But once the horse is ready to go, I use a wooden step to get up. Hold the reins in my teeth. Don't misunderstand me. I could carry my food supplies by putting them into a duffle and slinging its strap over my shoulder. Awkward, but it works. It's easier to have them delivered, what with the food thefts that's been occurring. Do I have you to thank for the drastic drop in such thefts?"

Tom smiled. "Yes, my doing. You look like you're in good shape. Do you exercise much?"

"Have to be. I love to run. That's the one thing I've always been good at—physically that is. I run every morning. Ever since sixth grade track. I found something I could do and got good at it. Then I joined our soccer team. Seems I can't get a foul by touching the ball with my arms and hands. That's a joke. The touching bit."

Tom grinned. "I love to run too. Last few years, I haven't had—no, I haven't made time for it. To be honest, I let other things get in the way."

"You should come run with me. I'll put you in your place. I go out around six in the summer. I use a gym in winter. Snow and me don't get along well."

"Okay. Six, it is. Is the snow thing a matter of keeping your balance?"

She smiled and met Tom's eyes.

"Precisely. Also, I hate stairs. Well, not hate, but I try to avoid them as much as possible. Tad scary going down them when you can't hold on to the rails."

"I can't even imagine, Jenna. You're an amazing woman. I sure wouldn't have predicted you got your degree in physics, though. Unless mechanics help you work out how to do things."

"Spot on, Tom. But I learned much more, especially when I worked heavy math into the mix. I have to admit tht I'm rather intrigued with you. At first, I sized you up to being just another security guard, bully guy. All brawn, no brains."

Tom laughed. "No one's ever said I had brawn. I barely passed the physical tests to get into the special operations.

Lowest score accepted on record. I think they were more impressed with my shooting skills. Say, did you hear that the Starburst returned from exploring Brussels? I got to see their presentation."

"Yes, I watched a replay. Paradise. That's what they're calling it. I'm hoping I'll make the cut and immigrate there one day. After they get towns up and running. I know I can't be one of the pioneers. Still..."

Phillis walked up. "Hey, you two. We're closing. It's midnight."

"No, it can't be," Tom said. "We just got here. Must be seven." He glanced at his watch, his eyes opening wide. "You're right. Wow."

Phillis giggled. "Come back again."

Tom observed Jenna, as she used a foot to retrieve her phone, passing it over the register before stowing it in her pocket. After slipping on her shoe, they said good bye.

Irene said, "Thanks for the tip, Jenna. You come back soon, ya hear."

"You know me. I will," Jenna said.

Tom added, "Me, too. What an exceptional place you have here."

He saw a smile appear on her face.

As they neared the door, a short woman stumped in the door. No, she had black pad-like socks on that allowed her to walk on her stumps—barely and awkwardly.

"Stumpy," Jenna whispered when they were outside. "You gonna come run at six?"

"Yep, unless my services are needed elsewhere. Never can predict that. Otherwise, I'll be there. Thanks for the treat. Incredible place."

"Incredible people," Jenna said.

Chapter 8 Falling in Love

Tom couldn't get Jenna's image out of his mind. Six came quite early for him. Someone knocked on his door as he tied his shoes.

"One second," he yelled, hoping it was Jenna.

"Beginning to think you weren't going for a run. Morning."

"Yeah, just getting ready. Okay. Where're we going?"

"Down Leland to Montrose Beach. Then along the lakeside and back. Hope you can keep up."

"Oh, you're on, beautiful."

She wore a tee shirt and shorts, along with jogging shoes. No socks. She'd tied her long hair into a ponytail, and he wondered how she could do that. In fact, he wondered how she could do most everything.

They jogged down their avenue and past the new Med Center, into Montrose Park proper. Tom couldn't help seeing her bouncing bosom, but tried not to stare. They matched speed, though Tom's long legs would allow him to speed past her if they raced. He perceived a distinct slowdown when they hit the sandy beach. Soon, he realized the soft sand made it difficult for her to keep her balance.

He said, "How about up on the path? Sand is getting into my shoes."

Tom sensed her relief with his suggestion. Then he realized each was testing the other. He smiled. For an unknown reason, he wanted to impress her. After the run, they walked along the lakeside, cooling down.

"Do you like to swim?" she asked.

"Yes, when I can make time for it and have a pool. I've

54

gone in the lake, but it's too polluted these days. How about you?" *Damn, that's a silly question. How's she gonna swim?*

"I like to go at least once a week. There's a gym club not too far away with an Olympic size pool. It's relaxing. Mind you, I paddle along with my feet. I often go Saturday mornings. Fewer people."

"Fewer stares?"

"You're good. Yeah, fewer stares. Wanna come?"

"Yes, but I'm not a member."

"I can bring one guest."

"You're on. Thanks. I didn't realize how out of shape I've become these past few years. Always worried about money. But not anymore. You said you work for GPan. Honestly, I can't imagine what you do. Must have something to do with math and physics."

She smiled. "Top secret. Can't tell you. But I work out of my apartment. Are we on for tea after supper?"

"I'd like that. I'll text you if something comes up and I can't make it. Oops. I don't know your number. Heck, I don't even know how to enter a contact number on this new phone. Major Callahan set it up for me."

"Oh, brother. Get it out."

She sat down, took off a shoe, and retrieved her phone.

"Set yours beside mine and watch me. My foot, silly."

Tom flushed. She'd caught him staring at her bosom below him.

"One button. This one. Presto. Our phones just shared numbers. It's that simple."

As Tom retrieved his, she stowed hers and put her shoe back on. Tom wanted to help her stand, but again had no idea how.

At least he opened their main door for her. As before, she stood before her door, removed a shoe, grabbed her key between her toes, and unlocked her door. Again, he watched her movements in amazement.

"What? Never seen a woman opening her door before?"

"You're gorgeous. See you tonight." Tom deflected and entered his own apartment.

He had a spring in his step when he reported to Major Callahan.

"Anything happening today?" he asked.

"My, aren't you chipper this morning. No, not really. Say, your neighbor. Jenna Sweet. I checked with my contacts at GPan. She is on their payroll, but what she does for them is classified I doubt the CEO even knows. Did you find out anything?"

"No, she said her work is classified. She works from home. That's all I know. She's an amazing woman, though."

"I think you might be falling for her."

Tom's face felt feverish. "We just met."

Both received a text from Art, and they rushed to his office.

"Ah, got some news. President Snowden has abolished the Congress. Says there's no need for them any longer. If new laws are needed, she and her various departments can invent them."

Liz said, "I've been expecting that since she got rid of the Supreme Court."

He continued. "We've only got a weak DC office, but they fear for the safety of the Congress men, women, and their staffs. Especially since several congressmen are protesting her decision. I've offered to send you two to help guarantee their evacuation from DC. Mind you, it's these people who let the swamp take over. Don't take any risks. Their lives matter little now. Still, it won't look good if they are all murdered. The one thing DC has is jet fuel. That's our pay. Wheels up in an hour."

Tom had to dash home to fetch his gear. But when he returned with only a couple minutes to spare, Major Callahan

56

met him with a ghastly stare.

"Trip's off for now. They are all dead. Senators, representatives, staff. Someone unleashed a toxic nerve agent. They never had a chance. My job is to gather Intel and figure out who did this. Once I do, you're up."

"Good lord! All of them. Okay, let me know who my target is. Damn."

Tom fidgeted all day. He couldn't stop thinking about Jenna.

Major Callahan worked her connections and ignored everything else around her.

Five o'clock came, and Tom took the fast lane of the MTES north to his place. He tossed a dinner into the microwave and changed into civilian clothes, a plaid shirt with snap buttons and shorts. He walked around waiting for his watch to show six. Then he knocked on her door.

"You look great. My treat tonight," he said.

"Hair's damp. Washed it. Talk about a chore. You should try it some time. Wash your hair using only your feet. On second thought, don't; you might fall."

"Hey, isn't that something you have to watch? Falling, I mean. You don't have arms to catch yourself or anything."

Jenna smiled. "Yeah, falls are really nasty for us. Phillis has the bruises to show for it. I can't tell you how many times I've taken a spill. Mostly when I was in grade school and still learning to adapt. A fall does hurt. I do my best to be careful."

At the tea garden, Irene said, "Hey, Jenna. Tom. Saved the same spot for you. Okay?"

Tom saw a sparkle in her eyes, but didn't grasp what it meant. He found he was staring at her hooks, wondering how she could do anything with them. If only the economy hadn't tanked. He'd seen fantastic prosthetic arms on soldiers who lost limbs. Now, such things exceeded anyone's pay, except for those who worked for one of the Galactic corporations. For a moment, he wondered what Irene could do for a corporation. Then he realized that as far as society was concerned, these women were all broken pieces. He felt sick.

Jenna picked up on his discomfort and asked about it.

"It's just normal people think of these women as somehow broken pieces. Yet, they are making a real go of this place. Not what I think a broken piece would do."

Her face turned serious. "Yes, welcome to our world. They give us unwanted sympathy and pity. Oh, you poor thing and similar crap. Yes, we have physical challenges that norms do not, but that's all. Some more than others."

"Don't worry, Jenna. I don't pity you or any of them, but I feel bad for what happened to them. I'd like to help you and them when you need it. Isn't that what a normal person would do? Help others when they need it?"

"Only when we ask for it. Don't forget that. Our feelings are particularly sensitive to that. Did you hear what happened in DC to the entire Congress?"

"Yeah, I was minutes from a flight to DC to protect them. Got called off. All dead from a nerve agent. If we can identify who did that, you can bet I'll be on the next flight to DC to eliminate that animal."

"I hope you get the chance. That was awful. I'll bet anything President Snowden is behind it somehow. Probably avoiding getting her hands dirty."

"Say, if we go swimming Saturday, do we run first?"

"No, silly. That's too much exercise for my legs in one day. Pool opens at eight. It's a twenty-minute walk on the MTES. Knock around a quarter til."

"You're on. Say, did you ever study topology?"

Later, she asked if he had any siblings.

"I've an older brother, John. He's married and lives in Phoenix. Has a daughter."

He showed her a picture of the family.

The pair ordered and reordered and reordered until Phillis interrupted.

"Guys, we're closing. It's midnight."

Tom glanced at his watch in total disbelief. When he looked up, Jenna grinned at him.

As he paid their tab, he said, "Irene, add in the same tip Jenna always gives you, if that's enough of a tip."

"You sure? She always pays double the tab."

"Make it so, Scotty," Tom said.

"Another Star Trek fan," Irene said, a huge smile on her face. "I loved that show. Always dreamed of one day going into space. Now, it'll never happen." She waved her hooks.

"You ladies manage everything else. Don't say it's never going to happen."

As they left, Jenna said, "Now that was a wonderful thing to say to her. Reality is harsh. Probably no chance we'll ever get into space, but we can hope. You're impressive, Tom Durbin."

Such continued to happen the ensuing nights. They would chat until Phillis announced the midnight hour. Each time, Tom left in total disbelief, because only minutes before they'd ordered their tea and muffins.

Saturday morning came. When he picked her up, she had her pack slung over her right shoulder.

"Let me know if you need me to carry your pack."

"Okay, but I don't. You don't need me to carry yours for you, do you?"

Tom grinned. "Touché."

When they reached the entrance, he opened the door. Once inside, she flashed her ID card to the security guard.

"Morning, Jenna. Bringing a guest?"

"Yeah. See ya, Mike."

"Men go that way. Women this. Mind you, I'm slow with clothes. Meet at the pool. Can't get lost," she said with a grin.

Tom changed and found the pool. The chlorine odor cleared his sinuses. He guessed the pool must be new. Well maintained at least. Since he had no idea how long Jenna would take, he dove in and swam a couple laps before popping out, dripping water onto the concrete.

Then he saw Jenna coming out of the women's locker room. She wore the scantiest of bikinis. He couldn't help but stare. She had tucked her long hair under a white cap.

"Yeah, I know. They're enormous. Their only benefit is they act like a life preserver, though they also add enormous drag friction to any forward motion. I see you've taken some laps. Good. It takes me a long time to get changed. Sorry about that."

"Nothing to be sorry about, Jenna. You did it yourself. That's what matters. I'm curious how you can swim."

"I have to be careful getting in and out. A fall here can be brutal. I darn near broke my nose when I first came here."

"I'd offer to help, but I haven't a clue how I could."

Jenna eased her body into the water at the low end. "I back paddle and front paddle. Never have figured out the butterfly stroke."

With that, she flopped onto her back and floated along, her legs kicking to propel her. Her large bosom kept her top half above water, but they also added turbulence to her motion, slowing her down. Then she rolled over and frog kicked. She moved faster this way, but again, Tom saw her bosom did its best to prevent forward motion.

Still, Tom saw Jenna enjoyed swimming, and he swam alongside her.

"I see what you mean. But you are swimming despite the drag. Have you ever tried to calculate the drag they're making?" *Now that's the dumbest thing I've ever said!*

Jenna laughed and treaded water. "Actually, I once

calculated that. More of an estimate, though. How does one weigh these or compute their geometric shape? I can tell you this. If I had arms, I'd never win any swimming race."

Both grinned. Later, she said, "Okay. I've done enough. You can swim more if you wish. I can watch."

She avoided the ladders and he could see why. Tom watched her move to the shallowest point and slip her butt up onto the concrete. Then she brought one leg up and followed by the other. After an awkward bit of motion, she reclaimed her feet, smiled at him, and sat on a side bench. He swam a few laps and called it quits, guessing she'd be shivering by now. She was.

As she headed into the women's changing area, she said, "It will take me quite a while to shower and get dressed. Particularly my hair."

"I'm not going anywhere," he said.

She reappeared an hour later with the bag draped over her shoulder, her lush hair still dripping down her back.

"Sorry it took so long."

"Don't be. Again, I'm impressed that you're able to do all these things. Damned impressive. I know. You don't have a choice. Still, I'm impressed you don't let it stop you from living and doing things. You're one amazing woman, Jenna Sweet."

As they walked home, Tom took the next gamble.

"Say, do you have a boyfriend or a fiancé? Seeing anyone?"

Tom held his breath, not daring to breathe.

Jenna stopped and stared at him for a moment.

What have I done this time?

"No to both, Tom. Get real. What man will want to date me, let alone marry me? None. I gave up such ideas years ago. What about you? You still mourning the loss of your wife and son?"

"They'll always be in my memories, but like Major

61

Callahan said, time heals all wounds. Jenna, I'd like the chance to get to know you more. I can't stop thinking about you. Our talks for hours at the Tea Gardens—just fantastic. That's never happened to me before. I can't explain it. I've much to learn about you. Just hope you'll give me a chance."

"I have to admit that hasn't ever happened to me either. Our six-hour talks seem to minutes. You're an interesting man. You've got my attention. Don't worry so. I'll let you know if you step on my toes. I suppose it's awkward for you too—dealing with a physically challenged person."

Tom, who'd forgotten to breathe, exhaled. "You can say that again. Sometimes I just don't know what the right thing to do or say is. The last thing I ever want to do is offend you."

She smiled, nodding.

"Changing the subject, but what can we do for dates these days? All the movie houses closed years ago. All the fancy diners have closed," he said.

She giggled. "I've been thinking along those lines too. The only thing I've heard of is a few rock dances. There's also a fetish nightclub, but I wouldn't fit in there. I'll ask around, but there's not much to do these days. What's our world come to?"

"An enormous mess. Me too. I'll ask around. But I love running with you. Swimming was fun, too. Maybe we could rent a boat and sail around the lake, except I've no idea how to sail."

"Me either."

When they reached their doors, Tom decided to risk everything. As they approached her door, he slipped his arms around her waist, pulling her in. He leaned over and gave her a passionate kiss. She responded in kind, throwing a leg up and around his lower back, the best she could do for a hug.

When he opened his eyes, he saw tears trickling down her cheeks. He panicked. *Now I've blown everything!*

"I'm sorry. I didn't mean to make you cry."

She sniffled. "It's not that. I've spent my entire life daydreaming about a man holding me and kissing me, knowing that was never, ever going to happen. And it just did. I can't keep my emotions from exploding on me. Sorry. I better get inside before I bawl like a baby."

Rather than let her struggle to unlock the door, he slid an arm around, found her keys, and unlocked the door for her. As she entered, he kissed the wet back of her hair.

"Don't forget we're heading to the tea garden at six," he said, as she vanished into her apartment.

Once inside his, he thrust an arm into the air, danced a jig, and then calmed down. *What's happening to me? I feel like a silly school kid.*

Chapter 9 The DC Trip

From thirty-three thousand feet, Tom texted Jenna, explaining he had to go to DC for a few days and not to worry.

He'd just cleaned up when Major Callahan called.

"We've found who murdered them. Report in now. Bring your gear and clothes for a few days."

Once he arrived, two duffle bags in hand, CEO Art Townsend briefed both. Tom noticed the Major's hair was wet, guessing she'd had to rush in, too.

"Okay. The GD field offices in DC and Alexandria uncovered those responsible for the nerve agent murders. Two men are part of the Deep State—the men who believe they know best. Top CIA personnel were called out for similar conduct back in 2020. The station chief in DC ordered the hit. He's one of Snowden's backers. One of his agents carried out the attack. But that entire field office is guilty of aiding the crime. In fact, Arlington suspects they have more nerve agent attacks planned. They're storing a stash of the stuff in the basement of their CIA building in DC."

The phrase "smelly Walmart people" flashed in Tom's mind. He'd heard that said about those who voted for President Trump years ago. As a twelve-year-old boy, he didn't know what that meant, though it was often in the news. In his eyes back then, Walmart seemed gigantic, filled with more toys than he could dream of having.

Liz said, "The whole CIA office is involved? We'll need an army to flush them out."

"Just the opposite. DC's come up with a genius plan. They'll fill you in when you get there. Good hunting."

"Don't we get any details?" Liz asked. "I hate going in

blind."

"If I had them, I'd tell you. All I know is they've pulled in a special op man called Riley O'Hara. This will be his show, but he wants the best sniper GD has, and that's Captain Durbin. Now get going. Jet's awaiting you."

The two rushed to New O'Hare. The same Lear jet awaited them, engines revved. They just got onboard when the plane began taxiing. Hence, Tom could only text Jenna once airborne.

"You have a girlfriend," Liz said over his shoulder.

Tom flushed. "Yes, I believe so. Was taking her out for tea tonight. Ah, well."

"Tea? Oh, brother. Sounds boring. You must bring her to one of my boyfriend's parties. I wonder what the DC plan is? And why I didn't need to bring my drone packages?"

Tom shrugged and dozed, dreaming of Jenna.

They landed at a private field whose runway barely handled the jet. The front wheel ended up three feet from the end of the concrete. Crew stood on the grass, ready to turn the plane around by hand. A man waited for them with a gas-powered van.

"Hi. Major Callahan, Captain Durbin?" he asked. They nodded. "Into the van. Quickly. Don't want prying eyes to see you."

With no windows, the pair jostled along, wondering if they were even on a road. As the vehicle began slowing down, a hollow noise echoed in Tom's ears.

"Think we're heading underground. Parking deck, maybe," he said.

The van stopped. A man opened the door. "Captain Durbin? Major Callahan?"

Both nodded. "Chaps, I'm Captain Riley O'Hara, demolitions expert. This way. I'll explain me plan."

His thick British accent forced Tom to pay close

attention to what he said. He led them to a small room with building schematics taped to a whiteboard. Next to it was an aerial view of several city blocks, blown up to twenty-inches square.

"Have a gander. That be the CIA building," he pointed to the center of the view. "What a balls-up we got here. I need you aces to keep 'em plonkers pinned down inside while I do me work. Sneaky toffs put a tracker on the trigger man. Head nutter never leaves the building. Principal exit point is here. This door. Captain, you terminate any nutter who comes out that door. Major, the toffs provided these drones. Yeah, those are guns. Probably nicked them from the army. .30 cal deer loads. Thirty-six rounds per drone. You fly 'em around the side entrances just in case the nutters try to evacuate once the Captain starts nailing 'em.

"The point being, I'm down here." He pointed to be basement schematic. "Here's where they stashed the gas. Real plonkers. You'll hear two booms. First one's a hot one. Destroys the agent. Second one. Really big boom. Takes out these support beams. Marked them with red X's. Dog's bollocks, it all falls."

Tom scratched his head. "Let me see if I got this right. You're going to collapse the building with everyone inside?"

"Aye, chaps. You keep 'em pinned inside. Your toffs don't want anyone escaping. They bugged the plonker who gassed your people just to make sure he doesn't bugger off."

"How are you getting inside to plant the charges?" Liz asked.

"Trash man. He goes down there once a week. Only tomorrow, I'll be driving the lorry. Got a bloke who will cover me. Take these burners. We'll stay in contact with them. Fish and chips are back there, along with two cots. Get some sleep. Wake you when it's time for action."

"Are you from the UK?" Liz asked.

"London. Got trapped over here when everything tanked. If I do this job, they'll fly me home. Guess the posh still has jet fuel."

At nine the next morning, Tom settled into his concealed nest two blocks from the CIA headquarters. He'd setup on someone's pool deck about three stories up. From here, he had an unobstructed view of the walkway from the main doors. He'd been given a handheld device. Its blinking red light came from the bug on the man who'd murdered the Congress people, showing the man was inside the building.

"All you have to do is watch. If the man comes outside before the boom, terminate him," the demolitions man said.

Liz had monitors set up behind several tall umbrella shades. One by one, she launched the drones, positioning them some distance from the side doors. Then she spoke into her comm device. "Drones in place. Ready for action."

Tom focused on the blinking light, his rifle loaded and positioned. He imagined Riley going from post to post, installing his charges. Time passed. He found it more difficult than ever to keep his mind clear of thoughts, focused on the job. The smiling face of Jenna kept appearing.

The blinking light moved. Instantly alert, Tom followed its motion. Convinced the man might head for the doors, he trained his scope on the double doors with the CIA logo on them. The doors moved. Tom saw the murderer stepping outside, lighting a cigarette while juggling a package. Slowly his finger moved until the rifle fired. With the silencer and brake, only a popping sound could be heard. He doubted anyone near the building would have detected it. Through the scope, he spotted reddish material on the door. The murderer of the Congress people lay terminated on the CIA steps.

Liz paid close attention to her monitors. His slaying would trigger action within the building. She rather hoped some would come outside. Major Callahan wanted to try out the fancy automatic rifles attached to the drones. She had nothing quite this sophisticated and resolved to ask if she could take one home.

"Few more bloody minutes!" Riley's voice broke their comm's silence. "Keep the plonkers inside."

Tom saw the doors moving. He fired another round into the door. He suspected the 300PRC round would penetrate the door, unless it was armored. Wood splintered. A body fell out, lodged between the two partially opened doors. Since he didn't move, Tom didn't fire again but watched for movements.

The sound of the 30-30's firing a few rounds brought a smile to his face.

Liz called out, "This is *so* cool!"

"'Nother minute," Riley yelled.

A muffled boom caught their attention. Ten seconds later a series of loud booms vibrated the still waters of the pool beside them. Tom looked up from his scope, which had too narrow a field of view. Just as Riley boasted, the entire building imploded. Floor after floor dropped on the one below it, all in a surreal slow motion. As the roof reached near ground level, an enormous dust cloud rose, obscuring all from view.

"Wow!" Liz said. "Landing drones now."

Tom packed up his equipment, stowing them and the sniper tarp in his duffle bag. He helped Liz stow the three drones. While she carried two, he grabbed the third packed unit, and they headed back to the underground lot.

Riley met them. "Nice boom. That'll be my ticket home."

"Say, can I keep one of these drones?" Liz asked.

"What the toff don't know won't hurt them, eh? Always say it flew off somewhere."

The pair climbed into the van, though Liz "accidentally"

carried one of the drone packages inside with her. Soon, the bumpy ride took them to the private landing strip. The pilot and ground crew had manhandled the plane, turning it around.

"All gassed and ready to go. Hope there's enough runway, gang," their pilot said.

Tom swallowed hard. He could see the end of the concrete ahead, awfully short!

He held his breath until he felt the plane surge upwards. Only later did the pilot relay they made it with about a foot of runway left.

When they returned, Art met them.

"Well done. Apparently, those people were President Snowden's enforcers. We expect retaliation, but as of now, she doesn't know what actually happened. The news reports that a building flaw caused the collapsed. Stay alert for trouble. Take Monday off."

Chapter 10 Sorting Things

Tom and Jenna returned to the tea garden Monday evening. They hadn't said much until Patty brought them their initial order.

"How did your DC trip go? And did you hear about the CIA office building collapse? Structural failure, the news site claimed, but I don't believe that. Killed about a hundred operatives, including their station chief. President Snowden claims this is the worst calamity to ever hit DC," Jenna said before stopping to sip.

"Like clockwork. I terminated the man who used the nerve agent to murder our Congress people. I can't believe our own CIA wiped out Congress. Unreal."

Jenna grinned. "Ah, ha. Thanks for getting justice for those victims. I thought you must have had a hand in it. But how could a rifle bring down the entire building?"

"It couldn't. Takes an enormous boom to do something like that."

"I did some calculations. Looked into building demolitions. My guess is that someone took it down with explosives. Someone caught it on their old cell phone and posted it."

She brought it up on her phone, sliding it over so he could watch it. "Textbook demolition of condemned buildings."

"Yes, I had a good view of it. News is being spread via the internet. Makes sense, since the TV networks lost all their revenue because of their non-stop lies and misrepresentations," Tom said.

"And their constant backing of the Dem Socialists

movement. I sometimes wonder if they aren't to blame for the world mess we're in today."

"Polarized our country for sure. But the whole world? I doubt that. At my university, most professors had their own agendas. They'd preach climate change would destroy all life on earth by 2031. We're still here, though things are a mess."

"My profs kept insisting people should get equal pay. Like there was no difference in abilities or skills. They tried to get me to join their crusade. Jenna, don't you want to get paid as much as any other worker? A living wage?

"I laughed at them. Look, just why do I deserve to make the same pay as a corporate CEO? Or an oil rig worker? Or an electrician. It's ridiculous. They should pay people for what they produce. I watched many of my fellow students buying into those ideas. Because of what my body lacks must be why I didn't join them. Just like I don't want sympathy or pity."

"Glad you didn't. No, the governments of the world brought this on us with their fiat currency. Money based on nothing but faith that it represented something of value that could be exchanged for other things of value."

Jenna interrupted. "No kidding. For our country, it began when they abandoned the gold standard of the dollar. The value of a dollar crashed. I saw a graph of it. Today, that curve is tangentially approaching zero."

"I saw that, too. The Fed just kept printing more and more money, without end it seems. Propping up the economy and stock markets."

She said, "I think the last straw was the Dem Socialists push to make us all equal. Remember Black Tuesday? In one day the stock market lost seventy-five percent of its value."

Tom chuckled. "A week later the stock market ceased to exist. Banks closed right and left. Everything dried up. That's when Dad's hardware store had to close. He couldn't get new products to sell, and no one could afford to buy anything. Dad just locked the doors. Later vandals broke in and redistributed his remaining inventory."

"What's he doing now?" Jenna asked.

"He's fifty-one and sitting around the house driving Mom crazy while waiting."

"For what?"

"To hear if he has a chance to immigrate to Brussels or Pylon. When I started with the CPD, we checked on that. Had him apply. But with ten billion people on Earth, it's not likely he'll get chosen. There's too many who are younger."

Jenna sighed. "I know how he feels. I did everything imaginable to get myself chosen to immigrate to Brussels. Never going to happen. No arms. I'm a hundred years too early in the new world settlement process. That's what they said. Wait until towns, services, and utilities are set up. What about you? Do you want to immigrate to a new world?"

Tom sighed. "Not really. I don't have a pioneering spirit. I can't see myself plowing fields, building houses—any of the jobs that would turn a virgin world into a civilized one. Like I said, I've sold my soul. Now what do I do? I kill evil people. For a living. But between us, I'd rather teach kids mathematics. I'll be dead long before they're ready for school teachers on these new worlds."

"Hey, that's worth striving for. Teaching kids math. I've thought about teaching physics, but no one's given me a chance. Maybe one day. What about having more children? If you got married again, I mean."

Tom noticed her cheeks flushed. He smiled, thinking of little Jason. "Yeah, I'd like that. A whole lot. I didn't know what I was missing until we had Jason. I have an affinity for kids. To help them learn to be the best. What about you?"

She clenched her jaw. "Don't know. Exactly. I—er, I had the doctors check. My genes are defective. If I had children, its fifty-fifty if they'd have arms. I've downloaded videos of other

72

armless moms who show how they feed and care for their babies. I know I could do that. It's just. Well, you know."

"You are the neatest, smartest, sharpest person I've ever met. Arms don't matter to me. It's the person who does. If you had children, I'm sure they'd be just a fabulous as their mother is. Heck with genetics."

"But you've never seen how I have to do things. How weird it must seem. How slow I am."

"You get the job done. Isn't that what matters?"

"Yes, but—"

"Say, since we first met, I've wondered what thing about not having arms frustrates you the most? I've tried imagining what you daily life must be like, but—"

"You can't." Jenna finished his sentence.

His face felt fiery. "Yeah, right. You don't have to answer. Just curious."

"Getting dressed. Some days, I wish everyone could just go around naked. Honestly, often it takes me an hour to get my clothes on and look presentable. You've not seen me wearing dresses because it's hard to zip them."

"Back zippers?"

"Bingo. I've figured out ways to do it, but getting dressed takes forever. Sometimes I get pooped, I have to take a break before I can finish it. It took me an hour to get into that bikini Saturday and then get my street clothes on over it. All the other things—I don't mind being slow with them. Worst nightmare is someone comes knocking on my door before I'm dressed. Who's gonna wait for an hour while I get dressed to open it?"

Phillis walked up. "I have to have help to get dressed. I hope one day I will be able to do it myself, but I'm not holding my breath. We're closing in a few minutes."

Jenna smiled and nodded.

"I swear these people have a time warp in here," Tom

said. "We just got here. Can't be seven yet."

Phillis giggled and nodded her head towards a wall clock. Tom shook his head.

As they strolled homeward, Tom slipped an arm around her waist. She didn't resist and leaned in towards him.

I wonder if she is testing me. Hinting at how hard it is for her and what it would be like if we got together.

Again, he kissed her goodnight after opening her door for her. She returned his kiss, pressing her body into his. His arms encircled her.

When they parted, she whispered, "Want to come in and spend the night?"

"You bet. I love you. I can't get you out of my mind."

As Tom followed her inside, he noticed the layout of her apartment was a mirror image of his. The only spatial difference: nothing was higher than his neck. Her pictures stood on an end table, whereas he'd put his family photos on top of the dresser.

"This way. Bedroom. I'll let you undress me, unless you want to wait a half hour while I do it," she teased.

As they entered her bedroom, he saw two machines, one close to the bed and the other on the floor. Jenna's face turned crimson and their eyes spotted them.

"My man-substitutes," she managed to say. "I have urges too."

"Of course. Glad you found a way to handle them."

With that, he kissed her again, pulling her attention off her embarrassing machines. He undressed her and watched how she pulled the covers down with a leg as he disrobed.

Later, their passions satiated, Jenna began crying.

"Oh, no. Did I do something wrong? I'm sorry," Tom said, his mind frantically trying to recognize what awful thing he'd done.

"No, it's not you. It's me. I can't describe how wonderful

that felt. Your hands over my body. I'm crying because I'm happy, and I can't control my emotions right now. I love you, too. I never, ever believed I'd ever experience what we did tonight. Never. Not even in my wildest dreams. You've given me something I'll cherish for the rest of my life."

His finger wiped her tears away before kissing her again. He pulled her close. Dawn came too soon.

"I have to get to work. Maybe one day I can watch how you manage to get dressed. But I love how you look this way," he said, as they woke late.

Jenna smiled. "Once you see, you'll not want me around."

"Wanna bet?"

He leaned over and kissed her.

"Six tonight."

Chapter 11 Out of Gold

When Tom walked into Major Callahan's office, she glanced at her watch.

"Yeah, I know I'm late. We overslept."

"We?" she teased, raising her brows.

"I've found someone. Didn't think I ever could again, but she'd incredible."

"In that case, I'd like to meet her. Say, my boyfriend is throwing a party Friday night at his north side mansion. Why don't you come and bring her?"

"I'll ask her tonight. What's new today?"

Her smile faded. "We're on high alert. President Snowden's gold supply just ran out. They've emptied Fort Knox. She was using gold to pay for the free food she handed out. That's why we're on high alert. No gold to us; no food from us to her. Shit will hit the fan, as Art said this morning. Half our security guards are out protecting food deliveries to our people. Our job is to watch Chicago, ID hot spots, and prevent looting."

***

President Snowden sat in the Oval Office, staring at the latest report. She looked up as her Secretary of State, Axel Brookworth, her top aide, entered.

"How can this be? We're out of gold and silver?"

"Aye. Just checked on it myself. Vault's empty."

"I just ordered the Feds to print another two trillion dollars. I'll make a speech tonight, doubling everyone's pay. That should buy us time. Any progress on how we can take over the largest farms? I can declare a National Emergency and confiscate them. Do we have anyone who could run them if we do? How about the shipping nightmare? We're using up the country's fuel reserves far too fast for my liking."

"The loss of our many CIA operatives hampered our efforts more than I'd like. It's those damned Galactic corporations. Our takeover should have worked out except for their surprise appearance."

"Turns out," she said, "it was far easier just to print more money than to confiscate billionaires' wealth. And with the value of a dollar this low, we've ensured their wealth doesn't amount to much any longer. Let them spend 10K for a loaf of bread."

"Which brings me to another angle. Isn't it about time we fired up the Antifa crowd? Let them go after Corporation food supplies."

"Good idea. But attack the Corporations, not the food supplies. We need the food. We'll lose control of the people if we can't feed them. Make it happen. Use the Internet. Fire them up. Have we figured out who destroyed our CIA people?"

"Langley is sure Corporations had a hand in it. But no proof. And we lost our entire supply of nerve agent."

"Every time I turn around it's those damn corporations interfering with me. We gotta put a stop to them. Maybe call out the army. Crush them with our tanks."

"Madam President, that's not feasible. They've popped up offices in all major cities around the world. We don't have enough fuel to launch such a widespread operation."

"Have Antifa do it for us."

***

While the Major and Tom monitored the many screens looking for trouble outbreaks in Chicago, her IT support man knocked.

"Major, listen to this." He called off a URL. "Snowden is calling for all Antifa to attack their local corporations. What should we do?"

"Thanks. I'll relay it to the CEO. Best send out an alert

to all Galactic corporations. They might not have seen this. Good work, Dave," she said.

When she returned from discussing the situation with CEO Art Townsend, she grabbed her drones.

"I'll fly drones over key areas of Chicago. Try to give us early warning of any Antifa groups coming our way. GPan and GD are the most likely targets. The other corporations are still manning up."

"Those are the lawless bunch of left-wing radicals, right?" Tom asked.

Dave said, "You can say that again. Vicious bunch of thugs, but cowards at heart. Have to wear masks because they're afraid they'll be identified and arrested for the crimes they're committing. You be extra careful out there, Major."

"Where do you want me?" Tom asked.

Major Callahan said, "Rooftop. In case they head here, I want you picking off the worst of these beasts. With luck, the CPD will hold them off."

Around noon, Major Callahan alerted Tom and the CPD. "Big group is marching up State Street by East Pershing now. They're firebombing buildings. CPD is moving to intercept. We need to set up a barrier around the old IIT campus."

CEO Townsend gathered his daytime guards. "Tom will lead you. Two dozen are to take the fast lanes of the MTES down the old I90 route. Set up a backup position near the abandoned IIT complex. I'll have the CPD fall back to meet you. Major Callahan estimates the enemy's numbers exceed a hundred. Arm yourselves with the AR15's. Remember, we take no prisoners. Go."

The men had already donned protective armor. While waiting, each had loaded up ten clips that held thirty rounds. Thus, no delay resulted. Tom grabbed his gear and rushed out of GD, two dozen on his tail. They raced down the fast lane of the MTES system, going much faster than the tiny electric cars that the CPD had.

Major Callan's voice came through his comm set. "I've asked Art to ask our local FBI office for help because more rioters have joined the crowd. We're facing closer to two hundred. They're burning CPD and civilian cars, and the police are falling back. They aren't equipped to handle such a crowd. Will you be able to get to the fallback point soon?"

Panting, Tom said, "We're running there now. Should make it."

"Jesus! Another swarm just joined them. There must be close to a thousand rioters now. We need the National Guard or army!"

Tom rush around the abandoned IIT buildings, signaling his men to take up positions. On down State, he saw the police jogging towards them. Angry yelling bounced off the buildings. Smoke rose from fires these fiends had set. As the police reached them, Tom yelled.

"Form a line. When you're out of ammo, fall back. We'll cover you."

One saluted Tom, surprising him. Another yelled, "Thank you guys!"

Before long, the mob drew close. Most wore black outfits and ski masks. A few brandished guns, but many carried Molotov cocktails. One of the closer rioters lit his bottle and leaned back to throw it at the line of men.

Tom's gun fired. At this distance, he saw the small hole appear in the man's mask and forehead. He dropped to the ground, the bottle shattering. Flaming gas ignited his clothes and spread in a circle around him, causing others to get out of the way.

As soon as Tom fired, the others joined in. 9mm shots rang out from the police, while the heavier .223's of the AR15's dwarfed them. Dozens of the rioters at the head of the mob dropped, but others returned fire. Worse, many more fire bombs arced, shattering and spreading deadly flames somewhat close to the line of defenders.

The police soon ran out of ammo. The mob wounded several police who lacked body armor. Tom yelled for them to grab their wounded and retreat. They didn't hesitate, while the GD security men continued firing.

From above, Major Callahan's stolen drone joined in, firing down on the middle of the mob. The drone only carried three dozen 30-30 rounds. Thus, she limited her fire to mob members who carried guns. She dropped twenty before her ammo ran out. She kept her other drones high up, unwilling to lose them to ground gunfire.

The security guards finished their three hundred rounds of .223 and reverted to their 9mm backup semi-automatics. Just as Tom prepared to retreat, reinforcements streamed onto State Street from many side streets and alleyways. Dozens of blue Don't Tread On Me flags fluttered in the light breeze. Attacked from several sides, retreat became the only escape for the Antifa mob.

After the State Street Battle ended, a woman wearing a blue uniform marched up to Tom.

"Greetings. I'm Commander Trumble of the Sons of Liberty, Chicago branch. Looks like we got here in time. Don't worry. My patriots are going from body to body, terminating any who still live. We're taking their guns, too. My card. Call us when you need us."

With that, she saluted and walked back past her troops. Sporadic pistol shots reflected another kill shot. Later, the coroner reported one thousand sixteen dead Antifa men and women, none older than thirty.

Worse, these monsters killed or burned alive twenty-six civilians who happened to be on the MTES as they passed. Sixteen buildings had fire damage, and a section of the MTES needed significant repairs.

When Tom and Liz returned to the skyscraper, CEO Art Townsend had news for them. Not good, though.

"I just found out our Governor-mayor Bebo ordered the FBI and the National Guard to stand down and take no part in the conflict. He didn't expect I'd contact the vigilante group, the Sons of Liberty. They arrived just in time. Also, nice drone work, Major."

"I thought," Tom said, "the FBI was supposed to protect us. Last I knew, the Guard had around a thousand members in the Chicago area. We could have used their help."

Art said, "President Snowden asked the Antifa groups around the country to mob Galactic corporations. Naturally, she wanted them to succeed, so no Guard or FBI. Surprised they didn't ask the CPD to stand down too."

Tom rubbed his face. "But why?"

"Food. They've very little access to food since we stopped deliveries. We're entering the critical take over phase, Tom. The future of Earth will be decided in the ensuing months. With luck, our Galactic corporations will take over and bring peace and prosperity to Earth. If we fail—well, you can see where Snowden's taking us."

"But won't ordinary people suffer if they can't get any food?"

"We're looking into finding covert ways to help, but right now, things will only get dicier. Practically everywhere, local economies are crashing. Today, no one is accepting a dollar as payment for anything.

"A dollar isn't a means of exchange any longer. GPan is minting silver and gold coins, getting them into circulation as a temporary means of exchange. Only a few have access to the new currency, the Galactic credit. They've been introducing the silver dollars to those suppliers who don't. With luck, that'll be enough to keep trade functioning.

"Tomorrow, the Pathfinder is due to land. They're returning from Pylon, Epsilon Eridani. Glowing reports from that world, too. Televised conference again. Around ten. Go home and clean up."

After he left, Liz began servicing her four drones. Dave, her IT man, walked in.

"Nice shooting, Major. Any chance we can get more of the gun drones?"

"Thanks, Dave. No, I stole this one from the DC group."

"I know guys in the fabrication department. If I show them this one, maybe they can rig up something like it on the other drones. Is the ammo really used for deer hunting?"

"Hey, that would be wonderful. Yes, 30-30 deer hunting ammo," she said.

Tom added, "Only the most popular deer hunting round ever made. Liz has more punch with her gun than those AR15's we used."

"Ah, but you can insert a new 30-round clip in seconds," the Major said.

All three laughed.

She added, "It's a tradeoff between total flight time and how many rounds it can carry. The heavier the load, the less time in the air."

Turning to Tom, she said, "Are you and your girlfriend coming to our party Saturday night? Dying to meet her. Six o'clock." She rattled off the address.

Dave said, "Isn't that in the mansion district?"

Lis flushed. "Yes, Phil's one of the Buffett's."

Chapter 12 The Party

"Don't worry, Jenna. I don't have a suit or anything fancy either. Wear what's comfortable."

"Well, I am worried. I don't know any of these people. Mansion district. God, they're all ultra-wealthy. We'll stick out like sore thumbs."

"But Jenna-darling, you don't have any thumbs," Tom teased, bringing a smile to her worried face.

"Okay, but I'm telling you we won't fit in. I'll be ready to go in time, but I have to start early."

When they headed out to the MTES for the long ride north, he wore tan pants and a snap button plaid shirt. She wore loose-fitting pants and a blouse.

"Took me an hour to get these darn buttons fastened."

"Well, you look fabulous. Your hair shines."

By now, he knew how much her long hair meant to her appearance.

"Thanks. Spent all afternoon on it. Were you in any danger when the Antifa attacked? I heard they fired guns at you."

"Not really. We wore body armor. The CPD didn't. Several got shot. Besides, they were using 9mm semi-automatics with short barrels and from at least twenty-five yards. Not much chance of hitting anything."

"Well, I worried."

"I'm more worried about Liz's party. Getting her to smile is like pulling teeth. She's always super serious. I wonder what we're getting into at this party."

"Did you have to say we'd come?"

"She's my boss, so it's best we do."

"Holy cow, is this the place?"

They stopped beside a small gatehouse. A tall fence encircled the mansion and grounds. Fancy evergreens lined the driveway leading to the front portico and entrance. Several electric cars sat parked in the small lot opposite the entrance. A man in a suit waited at the entrance doors.

He frowned. "Your name, sir?"

"Tom Durbin and guest."

He checked a list and frowned again. "This way, sir." He opened the doors for them.

They walked down a short hallway. Portraits lined either side, presumably other Buffett's. Ahead, string quartet music failed to drown muffled conversations. They entered a giant ballroom. Already many guests sipped from wine goblets, as waitresses in their scanty uniforms moved about carrying trays of crystal glasses and empties.

The women all wore fancy gowns and tall heels. The men, suits.

"Ah, here you are at last," Major Callahan's welcome voice floated over the talking guests.

She had her hair down and wore a blue gown. Tom blinked. He'd never seen her like this.

"And my fiancé, Phil Buffett. Phil, this is Captain Tom Durbin and his girlfriend."

"Jenna Sweet," she spoke up, suspecting Liz didn't know her name.

Phil's eyes undressed both guests. "Well, I can see a captain's pay isn't that great. But then, these are difficult times. Hard to purchase the bare necessities of life, isn't it? Liz and I are in line to immigrate to Brussels. I can't wait to escape all this madness. Can you believe what Earth has come to? Barbarians at the gates everywhere. Too bad you can't immigrate there with us, Tom. I've heard they don't accept handicapped people. No offense, Miss Sweet."

Tom thought Jenna's eyes shot darts into Phil's, but she maintained her fake smile, as did Tom.

"I hope you enjoy our party. I suppose Tom can hold your drink for you. The quartet will play Viennese waltzes later. Perhaps you can dance with us. Say, we could have a very special guest tonight. I asked GPan's CEO Paddock to invite the man who made immigration possible. Dr. Karl Oppenstein, inventor of the ion engine. Without that, it'd take a lifetime to reach Brussels. Thanks to his invention, we can get there in a year. I'm told Oppenstein is something of a recluse, but Paddock told me he'd pass the invitation along to the GPan inventor. I sure hope he shows up. I'm throwing this party in his honor. Most of my guests hope to make it onto the immigration list when they open it up."

"Wow, Liz. You didn't tell me Kark Oppenstein would be here," Tom said. "I'd love to discuss theories with him."

"Do that elsewhere," Phil said. "This is a party to honor him for making interstellar travel possible."

Jenna said, "I've heard he is quite the recluse. I'd be surprised to see him show up to this kind of party."

"Why?" Liz asked, treating Jenna with more interest.

"I'm sure he didn't invent the ion engine so the wealthy could buy fast spaceships and fly about the stars for fun. I think he wanted the help humanity survive better into the future. GPan says it takes real pioneers to populate a new world. There's no infrastructure there at all. Everything has to be built up from scratch—a fresh start and approach to making civilizations."

Liz chuckled. "I hope they put the power lines underground, along with gas and water. No more ice-caused power outages."

"Those who immigrate will have to do the digging," Jenna said. "Get their hands dirty. I don't suppose Phil knows how to wire a house or install the plumbing, toilets, and sinks."

"He'll be my spouse. I'm scheduled to be one of the initial security personnel guarding everyone else. But I'm sure Phil will help in some way," Liz said, defusing Jenna's innuendo.

She whispered to Tom, "Jenna's very pretty, but she's gotta be helpless. Are you sure about her?"

She sailed away before he could reply. Tom found a straw and held both their wine goblets.

"What did she say?" Jenna whispered moments later.

"She said you're very pretty."

Jenna seemed pleased with that. Wisely, he didn't relay all she'd said.

They mingled as best they could, but most of the well-dressed partygoers avoided them.

They'd been there an hour when Jenna said, "Are you ready to go?"

"I rather hoped Karl Oppenstein would show. I'd love to talk to him. I've many topology ideas I'd like to bounce off him."

Jenna laughed. "I hate to burst your expectations, but I'm very certain he's not going to show up at this party."

"How can you be sure? GPan invited him."

"Remember, I work for GPan. I would know if someone that important would be coming."

"You sure?"

"Absolutely."

"Okay, will you join me at the tea garden now?"

"Thought you'd never ask."

Without any fuss, the pair left. Around eight, they entered their favorite hangout.

Irene said, "Welcome, Jenna, Tom. We figured you might not come tonight."

Later that evening, Tom got down on a knee. "I love you. Jenna Sweet, will you marry me?"

She blushed. "Get up, you silly fool. Yes, I'll marry you, but only if you're sure about this. Although I've tried to be part of the immigration to Brussels team, Phil's right. Not much chance they'll let me. I'd be dooming your chances."

"I'm content to be wherever you are, darling. There's no one like you in the world."

"Well, get up. They're all looking at us."

Phillis walked up, grinning.

"Jenna, did he?"

Jenna blushed again. "Yes."

"I've asked for her foot in marriage," Tom said with an enormous smile.

Phillis giggled and nodded to the others. Only now did Tom see the whole tea garden gang watching them. They rushed over to congratulate Jenna and Tom.

They entered Jenna's apartment late that night.

As the pair sat on her couch, Tom said, "I don't know what to do with rings. Mom gave me her mother's wedding ring to use. These days there isn't an open jewelry store. It'll have to do for now. Hope that's okay with you."

"I'd be honored. Perhaps I can wear it on a toe, but maybe a necklace would be safer. But Tom, if you're marrying me, there's something I haven't told you about myself. Something you have to know."

"I can't imagine what, darling. Are you going to turn into a pumpkin at midnight or something?"

She giggled. "No, this is serious. I work for GPan."

"Yeah, secret projects and all that. It's okay with me, as long as you aren't in danger."

"It's not like that. No, they've given me a lot of Galactic credits. Like millions, Tom."

"I'm marrying a millionaire?"

She giggled. "It's not like that. I invented the ion engine. I'm Karl Oppenstein."

"What?" Tom said. His eyebrows rose. "You can't be him."

"I am. I invented the ion engine, but I used a pseudonym. When I published my paper, no one would pay any attention to a paper by armless Jenna Sweet. My name sounds more like a porn star. No one would take my paper seriously. I used a fake name. Only a very few people know I'm Karl Oppenstein. It was part of my senior physics research project. For heaven's sake, don't tell anyone, especially Major Callahan."

"You aren't kidding, are you?"

"No. Not about this."

"Incredible. Man, do I have a zillion questions for you."

"Can they wait for tomorrow? I'd rather push you into my bed right now."

Later, as he watched her brush her teeth, he said, "I thought you were right-footed."

After finishing, she said, "I am, as often as is safe. I make heavy use of my legs. The doctors warned me I could wear out the cartilage in my hips. I try to use my left leg as much as my right. I sure don't want to get my hip replaced."

"I had no idea. If there's anything I can do to help, just say so."

"Neck massages help. Pressing my head down onto my shoulders to hold things often give me neck aches."

Tom did so.

"Ah, now this is heaven for me."

"I'm here for you. Always."

"My folks won't believe this—that I'm getting married. We must find a way to get down to Arizona to visit them somehow. I wish the economy would revive so we could fly down or they fly here."

"Yes, too far for one of those electric cars. Still, we'll find a way. Let me undress you before you fall asleep on your feet."

"Okay. I think Major Callahan is making a colossal mistake hitching up with Phil. Oh, this must be what heaven's like. Keep massaging me."

Tom grinned and did so.

Chapter 13 One Too Many

The two married on Halloween with CEO Art Townsend performing the ceremony. Neither set of parents attended, because of the economic chaos. Liz stood in as Maid of Honor, while Dave Shirts from IT acted as Best Man. Both signed the wedding license, along with the couple and Art.

Their honeymoon comprised spending the day at the tea gardens and a chilly stroll along the lakeside. But they did make phone calls to their parents, promising to visit when travel was again possible.

Tom moved into her apartment, but took a little time off work to build a secret room in which to keep his gun, ammo, and reloading equipment. When he finished, it looked like all the other walls in the apartment, but a secret switch slid a door open allowing him access. While cramped, just three feet deep, it ensured gun security.

"There you go. As promised. Our children can't get to the guns and get into trouble."

"Sometime you must take me to the range and show me how to shoot," Jenna said. "I did some checking. Found this video of a woman like me shooting all kinds of gun things."

"Wow! How does she do it? Ah, with her feet and toes. Clever woman. Okay, but let's wait until it's safe to do that much traveling."

"And when winter is done. I have an awful time with it. Hard to dress warm enough and still keep my feet available."

"You have me to help now."

Little happened during the winter, except Jenna became pregnant with their son. They chose Samuel Arthur for his grandfather and hers. They expected Sam to make his appearance around the first of July. While Tom welcomed this second chance to be a father, Jenna grew more worried as the months progressed. But their friends at the tea gardens encouraged her each time they visited.

Jenna spent hours researching how other women like her raised their children. Tom picked up used baby supplies from others at GD who no longer needed them.

May 10, 2036, became the anti-Second Amendment date. President Snowden took to the airwaves and Internet streaming to make her big announcement just as people awoke.

"With winter's end, gun control is our major remaining problem. Last year, thousands lost their lives to guns. Many more were wounded. Tragic. So needless. For years, my predecessors advocated for gun control, but to little avail. Today, I instructed the FBI to confiscate all guns in America. They have a list of all registered firearms, and those will be confiscated. But as we all know, criminals have guns, often stolen ones. I've issued Executive Order 1299, giving the FBI the authority to search every home in the US and confiscate any guns. Specially trained dogs will sniff out the firearms. Don't bother to hide them.

"We will make 2036 a gun-free year. Gun crimes will drop to zero! Our world will be much safer. A word of warning. I've instructed the FBI to terminate anyone who refuses to turn over their guns or who protests the confiscation. We will not stand for further gun violence. That is all."

Tom exhaled. "Jenna, I gotta get to work fast. This is a disaster in the making. I'll text you when I know anything."

With that, he rushed out, just as his phone received a summons from CEO Art Townsend to report to work, ASAP.

"It's finally happened," Major Callahan said, as Tom ran into her office panting from his run. "Good. You're here. Art and I have been expecting this for months. Shit's going to hit the fan."

Dave ran into her office. "Turn on Channel Nine News. It's happening!"

She flipped a switch. The reporter and cameraman stood a block away from a house in southern Chicago.

Four FBI men wearing body armor stood at the home's front door. Evidently, they leaked the location of this first raid to gain publicity. One had a megaphone.

"We're here to confiscate your guns. Let us in now or we'll break the door down."

The reply from a window sounded like a machine gun.

Tom whispered, "He has an illegal bump stock that fires all thirty rounds in seconds. Hey, he's a marksman. Took head shots. Their vests would absorb hits."

The remaining two men rushed the door, getting out of the line of sight of the window. One swung a heavy ram, shattering the door. The other fired a stun grenade through the opening.

Kaboom! An enormous explosion blew both FBI men off their feet. The camera recorded bits of appendages flying, before the cameraman realized he what was filming and swung the camera away from the scene.

"What just happened?" the reporter said. "On me." The camera showed his white face. "They just killed all four FBI men. That explosion. What was it? A grenade? And IED? We apologize for the graphic view just shown. That was unexpected. Wait. Here comes a SWAT unit."

The camera panned to the armored vehicle that pulled up, SWAT stenciled on its side. Ten men piled out, even more heavily armed than the original four FBI men.

"They're wearing bomb proof suits. At least that's what it looks like from here. Who lives here? Producer, find out who lives in this house. They're surrounding the house now. Another FBI black electric car is arriving. They're going to the nearby houses. Zoom in on them. I suspect they're evacuating residents."

A loud gunshot echoed. The closest SWAT member paused a moment. The cameraman zoomed in on the figure, then wished he hadn't. Too late. Viewers saw a sizeable hole in the face visor and red stuff on the inside of the man's faceplate. In slow motion, he dropped to the ground.

Tom said. "Shit. That was an armor-piercing round. Probably .50 cal. Maybe bigger. What's that guy armed with?"

CEO Art Townsend poked his head into the room. "Are you seeing this? What the hell is he shooting?"

"Armor-piercing rounds. At least .50 cal. Need more shots to better tell. Might even be anti-tank 40mm rounds," Tom said. "These guys don't stand a chance."

Liz said, "Ah, city records show Bill Kant lives there. Also suggests he's a member of the Sons of Liberty. Looks like the FBI wanted to strike back against those who helped us with the Antifa mob last year."

"Good. They're falling back," Tom said. "Wait. Guys, don't all go to your van—"

Another tremendous explosion knocked the cameraman off his feet, and he was a block away. When he put the camera back on the van, or what remained of the burning van, bodies lay scattered about.

"RPG. The man has a rocket-propelled grenade launcher!" Tom yelled.

Bang. Bang. Bang. Several small arms fire struck the ground near the cameraman and reporter. They turned and raced away.

Tom said, "He didn't want to harm the reporters. What happened here was designed to give us and the world a message."

"You can't take away our Second Amendment rights," Dave said. "Isn't that right?"

Major Callahan said, "Looks like it. This man, fourteen. FBI, zero. That's an obvious message. Boss, I will monitor other major cities. If you're right, we're likely to see more of this."

"Keep a close eye on it," Art said.

"Well, Boss, now I get why you had us sign over ownership of our weapons to GD. Foresight factorial."

Art smiled. "Indeed. That's why I get paid the big credits. They can't confiscate your guns. Officially, they belong to the corporations who've loaned them to you. Since we're an international organization, local laws don't apply to us. Snowden can't touch us."

Dave said, "You saw this coming two years ago?"

"Yes, son. We did. I expected it to happen sooner. Here in Chicago. We're the murder capital of the country since around 2020. There's been so many murders in South Chicago and on the west side that the CPD doesn't even bother to investigate them. Just haul the bodies away. So, yes, for years I expected our corrupt Governor-mayor Bebo to try something like this. But he didn't have the balls for it.

"Well, now the fun begins. It'll be all hands on deck for the next few weeks."

"Why?" Tom asked.

"We're contacting every member of every law enforcement unit in the world, offering them positions with one of the Galactic corporations as security guards with gold-backed pay and the ability to keep their guns. We need to screen each one to filter out the undesirables and spies. Liz, I hate to do this to you, but you must postpone your wedding. I need you on this 24/7. We've got thousands to screen here in Chicago and only a few days to do it. You're likely to see many resigning their positions after what we just saw. It's suicide to confiscate everyone's guns. Sure, some will meekly hand them over, but we'll see many more shoot-outs. We must offer these

94

men in blue an alternative.

"Dave, Tom, you assist her with the screening. I'll send another two dozen up to help you with it. FBI, CPD, ICE, Marshals. Anyone with a badge gets an offer, subject to screening. Make it happen."

"But which corporation takes them?" Tom asked.

"GD wants the best of the lot. We'll distribute them among the two dozen new Galactic corporations. Look at it this way. This is the major recruitment we've been expecting. Snowden's action just pushed us over the top. We are about to succeed around the world. Make it happen, gang. My office has collected a list of all law enforcement people in the area. Names and cell phone numbers. We'll use call text multiplier and send out the same message to everyone.

"It'll say something like this. 'How would you like to work security for one of the new Sol Empire Galactic corporations? Great pay in gold-backed Galactic credits. Great benefits and you keep your own firearms. If interested, text your name to this number.' I've people standing by to retrieve those incoming texts. They'll relay them to you, Liz. Your Intelligence Office gets to screen them. If they pass, relay their name and number to my office. We'll make the initial contact and handle the hiring details."

"But this means thousands of people to check," Liz said.

"Precisely. Like I said, you're gonna be busy. Tom, Dave, and others will join you and your staff." His phone beeped. "Ah, the messages have been sent. Now the fun begins."

"Fun for you, but a nightmare for me," Liz said.

***

"Well, Madam President," Axel Brookworth said, "the day's tallies are in. Grim. The FBI lost two hundred six agents, killed four hundred five resistors, and confiscated two thousand one hundred forty-five firearms."

"Not bad. In a year, we'll have grabbed a million guns. Wait, they lost hundreds of agents?"

"Yeah. Many are putting up a fight, refusing to give up their guns. Chicago lost fourteen agents, and the perp got away with his guns and took theirs as well."

"Well, hell. Let's order the local police, ICE agents, US marshals, everyone to help the FBI agents. Perhaps I should call out the local branches of the National Guard to assist."

"Keep that as a last resort. That won't go over too well. But there's another problem."

"These stupid people. Problems. Problems. Problems. It takes someone like me, like us, to show them the solutions they need. What is it this time? More food issues?"

"Er, no. Mass resignations are pouring in."

"What?"

"Someone sent this text to every law enforcement person in the country."

He showed the President the message.

"Those fiends. That's treasonous."

"But we can't touch them. They're a global set of corporations."

"Contact our supporters in the major cities. Have them find out who's behind this and put a stop to it by any means necessary."

"Yes, Madam President. We'll have it stopped by morning."

***

Overweight Governor-mayor Bebo read the message from President Snowden. And showed it to his top enforcer, a man known only as El Gato, a highly efficient sadistic man, who'd climbed the Mayor's ladder by terminating dozens of competitors and those requested by his idol, Bebo.

"We have a problem," Bebo said. "I checked an hour ago. My specially appointed CPD superintendents are still on the job and loyal, but almost all other personal have resigned today. I told Superintendent Johnson not to accept any resignations, but they stopped showing up for work anyway. He's got no one to round them up and force them back to work. Same is true for the FBI after that massacre. The only law enforcement people left are the men I handpicked for the top positions. Not good, El Gato."

"Boss, I've snuck a spy into this Galactic corporation hiring process. I aim to find out who is picking the people. Someone orchestrated that counterattack to our Antifa raid last year. I'm gonna make someone pay for that."

"Good thinking. Getting food for our people has become very hard. With the loss of all the pigs, maybe we can step up food thefts."

"Hey, that might bring that vigilante sniper back."

"We gotta do something soon. People are hungry."

"Are you going to use the National Guard to confiscate food supplies from Galactic corporation depots?"

"That's on the back burner. First, we must see how Snowden's gun confiscation works out. If most guns in North Chicago are gone, then our troops can do what they want with relative immunity. I'm not about to risk another Antifi slaughter like we had last year. Just find out who'd handling ripping off our pigs and put a stop to it."

"Gotcha, Boss."

"Now send in Honey Bunny Mounds. I'm stressed out."

In minutes, the young blond teetered into his office. Her six-inch stilettos made her match his height. Her dress couldn't have been shorter. But what set this former porn star apart were her monster breasts. El Gato once measured them when he arranged for Honey Bunny to become Bebo's stress-reliever companion. Bebo insisted on nothing smaller than an M breast cup size, but El Gato thought hers looked more like basketballs.

But Bebo enjoyed them, claiming they were stress relievers. El Gato preferred regular street-walkers.

"Oh, poochy, doochy. Honey Bunny is here." Her bosom bounced as she entered. The dress top barely covered them. "Such a stressful day. Let Honey Bunny make it all better."

He sat behind his enormous desk, designed to make visitors seem small. She thrust her bosom into his face, while rubbing his back with her hands. One of his hands slipped under her top, partly encircling one mammoth breast, while his other slipped up her legs. He let out a sigh of relief.

El Gato turned, smirked, and left. In the hallway and out of Bebo's hearing, he said, "Lord knows where I'll be able to find more like her. Wanted: titanic boobs. Not a likely ad." He chuckled when a new thought struck him. "Got our own Med Center. I'll have the doc make one. Problem solved. People will do anything to have a free house and a full stomach."

***

Early in June, Art summoned Tom to his office.

"It's come down to this, Tom. Snowden has to go. She's calling up the Army to confiscate firearms. True, half the soldiers have left: terms up and resignations. But there's enough left that might allow her to succeed in removing millions of guns. Criminals will still find ways to get them, but honest people won't. This comes from Sol Empire-wide GPan CEO Wang Chan himself. Terminate Snowden."

Tom said, "Wow. That's quite a challenge. She's in the White House, a veritable Fort Knox. There are still many Secret Service agents around her."

Chapter 14 The Tasks

Once again, Tom found himself onboard the private jet, headed for DC.

Art had called. "I've lined up a Mr. Kent, who used to work for President Snowden before being fired. He claims she steps out onto the porch of the south entrance overlooking the South Lawn at least once a day. According to him, Snowden likes to breathe in fresh air for five or ten minutes, while reveling at the view. From the American Red Cross building's roof, you should be able to have an unobstructed line of sight. Problem is, it's likely to be a two thousand yard shot."

"I'll check it out. Thanks."

When the plane landed, Tom rented an electric car. He called the contact information for Mr. Kent.

"I've landed. Can we meet?" Tom asked. "I'm not familiar with DC."

"I'm at the DC GD building." He rattled off its address, but Tom had him repeat it, while he entered it into the onboard nav system.

Mr. Kent, now a security guard, met him at the entrance.

"You're staying with us. Let me take you to your room."

"Okay, but I want to reconnoiter as soon as possible. Wish we could take a helicopter ride over this Red Cross building. I'd like to see its roof."

"Hasn't been those for a couple years. No fuel. But would a drone view work?"

The next day, Tom stared at a DC map and the drone's image of the roof. After calculating distances, he found a workshop in the basement. Late that day, Tom finished building a special covering for his sniper nest. It blocked infrared scans and blended well with the gravel roof.

Mr. Kent created a forged ID card for Tom, saying he worked for ABC Roofers. Some Galactic credits exchanged hands, and Tom had a contract to repair a leak on the roof. First, he carried worker supplies up, further adding to the subterfuge. On the next series of trips, he brought up his new nest and sniper gear.

Based on Mr. Kent's information, President Snowden stepped outside in the early afternoons. For the next two days, Tom spent the afternoons hunkered down in his nest, watching her movements and calculating the shot. From this distance, she could move between the time he pulled the trigger and when the bullet arrived. Tom knew he'd only get one shot. If he missed, the Secret Service agents wouldn't let her outdoors again. He had to get it right.

His radar range finder gave the precise distance. However, wind speed played a strong factor in such long shots. Even if he could know the wind speed on the White House porch, what was it elsewhere along the flight path? Based on weather reports, they expected rain tomorrow, but the next day should be sunny. That meant he had to cover for having repaired the leak. Too many questions if he continued beyond the rainy day. Either that or drill a hole into the roof.

During the rain, he went up, presumably to check on things. When he came down, he reported he'd fixed the leak.

"I'll come back tomorrow after the rain and get my tools. It's pouring right now."

The next day, he arrived just after noon and began carrying tools down to the waiting electric car, which had the ABC Roofing logo taped to its sides. Then he crawled into his sniper nest, trained the scope on the porch, and waited.

Around one, President Snowden stepped out, gazing far and wide across the land she claimed as her own. Tom

100

squeezed. The bang couldn't be heard from the White House steps, nor likely from inside this building. He picked up his gear, folded the nest, and climbed back down. No one challenged him. He nodded to the security man at the door. Once in his car, he headed to the airport.

In the lot, he peeled off the logos and returned the rented car. Minutes later, his jet lifted off. Only then did Tom relax.

With the jet on autopilot, the captain asked, "Successful mission?"

"I hope so. Couldn't stick around to verify, but likely. News should cover it."

Hours later, the pilot woke Tom. "Hey, turn the set to Channel Nine News. You did it, man."

Tom turned on the TV. "...latest news. President Snowden has been killed. The Secret Service said she was hit by a random bullet someone fired high into the air. She was unlucky to be where the bullet landed. It's ironic. She pushed hard to confiscate all firearms. Yet a totally random stray bullet struck her down. More as information is released."

Tom turned it off and filled his mind with images of Jenna. He felt good in that he'd ended the reign of the Dem Socialist who'd destroyed the United States. What the country was now, Tom didn't know. Just more chaos, unless the Galactic corporations could bring order, but that would be a worldwide tall order.

***

"How goes it?" Governor-mayor Bebo asked, his eyes a haze from cannabis.

El Gato glared at him. *Drogado again.* "How goes what?" *No un mind-reader.*

"Making me more Honey Bunnies. I need lots more. Keeps stress down. Running state and Chicago. Takes a lot out of me."

"You were supposed to take your wife to lunch today or did you forget?"

"She's a coke head. Wouldn't remember it, anyway. Besides Honey Bunnies—now they know what a man needs. Where is Honey Bunny Mounds? Send her in. I need de-stressing."

He not know if I replace Miss Mounds. Hombre loco! He left, found Honey Bunny filing her nails, and told her, "El loco wants you now."

He gestured to the door. Valuing his position, he watched her teetering walk to make sure she went the right direction. Then he left the Governor-mayor's office in South Chicago and ducked into South Chicago General Hospital to visit Bebo Ritzker 's private surgeon, Dr. Merryweather. Now here was a real man. Not like the fat pig of a mayor. The two men shared a common passion for young girls, whom they abandoned when they reached fourteen.

South Chicago teemed with such girls, all looking for a way up the ladder. Promise them clothes and drugs and watch them jump at the opportunity.

"Hola, Dr. Merryweather."

***

Just then, intending to relay a message, the new nurse in training, Rae Lin, reached the other door. Why her feet had to be altered so she could only wear these tall heels eluded her. Other nurses wore comfortable flats. Nor did she grasp why the doctor demanded her breasts be enlarged. Already they were excessively big. Instead of relaying the message, Rae paused when she heard voices. She listened.

***

"Hey, El Gato. Got a freah crop in. Drop by tonight. Party time. What brings you to my surgery?"

"I'll be there. Bebo wants many more Honey Bunnies."

"Well, as you know, I'm working on making a new

bunny for Bebo. You can't get boobs that big overnight. Gotta slow-stretch them. She's not ready yet. She thinks she's becoming a nurse. Be ready for Bebo sometime next month. If you take her now, he'll complain they're too small. We don't want to get on his bad side."

"El loco is more loco each week. Maybe *una buena idea* to get several more Honey Bunnies started."

"As you wish. Say, I heard about your latest assignment. Have you found out who the GD Intelligence Officer is that's been causing Bebo massive headaches?"

"Sí. Got a spy in GD. It's a damned woman. Ex-soldier."

The doctor chuckled. "Bet that one's a real tough cookie. How soon are you killing her?"

El Gato sighed. "I should have just gone and done it. Instead, loco me, I told Bebo about Major Liz Callahan. 'Killing her does no good,' he says. 'Best put fear into GD people's hearts.' Give her a tongue necktie? I says. He says, 'No, fix it so she can't fly drones or do much of anything. Off with her arms. Yeah, that'll do it. No, wait. Armless Honey Bunny. Yeah, make her into an armless Honey Bunny. That'll scare the willies out of GD people.' I says it might their women, but not their men. He says, 'Then we'll just have to turn their men into armless Honey Bunnies too. Merryweather can use his new gender transformation surgical skills.' Lotta big words for turning man into woman."

"Now we're talking my language," Dr. Merryweather said. "Yes, we've perfected that process. I published a series of papers on the best surgical methods to carry out gender changes. This is the leading hospital in Chicago for such transformations."

"You're freaking me out, doc. Changing men into women. Must be ugly women."

The doctor laughed. "In the past, perhaps. But with my new whole-body approach to such surgeries, I can turn out

Miss Galaxies or Mr. Atlases."

"Whoa, keep your knives away from me!"

Both men laughed.

"Anyway, that's what Bebo wants done to her when I bring her to you. Armless Honey Bunny. Be a few days from now. Be prepared for her."

"Thanks for the alert. Yes, it takes advance prep work to have everything fresh and ready for such an operation. In gender transformations, to do it right, we use appropriate body parts from someone we snatch off the streets. Someone who won't be missed. South Chicago is filled with such men and women. But it takes a bit of prep time to find the right match."

"Ghoulish, man. Me, no part o' that! Cya at the party tonight."

With that, El Gato left, and the doctor followed him out.

***

Rae swallowed hard. Her eyes bulged. I've been a fool. I've seen Honey Bunny Mounds. That's why he's growing my breasts. Already I take a J cup, but Honey takes an O size. She told me. And he's distorting my feet. What have I gotten myself into? Got to get away, but how? Where would I go? Best play along and figure how to escape.

She flipped her long auburn hair back with her two-inch nails and returned to her temporary nurse station. Rae's stomach fought to release its contents.

***

Around midnight, El Gato slunk along the MTES route that Major Callahan followed to get to GD each day. His men had followed her for several days, proving she was a creature of habit. At each CCTV camera station, he fired his .22 silenced semi-automatic shattering the lens. No one could track him when he abducted the Intelligence Officer. He parked an electric car midway along the path, leaving plenty of blacked

104

out zones on either side of the car. He stowed a blanket in the back.

Back at his hideout, he prepared his dart with the knockout drug. He wore latex gloves. Once he'd neglected them and paid for that mistake with a numb hand for a week. This concoction came from Juarez, and he had lost count of the number of people he's abducted using it. Most were women and girls. Naturally.

Early morning, El Gato appeared to be reading a paper while sitting on a rest bench beside the MTES in the blackout zone he'd created. Like a cat, El Gato waited on the unsuspecting mouse—Major Callahan walking briskly to GD to start her day. Impeccable timing. He rose and followed behind her, closing the distance. When he reached her, he pushed the dart into her neck. By having her hair in a tight bun, he had unfettered access to it. He slipped an arm around her.

"What..." Liz struggled to say.

El Gato felt her legs give way and supported her weight as they continued moving down the escalator. When he approached the car, he pretended she was drunk and helped her inside. Seeing no one watching, he dumped her body and covered it with the blanket. The electric car moved off into the early Chicago morning. He followed a circuitous path to the hospital and surgical center, not in some attempt to elude CCTV, but because the MTES constructions this close to the heart of Chicago blocked off many streets.

He pulled into the underground parking lot and called Dr. Merryweather. Soon, the doctor and two orderlies appeared with a Gurney. Neither man said anything, as the orderlies lifted Liz out, placing her on the Gurney and covered her up.

As they wheeled her away, El Gato said, "Turn her into an armless Honey Bunny. Bebo's orders."

"Got it. Say, have you heard? President Snowden's been

killed."

"How?"

"Saying a stray bullet, but who knows."

"*Maldición!* I don't believe it. Not stray for *el presidente!* In the White House. Surrounded by Secret Service? *Diablos no!* It has to be the Assassin! Better go tell Bebo. Watch your back."

***

I've never seen El Gato this nervous. Could it be the Assassin? DC covering it up?

Dr. Merryweather shook his head and followed the Gurney. Once inside, he removed her clothing and slipped a hospital gown on her. He dumped her apparel down the disposal. After he alerted his surgical team, he washed up.

All assembled around him in the operating room. He said, "We begin with arm removal. Our objective is to leave no scarring. She wishes to look flawless, as though arm were never there. Breast enhancement comes next. We'll use the massive growth hormone first. Later on, we'll then insert the silicon. Remember, we're trying for perfection. A perfect, gorgeous body."

His skilled team began their work. None asked why they were removing perfectly good arms. Rather, they focused on his challenge to make it look as though there never had been any surgery. Others worked on her breasts, while one monitored the anesthetic application.

An hour later, Dr. Merryweather scrutinized the results. "Excellent work, everyone. Keep her doped up for the next few days, while the hormones do their work and shoulder healing begins."

Nurses wheeled her out and into a private room.

"Ah, Nurse assistant Miss Lin, you're now assigned to the patient in Room 303. Sit with her. She's being kept doped up for three days giving the healing a good start. We'll do further work on her bosom next week. She'll be hospitalized for a month, but once we wean her off the drugs, she'll need your help with everything."

Rae said, "303. Okay."

***

Rae found the room and sat down. Heavy bandages covered the young woman's shoulders with an IV in her left leg. Already the woman's breasts swelled. Rae's stomach knotted. She recalled what she'd overheard and knew this must be GD's Intelligence Officer.

Rae rushed to the bathroom as fast as she could in her six-inch stilettos. She flushed her breakfast and returned to her chair.

She's gonna be helpless. Her life's ruined. Monster breasts, too. Are they going to cripple her feet like mine, too? This is sick. Rae, you gotta do something or you'll end up being another one of Bebo's Honey Bunnies. They might even cut off my arms! Oh, God. What have I gotten myself into?

Another nurse entered. "Hi, Rae. Want to lend me a hand? Take her blood pressure and then attach the heart monitor sensors. Use her right leg. I've got to install these."

While the two set about their tasks, the nurse asked, "So, Rae, have you decided on what type of nurse you want to be? Surgical and trauma nurses are the highest paid, but I can't stand all that blood. I'd rather take care of them afterwards. In the emergency room, seconds count. I don't think that fast. How about you?"

The two chatted while doing their work. When the nurse left, she could monitor Liz's vitals from the nurses' station.

107

Chapter 15 Revenge

Tom woke when his plane landed. After a brief drive to GD, he reported to Art.

"I think I got her," he said.

CEO Art Townsend grinned. "You damn well did! Incredible shot! Everyone's talking about it. Heard the details from DC office. Well done. Take the day off. Go enjoy Jenna."

Tom needed no further encouragement. He used the MTES fast lane.

"I'm back," he called out as he entered their apartment.

Jenna, now very pregnant, waddled out to meet him, her face radiant. They hugged and kissed for many minutes.

When they pulled apart, she said, "President Snowden's dead. They claim a stray bullet. Was you, wasn't it?"

Tom smiled. "Had to put an end to her evil. In her few years, she and her Dem Socialists have destroyed our country."

"If we don't have any leaders, what will happen?" she asked.

"The Galactic corporations are supposed to step up and run the world. At least that's what GD claims. Guess time will tell. If only commerce could get back to normal. I miss fast food."

Jenna giggled. "So do I, Mr. Hot Shot. Ouch. Sam's kicking again. Tom, I'll be relying on you more and more. It's getting harder for me to do things. I'm becoming a blimp."

"But a gorgeous, loving, sexy blimp that I love," he said, hugging her again. "Only six more weeks."

Jenna sighed. "You've no idea what it's like. I took all morning to get dressed. From now on, buster, you get to dress me."

"Yes, my charming queen," Tom said, kissing her again. "And I'll give free massages too."

"Oh, melting my heart, eh?"

"That's the plan. You sit while I make us something to eat."

Jenna laughed. "You're hired. Could you do this all the time? No, wait. I'll tire of eating TV dinners."

Both laughed. "I know," he said, "I'm a lousy cook. In a few months, I'll take lessons from one of the best."

She smiled. "You know I might not have time, what with the demands Sam will make."

"I'm aware of that. Been there, done that before." He sighed. "Yeah, no getting around it. Those first few months are darn near sleepless. Cry, eat, diaper, sleep. Over and over every couple hours. But I'll be here to help lots. You'll be the best mom ever."

Jenna laughed. "Optimistic are you?" She sighed, "Yeah, it's gonna be the biggest challenge I've ever faced. I won't kid you; I need your help."

"You can count on it, darling. Anything for you. While I was gone, I couldn't stop thinking about you. I can't believe how lucky I am to have found you."

Jenna said, "It's the other way around. I never dreamed a man would ever want me." She shrugged her shoulders.

"Well, I sure do. Now to make us lunch. Fancy a TV dinner?"

She laughed.

The next day, Tom reported to Major Callhan's office. Dave, her IT guy, had a worried face.

"She's not in. Not like her to be late."

Tom said, "Give her a few minutes."

He returned to his office and looked over his email inbox. Dave interrupted him.

"Hey, Tom. She's still not here, and it's almost noon."

He looked up at the clock, surprised at the passage of time.

"Try calling her cell. Maybe she over-slept."

"Already done that. Went to voice mail. I'm getting worried, really worried."

"Okay. I'll check out her place. You contact her fiancé, Phil."

Tom rushed out. Since I've known her, she's never been this late. As he rushed along the fast lane of the MTES, his stomach tightened. When she didn't answer her door despite his pounding and yelling, his shoulders sagged. Something was very wrong. Hastily, he called Dave.

"She's not home."

"Phil hasn't seen her since yesterday. I'm sounding the alarm."

"I'll be back ASAP. I have an awful feeling she's in trouble."

Dave said, "Big trouble. On it."

When the out of breath Tom rushed into Major Callahan's office, Dave had all her screens up. His ghastly face spoke volumes.

"She's vanished. Found her leaving. CCTV has her walking down the MTES heading here, just like she always does."

Tom resisted the urge to ask how he knew the route she always took.

"At this spot, she vanishes. The surveillance cameras are out for the next three blocks. According to the logs, they went out after midnight. Someone shot them with a .22. Work crew found the brass when they went to fix the cameras around ten. But I can't find any trace of her after this three block section. It's like she just vanished."

"Abducted," Tom said. "She's been kidnaped. Alert Art. I'm not good at this Intel stuff, but let me poke around some."

110

Dave fired off a text message, while Tom verified what Dave had already discovered.

"Can you bring up a city map of this area with the three blocks in it?"

Dave's fingers flashed. The large-scale map appeared on one monitor. Tom studied it for a moment.

Art joined them, a worried look on his face.

"Dave, any cameras along this side street? If she was abducted, odds are they took her in the middle of the blackout zone. Perhaps had a car waiting. Look for a vehicle going either direction on this street."

"Got the time stamp when she moved past the last camera before the blackout. Let's see what we can pull up. Here, you go through the west side while I do the east side," Dave said.

An hour later, all three looked at an electric car with a single occupant rolling along the side streets.

Dave moaned, "Here's where we need Major Callahan the most. How do we follow that car with all the street and camera changes?"

Tom had a hunch. "Print me off a shot of that driver's face, the best you can get. I think I recognize it from a wanted poster in the CPD precinct. Run it through facial rec."

Minutes passed before Dave replied.

"El Gato. Eighty-nine percent likelihood."

"I thought so. He must be the kidnapper. Art, put everyone you have on tracing that car and finding her. I'm going after El Gato."

With that, Tom dashed home.

"Hey, El Gato has abducted Major Callahan this morning. I'm going after that mobster."

He strapped on his dual .44's and stowed his backup 9mm. Then he grabbed his sniper rifle pack.

"Be careful. Get her back, and come home safe," Jenna

said.

"I won't take any unnecessary risks. Don't worry."

"But I do worry."

After a parting kiss, Tom raced back to GD and checked out an electric car. An hour and dozens of meandering side streets later, he entered no-man's-land of South Chicago. The worst of the worst lived here. Drug pushers, addicts, sexual deviants of all types, extortionists—mobsters that would have made Al Capone proud to call South Chicago home.

Tom had a plan to find this elusive fiend. He stopped near a small group of thugs standing on a street corner watching workers installing more of the MTES system. Watching, not helping. He walked up to the group, sizing up each one. The tallest man stepped in front of him.

"What yo want, dude? We donna like your kind."

"This your street?"

"Yeah, what of it?"

"Where can I find El Gato?"

The others stopped milling around and paid attention.

"None yo business."

"I'll count to three. Tell me where I can find El Gato or I shoot. One. Two. Three."

He pulled out a .44 and fired, killing one of the men standing beside their leader. He cocked the gun, ready for another shot.

"Ain't tell'en yo."

Bang. Another of his buddies dropped. The remaining ones turned and raced away. The leader would have, except Tom latched on to him.

"Last chance. Where can I find El Gato?"

For emphasis, he cocked the hammer with his other hand.

"Okay. Okay." He rattled off an address.

"Now yo's being sensible."

Tom back to his car and got inside, still holding his gun. Two others rushed out, blasting at him with their 9mm semi-automatics. Like the ignorant thugs that they were, they held the guns sideways and in one hand. While it looked impressive, their shots didn't even hit the car as Tom drove off.

Once away from them, he entered the address in the nav system and activated it. These automated cars still amazed him. It drove him to the address.

Tom reloaded and got out of the car. In contrast to the nearby buildings, this one looked well-maintained. He walked up to the door, but noticed others coming out of nearby buildings, curious about the car. He knocked.

"What yo want?" a man said.

"Came to see El Gato. Take me to him. Please."

"Yo got appointment?"

Tom pulled a .44 out and pointed it at the man.

"Take me to El Gato. Now."

"All right. All right, but yo's a dead man walking."

He walked into a room filled with fancy electronics. Games and monitors, the best money could buy—back when a dollar had value.

Two strippers were doing a lap dance beside El Gato, who fiddled with his game console control. Tom recognized him.

Bang! A .44 lead bullet smashed through El Gato's head. Tom pivoted and fired another round, killing the doorman. He left the screaming women. A crowd had formed by the time he got back to his car. He got in and headed off before they realized what had happened. Then a hail of bullets rained after his car. A lucky shot took out the rear window. Two other slugs cracked rear plastic panels.

Tom didn't relax until he reached State Street and 59th Street, officially out of the gang infested south side. Once back at GD, he offered to pay for the damages.

"I terminated El Gato and a couple other thugs, boss. Got a measure of justice for Major Callahan. Any idea where she's at?" Tom asked.

Chapter 16 A Twist

Rae sat beside the drugged Major Callahan. She checked the various tubes and fluid flows. Often, she wiped the woman's face. Once, when Liz partially regained consciousness, Rae followed the doctor's orders and let Liz try a sip of ice water. After one sip, the medication kicked in again.

When no one was looking, she stole a glance at her chart. Rae knew enough medical lingo to know the chart ordered giant breast implants inserted once the cup size had reached a J, the same giant size as hers, way too big. Her stomach knotted. This also meant they would likely order her to get that surgery, too. Worse, the morning nurse has measured Liz while changing bandages and drain tubes. She logged ten inches or a J cup size on the chart. Rae knew that soon they would haul the woman back into surgery to have her breasts doubled in size.

Worse, farther down on the chart, Rae saw they scheduled the woman to have her feet reformed. Translation: arch altered like Rae's so she could only wear very tall heels. While Rae enjoyed wearing such heels—she used to visit fetish nightclubs—she also used her arms on handrails and to keep her sometimes teetering balance. The Major no longer had them, and Rae presumed life would be even more horrid if Liz had her feet reformed.

Rae had to do something soon. She had to get out of South Chicago before Dr. Merryweather ordered her to get the massive breast implants. After that, they would surely give her to the Governor-mayor as one of his Honey Bunnies. I'd rather die than be that! I have to get away. But how? Where? How can I save the Major? She's still needs constant care from a hospital. I can't just walk her out of here.

When the evening nurses came on duty, she headed down to get supper. Everyone walked past her because her tall heels enforced tiny steps. Now if she wore a tight fitting latex dress, then that would have been acceptable. In a hospital, she felt out of place, despite wearing a nurse-in-training uniform. At least they hadn't yet forced her to cut her nails. She dreaded that day, but suspected it would come. As she clicked along the polished floor, her large bosom bounced. Annoyed with that, she sighed. At least they aren't like Miss Mounds. Hers are grotesque. I can't understand why anyone would want that. Mine and now the Major's are too big as it is.

"Ah, here you are," the voice of Dr. Merryweather startled her.

She looked up at his smiling face. Her stomach tensed.

"Just grabbing supper. I've been with her all day. She woke up once. Sort of. I gave her a sip like you said. It's educational for me to sit with her. I'm learning a lot. I know what signs to look for."

"Yes, yes, I'm sure you're doing a fine job. I came to tell you the wonderful news. You're being rewarded for all your services to the hospital. The new breast implants just came in. Report to surgery at nine tomorrow morning. I'll have you back watching over your patient before lunch."

Rae's heart sank. "But who'll watch over her while I'm gone? The nurses are busy. What if she wakes up again? She's helpless now. I should be there for her."

"Admirable qualities in a nurse, Miss Lin. I've left word for the morning nurses to check on her every fifteen minutes until you get back."

"Oh. Well, thank you. Guess that will work." Rae couldn't think of any other way to get out of this mess.

"Don't worry. There's nothing dangerous with this surgery. It'll take several weeks to grow your breasts to their

116

ideal, perfect size and shape, one you can be proud of. See you at nine."

Rae choked and sipped water. I'll look like a freak, anyway. Wait, maybe they won't get big right away. Oh, he didn't say the Major would get them tomorrow. That's something. What do I do? Do I dare complain? What'll happen if I say I don't want them? She had no answers and couldn't finish her supper.

She returned to her patient's room and sat beside her until the night shift came on duty. Heels clicking, she headed to her tiny bedroom in the basement. Room and board came with the offer to train as a nurse. Why did I ever accept it?

At nine and dressed in a hospital gown, Rae lay on the operating table, surrounded by three nurses.

Dr. Merryweather entered. "Ready to take your next step towards perfection?"

Rae whispered, "No."

He laughed. "Don't worry. The locals will deaden any pain. This won't take very long. We're inserting the uninflated forms. Once you've healed, then we can begin inflating them until you've reached your perfect size."

"They won't be bigger today?" Rae said.

"No, we won't be starting the inflation for two weeks. Even then, we do it slowly, giving them time to adjust and adapt."

The operation began. She felt pinpricks and coldness. Rae couldn't see what they were doing, but it felt rather like someone poking her insides a little. An hour later, the operation ended.

"You can get dressed now and check on your patient. Just don't shower for a day. If you see any swelling or experience any pain, then let a nurse know. The implants are perfectly placed. In a couple weeks we can begin the final process."

She mumbled a thank you and dressed. Heels clicking, she headed back to her patient's room. On the way, she had to pass by Dr. Merryweather's office. She heard loud talking. It didn't sound friendly. She slipped around to the back door and put her ear to the door.

"Yes, I'm telling you that GD's top assassin just murdered El Gato. In his home, even. Walked in and shot him. Just like that. Then killed others on his way out. Bebo's furious. Bebo is sending out word to everyone involved with the Major to be on the lookout for the assassin. He will surely kill everyone who's done anything to her. Doc, watch your back! This assassin is both bold and deadly. If he finds out you had anything to do with the Major, he'll walk in here and kill you, too. Bebo said he'll send men to guard your place. Do you want more security here at the hospital?"

"Oh, dear God. Yes, yes, more security. In his own home? Didn't he shoot back?"

"No, he was entertaining young women. He walked in, asked his name, and shot him. El Gato had no chance at all. It didn't last a minute, if those freaked out girls can tell time. Guard your back, doc."

With that, he left. Rae stood still for a minute, her mind racing. An idea formed. She tiptoed around to his main door and knocked.

"Doctor? Is everything all right? I heard that man's loud voice. Couldn't help it, but I didn't get it all. Something about an assassin coming after you. Lord knows why anyone would want a talented doctor killed. Something to do with my patient?"

The color had faded from his face. He looked worried to her. She played into it, hoping his good sense was on hold.

"Yes, the GD assassin killed a friend of mine. I've no idea what that has to do with me and the patient."

"Doctor, I've an idea. Probably a silly one. But my

118

patient needs to be in a hospital for days. Why not transfer her to a hospital closer to her home? I could go with her and continue to monitor her recovery. When she's released, I'll be back. I know. Silly idea."

"Oh, no! Miss Lin, that's a wonderful idea. Yes, let's make that happen. And you don't mind going with her? You're adding to your nurse's training."

"I'd feel bad if I didn't. She's at least seen me when she woke yesterday. It would be good for her to see a familiar face. That's what the handbook says."

"Excellent. Thank you. I'll see your loyalty is acknowledged and part of your record. You get back to your patient. I'll make arrangements and let you know. Oh, and make sure you pack a bag. Expect to be gone about a week. Don't worry. We won't be starting the inflation process for two weeks. Plenty of time."

Rae flashed a smile and left.

***

He listened as her telltale clicks faded. "Sometimes that girl shows uncommonly good sense. Shame she's destined to become another Honey Bunny. She might have made an excellent nurse if we hadn't transformed her body."

He looked at the giant Chicago map on his wall.

"She probably lives up north. Let's transfer her to the new Med Center in Uptown by Montrose Beach." He wrote out the transfer orders and the indicated medical treatment. He recommended she be kept drugged for at least a week, ensuring healing was well underway. Nurse-in-training Rae Lin would accompany her and stay with the patient until the patient was released from the hospital.

He looked the papers over and then had another thought. He changed the patient's name from Major Liz Callahan to Beth Swift. Then he entered the hospital's system and altered her name on all hospital records.

119

After sending the transfer orders through the system, he paid Miss Lin a visit. As expected, he found her sitting beside the semi-conscious Liz.

"It's official. Transfer will be at ten tonight. You'll need your bag packed by then. For security, your patient is now being called Beth Swift. We don't want anyone attacking her or you or the transfer unit on their way to Uptown Med Center. I'm worried the assassin might try to harm your patient. I'm doing my best to protect her. Since I'm here now, why don't you go fetch your bags?"

***

Rae wanted to jump for joy, but kept a sober face. "Okay, doctor. I'll hurry as much as I can. I'm terribly slow. Thanks for watching and protecting her."

She enjoyed her tiny jab with the heels, but thought better of complaining about breasts. Once in the basement and packing, she mumbled to herself.

"Why does he want her name changed? That doesn't make sense. The assassin went after El Gato, who kidnapped her. Why would the assassin want to kill her? Besides, she will be helpless when she wakes up. I don't get it."

As she made her slow way back, she had another thought. Perhaps he's trying to hide the fact that he performed the operation. The assassin might want to come after him when he learns what's happened to the Major. That makes sense. Sneaky bastard. All men are sneaky, underhanded beasts.

Right on time, orderlies arrived. With Rae walking beside them, they wheeled the bed out to the waiting transport vehicle, a large electric van. She sat beside her patient on the ride north. One attendant sat opposite her, monitoring the patient's vitals.

She'd never been in this Med Center and followed behind them. Room 1040. She memorized the number. Once

120

the orderlies left, she glanced at Major Callahan's chart. Dr. Merryweather must have replaced her chart while I was gone. It says Beth Swift now. I had better play along.

Nurses entered. One said, "Oh, you must be Rae Lin, the nurse-in-training. Welcome to Uptown Med. It's very kind of you to have come with your patient. I'm sure Beth will appreciate your help when she wakes." She glanced at the chart. "Needs another week. Okay. Monitor her until I get more help. Then we'll find you a place to sleep."

Later, they brought a portable bed in for Rae. By now, her feet throbbed. Though she longed for a shower, she followed the doctor's orders and didn't. But she massaged her feet. When she closed her eyes, she exhaled. Somehow, she'd made things work out. At least the operation today hadn't made her breasts larger. She slept soundly and didn't hear the night nurses checking on Beth Swift.

***

"But why, Pooche Dooche, are we going to the hospital?" Honey Bunny said. "Are you sick?"

Governor-mayor Bebo Ritzker said, "No, Honey Bunny. I need to visit the doctor."

She scratched her head with one of her long red claws. "But I'm not sick either. Oh, do slow down. I can't keep up."

Bebo glowered at her for an instant, but then smiled and slowed down. His six guards followed behind him, guns drawn.

Despite the role she played, she wasn't a dumb blond as everyone presumed. She could see he wasn't about to let his guard down, not like El Gato had. In her opinion, that man grown too overconfident.

Her feet and knees ached when they reached the hospital, but she kept her fake smile. She clung to Bebo's arm for balance. The distinctive odors struck her nose the moment the outer doors closed behind them, a distant reminder of what she'd endured.

It seemed to her they wandered endless corridors before stopping at the office of Dr. Merryweather.

"You wait here, Honey Bunny. I have to speak to the doctor."

He pried her arm off him and went inside, shutting the door. The guards milled around some distance away. She wanted to sit, but didn't see anywhere she could. She ambled along, turned a corner, and spied a bench close to another door that was opened a crack. She heard voices, including Bebo's, and paid close attention.

"Don't worry, Bebo. I've taken care of the threat. I've had El Gato's victim transferred to Uptown but under a different name. She's now Beth Swift. I changed our records here. If anyone snoops, there's never been a Major Callahan in this hospital. Shame, though. I had begun converting her into another Honey Bunny, but a kind of helpless one."

Bebo said, "Now that's brilliant thinking, doc. You've earned your pay on this one. Here."

While Honey Bunny wanted to see what Bebo gave the doctor, she dare not.

"Thanks. Pleasure doing business with you. Your new younger Honey Bunny is coming along nicely. But to keep up the pretense with her, I had her go with the Major."

"But—"

"Don't fret. I've installed the breast implants. We have to wait two weeks for that to heal before we begin inflating them. About a month before she's complete and ready to join you."

"Well, all right. Can't rush medicine. But what about the others? Didn't El Gato tell you to make me lots of Honey Bunnies?"

"He did. It's hard finding the right candidates. I have another one coming down home stretch as we racers say."

Bebo laughed. "You only *bet* on horse races."

"True. But this next one will be a surprise."

"Oh, I can't wait! Clue. Clue."

Honey Bunny imagined his gleeful look and wanted to slap him hard, but remained frozen in her seat. That she was being replaced shocked her, though not unexpected.

"No. You have to wait. Just be careful. I don't like how close the GD assassin got to us, Bebo. If he can get to El Gato—"

"Overconfidence killed that cat. I've got six guards watching over this hospital 24/7 and a dozen with me. No assassin will get to us."

"Just be careful, Bebo. Rumor has it this GD assassin is damned good, and he had close ties to the Major. She was their Intelligence Officer. Some say they were inseparable. Perhaps it was foolish to have gone after the Major."

"Yeah, but El Gato assured me she never knew what hit her. She never saw his face and was unconscious when he dropped her off here. If you did your job, she never woke up here or saw any of you. She can't tell them a thing about it. Besides, she'll be helpless for the rest of her life. That's sending the kind of message to these upstart corporation CEOs. I'm the Governor-mayor. I run Chicago. I run the state. Mess with Bebo and suffer for the rest of your life."

The doctor chuckled. "Well, she certainly will. We don't make a functional whole-arm prosthesis. They're cosmetic only. If she was my employee, and I got her back like this, I'd be spooked and very leery of crossing you."

"That's the point. With that idiot Snowden out of the way—she did an incredible job of getting rid of many things— now I can get on with setting up the Ritzker dynasty in Illinois. Maybe I can expand and add southern Wisconsin and western Indiana to my domain.

"You know, I should try to find out the identity of the

GD assassin and capture him. Turn him into an armless Honey Bunny. Is that possible?"

"Capturing an assassin? I wouldn't touch that one."

"No, I meant gender change."

"Oh, well, yes. It's the very latest in surgical methods. The Dem Socialists pushed hard for its development. Took priority over finding cancer cures. Seemed backward to me, though. Yes, I kept up my training. This hospital is equipped to deliver these latest surgical methods."

"Excellent, doc. Just think how wonderful this world would be if we filled it with Honey Bunnies. Heaven."

Unless you're the Honey Bunny! She glared at the door. *This gig is nearly up. Still, I can't complain. It's kept me alive these past four years.*

Chapter 17 Reality Strikes

"Well, find her or I'll pull all the Buffett funding out of this corporation!" Phil Buffett yelled at Tom and Art, before storming out, slamming the door behind him.

"He is her fiancé," Tom hinted.

"It's been two days now and not a single clue," GD CEO Art Townsend said. He ran his hands over his face.

Dave knocked. "I've just checked with every hospital and medical center in Chicago. None has any patient named Liz Callahan. No Callahan in any of them. I'm running out of ideas to chase."

"Maybe killing El Gato was a terrible idea," Tom said, his jaw sinking.

"No, don't blame yourself," Art said. "Dave had already proved that El Gato dropped her off somewhere. He has video proof she wasn't in the car when he got to his home. Besides, we both know you had no way to capture him. If you'd tried to put him in your car, his gang would have killed you. It's a miracle you got out of there alive as it was. No, we just have to use our brains."

Dave said, "Why would El Gato want to take the Major?"

Tom ran his fingers over his lower lip. "We're looking at this all wrong. El Gato is Governor-mayor Ritzker 's right-hand man. Could it be he ordered El Gato to snatch Liz?"

Dave said, "Why? Oh, wait. She helped stop that massive Antifa mob last year. She and her drone killed quite a few of them. Perhaps he wants revenge or something."

"Maybe he's sending us a message," Art said. "If so, it's not clear."

"Right. If she's the message where is she? You'd think her dead body would be on public display or something," Tom said.

Dave said, "On it. I never thought to check the morgues!"

He dashed out of Art's office. He later returned with a sober face.

"Nothing?" Art asked.

"Nope. Another dead end, but that's a good one. She's not dead. Maybe," Dave said, though his voice slumped.

"We'll find her, Dave," Tom said. "What else can we try?"

***

Sitting beside her patient, Rae had time to think. The Major's new doctor had come, studied her chart, and examined her shoulders. He said she was healing well and that there would be little scaring. He complimented her surgeon, which caused Rae to smile. She'd resisted the urge to ask him to remove the breast implants. No way to pay for it.

I've gotten us away from the mad doctor. Now what? No one knows her real name. Yet. When she wakes—oh, dear God, she'll freak out! Then what? She can tell them her name. Maybe someone will come for her, but what do I do? They'll send me back.

A new thought struck her. Perhaps she has someone looking for her. Maybe she's married. Wait, he said Intelligence Officer. I bet GD people are looking for her.

The more she dwelled on that thought, the more she sensed that had to be true. And if so, would GD people reward anyone who found the Major? She imagined herself in their place. I know I would do that. Besides, this might be my ticket out of the muck.

The fourth day since the abduction came. Once the doctor and nurses checked on the Major and left, Rae pulled

126

out her phone. Her long nails hesitated above the screen. She took a deep breath and acted.

"GD Reception Desk. How may I direct your call?"

"I want to speak to someone about your missing Major Callahan. I know where she is," Rae said, sounding far braver than she felt. *Here goes my nursing career, if there ever was going to be one.*

A man's voice said, "Hello? Information on Major Callahan?"

"Er, yes. I know what happen to her. I'm with her, sort of her private nurse. I—we need help. I have her rescued this far. Please help us."

"Miss, where are you? What's your name? Are you in immediate danger?" Art said.

"I got us transferred to Uptown Med Center, over by Montrose Beach. We're in Room 1040. They have her under the name Beth Swift so no one could find her."

"Stay there. I'll have a team there in minutes."

"Okay. I'm supposed to be her personal assistant nurse. I'll stay with her. Always, if I can."

She heard voices in the background. Some sounded relieved.

"Team is on their way. Be there in five minutes. Do you need me to stay on the phone with you?"

"No. We're safe right now. Room 1040. Oh, I'm Rae Lin, nurse-in-training. Bye."

She looked at her patient. "Help is on the way, Major. Don't worry. Rae will look after you." After a pause, she added, "I hope."

Rae looked at the clock. The hands crawled.

Two men with guns drawn rushed into the room, while six other stayed outside. All wore the blue uniforms with gold trim. GD Security Guards.

"Oh, dear God!" the shorter man said.

"Damn!" the taller said. He took charge. "Are you Rae Lin? We're from GD. Major Callahan is our Intelligence Officer. You are safe now."

"What did El Gato do to her?" Dave wailed. "She'll be crushed! Does she know?"

Rae said, "I'm Rae. I got us away from them and here. No, she doesn't know. They've kept her drugged up. I'm at her side all the time, looking after her. Twice she's sort of woke up enough to take a sip of ice water. She shouldn't drink much until long after they let her wake up. She'll be in shock for a time, then massive grief. Can you rescue us? Take us somewhere safe?"

"Yes, of course," Tom said. "From now on, we'll have half a dozen guards just outside your door. Dave, it's best to leave her here until the doctors think it's safe to let her wake up."

Dave sighed. "A nightmare. She'll wake to a never-ending nightmare!"

"It'll be a shock all right. Don't despair. Jenna does just fine. Likewise, the others at the tea garden. But she'll need our support for a long time."

"Oh, yes, sirs," Rae said. "She's in for a terrible shock. Sometimes they never do come out of it. But she'll need constant care. That's why I'm here. I'm supposed to look after her as a nurse-in-training."

Tom said, "Dave, why don't you head back and give Art a full report?"

"Can you do that? I want to stay with her."

The forlorn face melted Tom's resolve. "Okay, stay. I'll report back. Rae, can you tell us what happened to her? You said you rescued her?"

Hesitant, Rae began telling them her story. As she did, tenseness eased out of her body. The dam of pent-up emotions and thoughts burst, and she rattled.

She ended with, "That's how I got us rescued. But now I don't think there is such a position as nurse-in-training. They were just using me and were going to do the same with Major Callahan. You have to help us."

Tom said, "On behalf of everyone at GD, thank you Rae Lin for rescuing our beloved Major. Well done. You are with us now—in good hands. I must report to our CEO."

"What's going on here? Who are you? What's with all the guns?" a man in white stood in the doorway.

Rae said, "He's her new doctor."

"Tom Durbin from GD. This is one of our top people. Her name is Major Liz Callahan, not the phony name they gave you. What is her medical condition? How soon can she be moved?"

"What? Her chart says Beth Swift. Accident victim."

Dave blurted, "She was kidnapped and mutilated with a scalpel! She's our top Intelligence Office."

"Okay. Okay. Nurse, get someone to change this patient's name. Well, I'm not allowed to give out patient information to non-family members."

Tom glared. "Do you want me to bring GD CEO Art Townsend down here with a SWAT team? What's her condition? How soon can we get her to safety?"

"I am legally obligated to say that, but with no more legal courts I don't know why. She's undergone surgery to remove her arms. An accident, her chart says. Beth, er, Liz, is healing very well. Should be no permanent scaring. Whoever did the surgery did a masterful job. As far as keeping her comatose, I'm not all for that. We followed the transfer chart's suggestions to keep her doped up for a week.

"If she were my patient, I'd bring her out of it now. Be prepared for a shock. Best get that over with as soon as possible. Then she can heal. She should be here at least a week until we remove the drain tubes. You could move her now, but

I'd like her to be under my care for the time being."

"Okay. We'll abide by your expertise. But bring her around as soon as possible. We need to talk to her and find out what happened," Tom said.

"You haven't been around trauma victims much, have you? Well, you might not get much out of her. Because of the accident and the system shock of what's happened to her body—those often cause short term memory losses."

He glanced at the wall clock. "I'll have her conscious around noon. Is Miss Lin going to be staying with her?"

Rae spoke before anyone could. "Yes. I'm supposed to be with her. Always. She'll be helpless and needs me."

"Okay. Except Rae, the rest of you leave while we do our work," the doctor said.

Dave and the guards stayed while Tom returned to GD, but promised Dave he'd be back before she awoke.

Rae watched the doctor closely, but he noticed her.

"Yes, we can use lighter bandages, Rae. Isn't that what you're thinking?"

Rae flushed. "Yes, doctor. That'll make it easier to handle her needs. When she wakes up, I mean. She'll be helpless."

"She must adapt to using her feet. I don't see any drainage this time. I believe it's safe to remove the tubes. Less to get in the way. Yes, nurse, remove the morphine drip. She's not likely to experience much pain. Dull throb in her shoulders at most. We'll need a vomit pan. Yes, change the catheter bag. I don't want her walking today. If she relaxes, then we'll remove it in the morning."

Rae spoke up. "Is that because shock might cause her to faint while walking to the toilet?"

"Exactly, Miss Lin. She'll have balance problems for some time. And she'll try to use her arms. It's an instinctive reaction. Keep a steadying arm around her. We'll begin

130

physical therapy tomorrow, if she calms down. I don't want to release her until she's able to move around without falling. That's what we must watch now. Without arms to break her fall, she could hit her head hard enough to kill herself. And we don't want that, do we? Her recovery depends on getting nourishing solid food in her. She'll be weak when she wakes. Woozy. Maybe dizzy when she tries to get up. Today, we let her recover from the intense shock. With luck, she'll keep ice water down. If so, solids for supper. Small amounts in case shock upsets her stomach. She should be released in a week, could be sooner depending on how she reacts."

"Okay, we're done here. Rae, you're in charge of her. Press the Call button when she wakes up, though I suspect we'll all know when that happens."

He left and Dave returned. "I heard all that. She's gotta be okay, Rae. She's just got to be. I can never thank you enough for what you've done for her."

Together they waited in silence. Tom joined them. Later, Art dropped by, pulling up a chair by the three. As the doctor predicted, Major Callahan regained consciousness near noon.

Her eyes flickered. She tried to sit up, looked down at her empty shoulders, and screamed as loud as she could.

Chapter 18 Recovery

For a moment, Liz couldn't grasp what her eyes sent her. No arms. Gone. Vanished. But they were just there a moment ago when she rode the MTES. Bandages, the odor of the room, the hospital gown. Her mind finally registered. She screamed louder than she'd ever yelled before. She gasped and screamed again. And again. If I scream enough, I'll wake up from this nightmare. Scream, Liz. Wake up!

I feel weak. My throat. Sandpaper. Water. Oh, God. I can't hold the cup.

She screamed again, though not as loud. Rae responded first, figuring Liz needed a sip. She moved the cup and straw towards Liz's mouth, her long red nails visible.

Her. I've seen her before. Somewhere. Fuzzy. Water. Water. Oh, God. I'm helpless.

"One sip only," Rae said.

I need a gallon. She's only letting me have one sip. Bitch. Oh, Dave, Tom, Art. Who are those others running into the room? Her next scream died in her throat.

"Hello, Major Liz Callahan. I'm Doctor Blythe. You're safe now. In Uptown Med Center. You've had quite a shock."

This doctor was alert. He saw the convulsion beginning and brought the vomit pan up with one hand while raising her up with the other. Liz vomited gunk.

"Good going. Now, Rae, let her have one sip of the ice water. Liz, you can have more as soon as it stays down," the doctor said.

"More. Sandpaper. What happened to me? I'm helpless. My life's ruined!"

This time Rae spotted the convulsion beginning and

hastily brought the pan back just in time. Then she wiped off the woman's face. "It'll be all right. I won't leave you."

Liz just sat there on the bed. Her eyes looked at Rae, then Dave, Tom, before resting on Art. She whispered, "What happened to me? I've seen her before. Vaguely. Long red nails. What happened?"

"That's what we were hoping you could tell us, Major," Art said. "Take your time."

"I remember walking. MTES. Yes, heading to work. Something stung my neck. Next memory is waking up now. My life's gone! What happened to me?"

Tom sighed, while Rae let her have another sip of ice water.

He said, "As best we can tell—thanks to Dave who was relentless in the search—El Gato kidnapped you. We think he shot out the surveillance cameras in a three-block section the night before. He had an electric car parked in the middle. We found a discarded thorn with a drug and blood on its tip. The DNA proved to be yours. Dave found the circuitous route El Gato took, but we never found where he dropped you off. Must have been that Med Center where Rae worked.

"When I found out El Gato took you, I went into the heart of South Chicago and terminated that monster. But it's Rae who saved you. You should tell her what you did," Tom said.

After giving Liz another sip, Rae related her tale, explaining how she'd overheard them talking and got the idea.

"It was easy to plant the idea of transferring us here."

That she now had as large a bosom as Rae didn't register in Liz's mind. Yet.

Rae finished up, "I stopped them from making your breasts gigantic and crippling your feet like mine are. That's something, at least."

The doctor said, "Okay. I think that's enough talking for

one day. Let's let Liz get some rest and her strength back. She's on the road to recovery."

Liz yelled. "Recovery? I'll never recover from this. My life's ruined! They'll never let me immigrate to Brussels. I'm helpless. I can't do anything anymore. I'm useless."

Liz broke down. Though she tried to suppress it since Art was here, her grief exploded. Liz cried, sobbing harder than she ever thought possible.

The men left, though Dave insisted on sticking around.

Rae dabbed her cheeks often and allowed Liz to cry. She knew it was useless to say anything to Liz. No words could comfort her or give her arms back. Words couldn't make it okay. Rae also knew grief recovery went in stages, the first being grief over the massive loss. Now and then, she held the straw up to the woman's lips. Without thinking or breaking her sobs, Liz sipped and continued to wail.

In time, her sobbing yielded to sniffles. Rae held a tissue to her nose, then another and another, before offering more water. At last, Liz stopped crying.

"I'm ruined. My life's destroyed. I've nothing left. I'm helpless. I can't do anything for myself. I gotta pee, and I can't even do that anymore."

"That's why I'm here," Rae said. "Up you go. I got my arm around you."

"I'm weak. I can't keep my balance. Rae, don't let go! Oh, God. I feel sick again."

"Sit. There you go. We made it."

Rae helped Liz sit on the toilet. Liz stopped shaking. Muscle tensions eased.

"Gown's come loose. Take it off," Liz said. "I want to see what's left of me. Lord, what did they do to my breasts? They're gigantic."

Rae chuckled. "Same size as mine. You'll need a J cup bra, assuming we can find a store that has them. But you should see Honey Bunny's. They dwarf ours. That's what they wanted to do to both of us. Make ours like Honey Bunny's monsters. I've no idea why. Makes no sense. We're not porn stars. The doc even inserted new implants in mine. I got us away before he started inflating them."

"Can I sit here a while? Sip?"

She took several sips.

"My life's ruined. Gone. Over. Why didn't he just kill me? That'd be better than this—this helplessness." She began crying again.

Rae spotted a nurse bringing in a food tray.

"Let's get you back to the bed. They've brought you something to eat. Probably not steak or anything. At least they have food in here. Last year, I had nothing at all. That's when they recruited me to become a nurse-in-training, but that must have been a lie, too,"

She eased Liz back to the bed.

"All soft stuff. Wonder if the broth tastes good," Rae said, offering a sip to her patient.

A half hour later, Liz ate about half, but felt exhausted. Rae tucked her in and watched her fall asleep almost at once.

The next morning, Rae helped Liz use the bathroom and fed her breakfast. This time, scrambled eggs but no toast.

"Coffee!" Liz said. "Gotta have coffee."

The doctor paid a visit. "Eating solid food. It's staying down. Excellent progress, Miss Callahan. Keep this up, and we'll be releasing you in a couple days. Need a bowel movement and no more bandages first. Rae, make her walk around the hall today, but don't overdo it. I'll check on you this evening."

After he left, Liz said, "I feel a bit stronger today. Not as dizzy. What's the point? I can't live like this. Helpless with everything." Again, she began crying, softly this time.

Around ten, visitors arrived. Dave and Tom brought her

fiancé, Phil, to see her.

"Knock. Knock," Tom said. "Phil's here. He's been worried about you. Hounded us every day until we found you."

He wore an expensive grey suit and red tie. "Liz? God damn it. It's true, then. You've lost your arms. You're helpless now. So much for immigrating to Brussels."

Tears flooded down her cheeks, but he continued. "Since I still want my chance to immigrate, our wedding is off. I'll find another woman to marry who'll give me that opportunity. No hard feelings, Liz. You understand. You can't do anything for yourself any longer. See you around—maybe."

With that, he walked out of the room and her life. Liz sobbed while Rae dabbed her cheeks.

"What a louse!" Dave said. "Heartless bastard. I brought you a vase of flowers to bring a touch of sunshine into your stark room. Hope you like sunflowers."

Liz looked at them. Her crying lessened.

Tom said, "I've some news. I've talked this over with Jenna. She insists Liz moves in with us for the time being. She wants to help you learn how to do everything with your feet. It's not the end of the world—just a very different, new beginning. Her words. Whenever they let you out of here, we'll stop by your place, pick up things, and move you into my place. Oh, Rae, you're invited. Jenna's about to have our first child. Just a few more weeks. Another pair of hands is most welcome. CEO Art Townsend is recommending you take a fully paid position with GD. Personal assistant. Your pay starts at three thousand Galactic credits per month."

Rae's eyes bulged. "Really? I can work for GD? Real pay? Credits that are worth something? Wow! Oh, wow! Liz, I told you things would work out. Thank you all. I can't believe it."

Liz said, "Why are we even bothering with me? I've lost everything I ever wanted. I'm helpless now. Brussels, gone.

Fiancé, gone. Job, gone. I wish I was dead." She began crying again.

Rae noticed how dejected Dave looked. Even Tom appeared dumbstruck with her reaction to the news. She motioned them to step outside.

"Guys, she doesn't mean stuff right now. I've studied grief and loss a bit in my nurse training. There's a cycle she has to work through. We need to let her work through the many stages. Upwards, that is. It's possible she could go into apathy and wait for death to come, but I won't let that happen. Give her time. She'll rise to anger. That will be an excellent step. Just keep on being here for her. Your wife hasn't arms, too?"

Tom smiled. "Yes, born without them. We have friends who lost their arms or hands or legs. They run their own shop. The Amp Tea garden. Jenna and I go there often. If anyone can help Liz learn to be independent again, it's Jenna. Thank you for caring for Liz."

Rae smiled and returned to her patient's side.

"We'll stop by your place, Rae, and let you pick up your things, too," Tom said.

"Everything I own is in my pack there."

"Huh?"

"Been living out of the basement of a hospital. Free meals and lodging while I tried to help the patients."

"Don't you have family somewhere?" he asked.

"No. I detest men. Dad beat Mom until she died. The police killed Dad, and I ran away. Had to find a way to survive this past year. No, all I have is right here. But with this new real money, maybe I can buy some things. Now, guys, you best leave us. I'm supposed to get Liz up and walking, if you ever want her out of here. She's supposed to get physical therapy, but Jenna's help will be better."

The next morning, Dave brought fresh flowers for Liz. He had stopped by her place and picked up a change of clothes, assisted by Art's secretary.

"Morning. Flowers and clothes," he said as he arrived.

"Top won't fit her, but we'll make do. She needs them," Rae said.

"Did she do enough walking yesterday?"

Rae glared at him. But since he brought clothes, she sighed. "Well, yes. Doctor thinks she can be released tomorrow, as long as she's staying with Jenna who can show her how to do things. You best go so I can get her dressed."

"Okay. I'll be back this afternoon to see how she's doing."

He can't miss seeing how red Liz's eyes were, Rae thought.

While Liz had a few dresses, most of her apparel consisted of GD uniform issues. And that's what he'd brought. The top didn't fit her enlarged bosom. Rae checked the bra. It's C cup wouldn't do. She rummaged through her pack and brought out her spare.

"Yeah, you'll need new bras. My J cup mostly fits."

That brought on a fresh round of sobs, which Rae ignored. She decided putting one of her own tops on Liz would clash with her pants and shoes. Using a bit of ingenuity, she made the uniform top work by using a shoestring to fasten the top halves together. She loosely tied the shoelaces, knotting them.

"There, you can slip them off to use your feet when you have to."

Liz cried again. "I can't do anything with them. Why don't they just terminate me? I can't live this way."

Once the sobbing died down, Rae made her do more walking.

The following morning, Dave and Tom arrived early, ready to help take Liz home. Rae had her dressed.

She said, "We're just waiting on the doctor. I know.

138

Looks like her bosom is bursting out of the top. But that looks better than wearing one of mine that clashes with the rest of the uniform. She'll need new clothes."

The doctor walked in, accompanied by a nurse with a wheel chair.

After checking her over, he said, "It's been a pleasure monitoring your recovery, Miss Callahan. I'm releasing you, but I want to see you for a checkup in six weeks. Isn't it incredible how far modern surgery has come? Our tech has more than doubled healing time. A decade ago, you would have been bedridden for a month to be as healed as you are now after about a week. Heck, even gender transformations are a snap these days.

"Rae, watch her. If you see any signs of bleeding around her shoulders, get her back here as fast as possible. Otherwise, Miss Callahan has no restrictions. Just make sure she gets physical therapy and learns to adapt as best she can."

"Can't you just terminate me?" Liz blurted out. "I can't live like this."

"In time, those feelings will pass. Now let's get you checked out. I'm sure your friends want to take you home."

Minutes later, Rae helped Liz rise from the wheelchair. While the men carried Rae's pack and a few toiletries for Liz, Rae kept a steadying arm around her charge. They stepped onto the MTES.

They'd gone a block when Rae, Dave, and Tom noticed Liz's legs. The initial little shaking escalated into very visible trembling.

"I have to sit!" Liz cried. "I'm terrified! I can't take this. Oh, God!"

Her bleached face said much as they found a resting chair by the MTES at the corner. Her legs bounced around out of control. Her eyes darted about in a wild pattern, focusing on nothing.

Dave turned white. "What's happening to her?"

Tom said, "Terror. I've seen that before. Can happen to soldiers. Stark terror. It'll pass. Liz, take deeper breaths."

The leg vibrations died down, and a little color returned to her face.

"I've never been so scared. Terror. I don't show emotion," Liz said. "Never. I can't show it. But I am. My legs almost gave out. This can't be happening to me," she wailed. "There's no hope left. None at all. There'll never, ever be any hope for me. Not ever."

Dave gushed, "Liz, don't say that. I'm here. I'll always be here for you. So will Rae and Tom. Jenna will show you everything. You just need time."

Rae said, "She's in despair, Dave. It's part of healing. She's not even hearing you now. Let's get her home."

She nudged Liz up. They stepped back on the escalator.

"God, I'm scared. I've never feared anything in my life. Nothing. But now I'm afraid of the MTES. I can't stop myself from falling. My stomach is in a knot."

Rae said, "I bet that's a natural response."

"I keep trying to use my arms. Keep my balance. But I can't. Don't let go of me. I'm scared. What's happening to me? I've never been afraid of anything. The guys—they're looking at me. Think I've gone psycho or something."

"You're doing fine. Watch your step here."

"South Chicago. Full of thugs. We should just terminate them all. The bastards. I hate them. Hate them all. If I could ever fly my drones again, I'd fly in there and kill every last one of them!"

Tom saw how angry she'd become. "I killed the guy who abducted you and ordered them to mutilate your body. El Gato is very dead."

"Well, I want to kill all of them. There's not a good person in all South Chicago! Not a damned one!"

Rae said, "Well, I was from there. But I agree. They're all a bunch of filthy beasts."

Liz sighed. "My shoulders throb. A little. Is that normal? I keep feeling my arms, too."

"Phantom limbs," Rae said. "I heard that's a common thing."

"Well, it shouldn't ought to be. Damn it. It's hard enough trying to cope without always feeling as if they're still there. Where are we going?"

Tom said, "To our apartment. Jenna's waiting for us. She'll help you learn new ways. Dave and I—we're glad you are alive. We thought you were dead."

Liz yawned. "Well, might have been better if I was. What kind of a life can I have? A boring one, I suppose. Just sitting around all day."

Dave said, "But we want you back at GD as our Chief Investigation Officer. We need you."

"Don't think that's gonna happen, Dave," she said.

Chapter 19 Learning

Rae's first comment upon meeting Jenna spoke volumes. "Gosh, you are *very* pregnant!"

Jenna laughed. "I spend all my time on the potty these days. Welcome, Liz. I'm sorry this happened to you, but I promise I'll teach you everything I know. I'm making a collection of videos I found on the Internet of how others like us do normal things."

Once settled in, Jenna explained to Rae, Liz, and Dave, who refused to leave, "You'll get frustrated a lot. I still do. Carrying things is problematical. And getting dressed is the hardest thing to do. Just remember, we take many times longer to do something than those with arms do."

Jenna had Tom dump a sack of pinto beans on the floor and set a bowl beside them.

"We have to build up strength and dexterity with toes in order for you to handle silverware. Pick up each bean and put them in the bowl," Jenna said. "Expect to be frustrated, Liz. There's no way around that annoying emotion. I have it every day. Feeding yourself is where we're starting."

Seeing Dave fighting his urge to help Liz, Jenna added, "And no helping her. She's got to learn how to do most everything all over again like she was a baby. The sooner she does, the sooner she'll get her self-respect back. Rae, you can give me a hand making lunch. I must start at least an hour before we want to eat."

***

Liz struggled to pick up a bean with her toes. She clenched her teeth. I must do this. Don't show emotion. Don't start now. This is impossible.

142

"Dave, promise me one thing," Liz whispered.

"Sure."

"If I can't learn to do stuff, promise me you'll shoot me. One clean shot to my head. Promise me you'll do that."

Dave grimaced. "I love you. I can't do that. Besides, I know you can learn to do everything. Jenna does everything. It's gonna take time. Lots of time. You can do it. You just got a bean in the pot."

Liz glared at him. "*One* bean. How many minutes did that take?"

Jenna must have overheard her. She said, "Liz, ignore time. Forget how long anything took. Time doesn't matter. Focus only on the fact that you did it. That is the only thing that's important. If you can hold a teacup, I have some women I want you to meet."

"Phillis?" Tom spoke up.

She nodded. "Phillis lost her arms just over a year ago. You can see how much progress she's made, but only when you can hold a cup and sip."

***

A few nights later, the group walked the short distance to the Amp Tea Gardens. The eyes of Rae, Liz, and Dave opened wide in disbelief.

From Irene's hooks to the empty shoulders of Phillis to the peg leg of Patsy, the three gaped until Jenna whispered it wasn't polite to stare.

Phillis walked up to take their orders, but Jenna introduced her to Liz and then the others.

"Liz just lost her arms over a week ago. Any tips for her?" Jenna asked.

Phillis grinned. "Yeah. Practice. Practice. Practice. Don't give up. We can't afford that luxury. I still can't get into the dress on my own. I need Irene and her hooks to zip me up. We all work on getting Irene's hooks on her each morning.

Team effort. You're in good feet with Jenna. She was born like this and is a pro at doing everything. It's been over a year for me, and I still can't do half the things Jenna can and that I must learn how to do. What I hate most is people staring at me and giving me their gooey sympathy."

Rae listened to Phillis and tried not to stare. Once Phillis submitted the orders, she returned to talk to Rae.

Phillis said, "You look absolutely amazing. Love those heels. I used to wear some like that. Before that man wiped out my arms. Damn men everywhere. Every Friday night, I'd dance away at the Fetish Night Club."

"Wow. You must have been stunning in a tight latex outfit and heels. I used to go there too—that is, before the big crash. That's when Dad beat Mom to death and the cops shot Dad."

"Golly, you've a story too. Got time to chat more? I just take people's orders. Can't carry them. Ah, best let Patsy serve them first."

Phillis nearly laughed at how Rae, Liz, and Dave tried hard not to appear to be staring at the one-armed, one-legged Patsy and her peg leg. After Patsy left, and while the others nibbled on their muffins, she chatted with Rae.

"Yeah, I have this sleek black latex gown that showed my every curve and matching six-inch Oxfords." She sighed. "Can't wear them anymore. No way to put them on. Gosh, I love your nails too. You're the most gorgeous woman I've ever met."

"That's a damn shame you can't dress up fetish once in a while and go out for some fun. Guess life's gotten awful serious for both of us." She relayed what happened to her after she ran away and got entangled with Dr. Merryweather.

Phillis grinned. "Well, I find them very sexy. I always wished mine were bigger. Come over sometime. I can show you what I used to wear. What happened to your fetish outfits?"

Rae sighed. "Lost them when I ran away. I just got hired by GD to help Liz. I have real money now. These are Galactic credits. If only stores opened up again. Hope they do. Cause we're desperate for things Liz can wear. Here. Let's trade phone numbers."

Phillis sat down on the floor and pulled hers out of a dress pocket.

"Hey, you're good," Rae said, bringing a smile to the armless woman's face.

"Some things. Not all. Much to learn. Sometimes, I get incredibly frustrated. Want to be friends?"

"You bet. Maybe even more," Rae hinted.

"I'd love that," Phillis said, displaying a giant grin. "Oh, another customer. Back when I can." She winked at Rae, who winked back.

Liz got her teacup to her lips for a sip. She sighed. "Guess my life has been forever changed."

"It'll be different," Jenna said. "But I've never let our handicap stop me. It's been my observation that everyone needs assistance with something. It's just our needs differ greatly from those of Dave, Tom, and Rae. Or even Patsy or the cooks. Irene's darn handy with her hooks. She can carry things that I can't. But she needs help getting them on and off her stumps, which we don't. Tom can barely cook us a TV dinner. I do most of the cooking. I can't carry heavy things, but Tom can. Get comfortable needing assistance with different things than you've been used to needing."

Liz flashed a fleeting smile. "Get used to my life being changed forever."

Rae butted in. "Well, that's the honest answer. Only a fool would claim nothing's changed. It obviously has. Phillis says it's taking her a long time to learn how to do what she used to do. She's making progress and isn't looking back. She's one heck of a person. I really like her. We've a lot in common."

Later while walking home, Liz said, "Damn scary being out here like this. I feel helpless. But I enjoyed meeting those brave women. Will we do this more often?"

Jenna laughed. "Tom and I spent nearly every night there until I became a blimp. While they appear optimistic, Chicago winters are very hard on us, particularly those missing a leg. Peg legs and snow make an awful combination while it's hard for us to don heavy parkas. I switched to a heavy cloak because it's easier for me to swing over my shoulders."

"It's even trickier in the snow in these heels," Rae said. "I'm seeing what you mean, Jenna. Each of us needs help with different things. Liz, I can't navigate snow covered sidewalks without someone's arm steadying me. Isn't that interesting?"

Interested is how Liz felt during the next few weeks. One by one, she viewed all the videos Jenna had downloaded for her. When Jenna went into labor, Liz found she could pick up the pinto beans without too much frustration. But she couldn't imagine dealing with giving birth like Jenna was. Tom whisked her off to the Med Center and called hours later with the news that Samuel Arthur Durbin had joined the family.

When the three returned home, like a pair of hawks, Rae and Liz observed Jenna to see how she managed caring for a baby. Tom put one changing pad on the floor and the other on a counter, a pile of clean diapers by each. This brand had Velcro fasteners, which Jenna could handle. Both women stared in amazement as they watched Jenna struggle to get Sam into a nursing position, by making a cradle from one bent leg.

Jenna said, "Gosh, so many new things to figure out how to do. You're not alone, Liz. I can't believe it. I never dreamed I'd ever be a mother." Her eyes watered, and Tom dabbed the eyes of the proud mother.

***

As things settled down, Rae spent every midday and early afternoon at Phillis's apartment, which she shared with the others. Often the pair slipped into Phillis's bedroom, sat on the bed, and talked.

Rae admired Phillis's fetish outfits. "Why can't you wear these fabulous heels?"

"Balance. Way too hard for me to keep my balance in them. Besides, how do I get them on? I can't ask Irene for help. Her hooks have their limitations."

Rae giggled. "Maybe one day we can play dress up. I'll help you get into your outfit and heels. I'd love to see how you look in it. Smashing, I'll bet. Super sexy."

Phillis flushed. "That would be fabulous. Some days, I sit here on the bed and stare at the gowns, remembering all the fun and feelings I used to have wearing them. But we're about the same size. Perhaps you could squeeze into the blue one. I'd love to see what your breasts look like. Mine are pitifully small."

"I'd love that, too." Rae leaned over and kissed Phillis, who pushed into Rae, returning the passion as best she could.

A tear formed. "What's wrong?"

Phillis said, "I can't hold you. I want to hold and squeeze you tight."

"Well, let me do that for us. You're fantastic as you are. We'll figure something out. You could be Miss Galaxy."

Phillis laughed. "Now I know you're high as a kite."

"High on you."

Rae winked as she countered. That led to more kisses and later, passionate lovemaking.

Thus, as autumn approached, many lives had improved.

Chapter 20 Interlude

Jenna and Tom encouraged the relationship between Rae and Phillis. Both could see good reasons that match would work. Dave spent untold hours with Liz, giving her constant praise and encouragement, along with the weekly flower bouquet. Jenna and Tom felt certain Dave was in love with Liz. Tom had seen it back when she was engaged to Phil. As winter came, they watched Liz focus harder than ever on learning how to do things with her feet.

"Doesn't she ever smile?" Jenna asked one chilly November night.

Tom chuckled. "Stone-faced Liz. She just doesn't like to show emotions. Been that way since I first met her. Whereas Dave wears his heart on his shirtsleeve. Give her time."

When the snows came, Rae and Phillis surprised Liz. Phillis dropped by each evening to help Rae in her tall heels navigate to the tea garden without slipping and falling. Then a half hour later, the others headed over for their nightly tea and chats with Dave keeping a steadying arm around Liz who still felt vulnerable when outside. Jenna pushed the baby stroller, while Tom lugged the bags of baby necessities.

***

Liz continued to see Jenna as a role model, secretly hoping to get as good as she was.

Over tea, Liz said, "Guys, bring me up to speed on the latest news. I miss my wall of monitors."

Dave said, "We finished vetting the mountain of law enforcement personnel. The ones that signed on when the gun confiscation fiasco began. Been manning up the other new Galactic corporations like Galactic Medicine, Galactic

148

University, Galactic Housing, Galactic Entertainment, Galactic Supplies, Galactic Manufacturing, Galactic Transport, Galactic University, Galactic Mining, and Galactic Agriculture. Several smaller ones are starting up too."

Tom said, "Galactic Entertainment or GEnt will be on the air next week. Everything from old movies and TV to the latest news. And we're seeing more stores reopening."

"'Bout time. I'm desperate for clothes that fit," Liz said. "What good are credits if there's nothing to buy."

"Watch GEnt." Dave said, "They'll be displaying a list of open stores. But grocery stores are a thing of the past. The food distribution centers have taken over. Gent will have an online order system set up next week. You make your order and it's delivered in a half hour. That's their new motto. No more walking to distribution centers and getting mugged on your way home with the goodies."

"Does that mean they're putting ordinary people of Chicago back to work for a corporation?" Liz asked.

"Sort of," Tom said. "We put each person who applies into the vetting queue. That's what Dave and I've been doing these past weeks. When they sign up, we take their picture, and Dave and I spend hours scouring their Social Media sites, searching Web records, police files, and news sources. Art's given us specific criteria to look for."

"Like what? Sort out the criminals?" she asked.

"It's much bigger than that. Those who were very vocal and active in supporting the Dem Socialist takeover are being rejected. Put into the Undesirable category. Turns out they're mostly the brainwashed youth."

"What happens to them?" Liz asked.

"They're the 'I'm entitled to free'—fill in the blank generation," Dave said. "CEO Wang Chan of GPan refuses to allow them to immigrate anywhere. If they want to work, two corporations might offer them employment. Namely Galactic

149

Agriculture and Galactic Housing-Maintenance division— glorified janitors. Wang said if they prove themselves there, they may reapply with other corporations."

"No one is accepting criminals," Tom added. "What's interesting are those Wang is pulling aside for future immigration to Brussels and Pylon. My Dad's been chosen. It's not an age thing. He's in training to run the initial supply shops and will be among the first immigrants to Brussels."

"Whoa! Congratulations!" Liz said. "Oh, wait. What about you?"

Tom chuckled. "I've no wish to immigrate anywhere. This young woman has captured my heart. And I've already sold my soul to GD."

"Hey," Liz said, "all those you've had to kill—they were evil. Destroying people's lives."

"Yes, but I still have to do whatever GD orders me to do. Anyway, those who are chosen to immigrate have to be physically fit and have specific skills they're looking for. Liz, I can't imagine landing on a new world that has no trace of civilization on it. No towns, no farming, no utilities, no nothing. Now that's scary."

Dave changed the subject. "Galactic University is overhauling all the colleges in the world. They dismissed all those professors who brainwashed students into believing capitalism was evil and socialism was the answer. "That was more than half. Now they're hiring others who've shown an ability to both teach and produce products. Those like you, Liz, who can actually do the work that they're there to teach."

"Used to, Dave," Liz corrected him. "Can't do much of anything now. Past tense."

"Not for much longer," Dave insisted. "You're getting better every day. Art says you're welcome back as soon as you're able."

"You're dreaming."

150

Tom said, "They're looking for good teachers for K-12, too. Galactic University is restructuring education worldwide."

"Are the corporations installing the US constitution?" Liz asked. "Freedom to speak your mind, carry a gun, confront your accusers—things Snowden outlawed?"

"Er, no. Democracy is a thing of the past. Corporations rule. What they say happens. What they ask you to do, you do, or face expulsion or termination," Tom said. "If people do their jobs, they are paid living wages and have a place to live in safety. We've traded our former freedoms for a potential comfortable survival. That's how I see it," Tom said.

Dave said, "But isn't that what most people want now? After these disastrous years? People want life to return to normal, whatever that might be."

"Yeah," Tom said. "Kelly and I used to worry about how we could make meals from a sack of flower. That's all we had to eat one week. Barest survival turned people into animals. Dave's right. People we've seen just want to have a comfortable survival right now. That might change in a few years."

Dave added, "Right now, the corporations are treating people with respect. Well, those that deserve it. They're trying to bring order back into the chaotic mess after the global economic and political collapse."

Liz said, "It wasn't exactly working everywhere when I was there."

Dave signed. "No, you're right. The Mideast, Southeast Asia, and Africa are in the worst shape, though South America isn't far behind. Overpopulation. Before the crash, Earth had more people than it could feed and house. Now it's getting worse in some places."

"Hey, it isn't all doom and gloom, Dave," Tom said. "I talked to a climatologist yesterday. He's applying for a position with Galactic University. According to him, global warming has slowed and appears to be reversing. Water levels are going down. Slow process, but it's happening. He says more ice is building up at the poles."

Liz cracked a brief smile. "Turning off all combustible engines worldwide will do that."

Tom laughed. "Yeah, no gas. No cars, trucks, planes. No pollution."

"No fun," Dave added. "I used to have this Mustang. Really hot car. Had to swap it for food a year ago. Ah, well."

Tom laughed. "Traded for these pathetic electric computer-controlled idiot cars. Some step down."

"Hey, they're self-driving. Don't knock it," Dave teased and then sighed. "If I got it back now, there's almost no place to drive it. Unless I want to go out West."

"Liz, do you think immigration to Brussels will solve the overpopulation mess?" Tom asked. "That's been bothering me."

Liz sighed, fighting back a tear. My chance vanished with my arms. "No way it will solve overpopulation. Spaceships take a year to travel the ten light years to Brussels. Assuming they can fit a thousand people on a ship, they'd need one thousand of those giant ships to move a million people. Overpopulation is in the billions. We need monster-sized ships or faster travel."

Jenna, who had been quietly absorbing the news, said, "The ion engines can't be speeded up significantly. Faster travel isn't likely. And there's a limit on the size a spaceship can be and stay structurally sound. Maybe technology will change."

***

Tom knew she'd invented the ion engines and thus knew what she was talking about. New tech had to be the long-term answer. The two had discussed this before. Ideas about hyperspace continued to be just beyond his conscious reach. But he believed the answer lay in topology. Dave's comment jarred him back to the present.

Dave said, "Oh, I heard those new flying boxes, the Electro-Magnetic Air Cars or EMACs as we're calling them, are gonna be the vehicle of the future. Galactic Transportation has just made a deal with the Cartwright corporation inventor to mass-produce them. Galactic Transport expects these green machines will replace all other vehicles. They are silent and fly. No roads needed, which is good since MTES is covering up the streets."

"He's right," Tom said. "Art told us GD will get six of them in January. Travel around the country might soon be possible again. Then we can visit Jenna's folks down in Arizona."

"Where it's warm in the winters," Jenna said with a wry grin.

Dave said, "Everything depends on the Galactic corporations getting up and running."

"There's a downside, Liz," Tom said. "South Chicago is still causing major trouble. Their thugs keep raiding food centers. We think they might have gotten their hands on some new phones and hacked their way into the Galactic credit system. GD investigators are working on it, but Liz, they aren't you. We sorely miss you and your super investigation skills."

"Yeah, well I sorely miss my arms."

***

Christmas came and went. Liz and Rae braved the cold and snow to go shopping. Both needed clothes that fit.

"Finally I look halfway good," Liz said. "Love these fleece-lined booties. I took Jenna's advice and picked up cloaks in several weights. Now to learn how to get them on."

Dave said, "Liz, you always look good, but I see your point. Now you look fabulous."

"Don't be silly, Dave. I'm severely handicapped. Say, I saw Rae's feet up close today. They did a job on her arches.

153

She really can't put her feet flat. She did find six more pairs of tall heels. Her old ones were falling apart."

"I think she and Phillis might get married," Dave said. "I saw them kissing again. Might be good for both of them, don't you think?"

Liz allowed herself a brief smile. "Yes, those two are made for each other, but I don't know if it's a good thing or not. I heard a GMed announcement that they've perfected a method for two women to have a baby. Baby girls only, though. Might be better for Rae to get her feet repaired."

Dave teased. "But Liz, dear, she and Phillis are into fetish outfits. Those shoes are part of that mystique."

"They can have it. I'm barely getting by."

"I think you're doing super, all things considered."

***

"Thank goodness for spring," Jenna said. "No more heavy cloaks to wrestle. Now we can take Sam out in the stroller. But I have to admit the new GEnt station is superb. Timely news and a terrific choice of flicks and music. And I love the new way to get groceries. Voice-activated ordering system and home delivery. What more could we want?"

"I worry about how you can carry the boxes inside if Dave, Rae, or I aren't here," Tom said.

"Like I used to before I met you. Sit and push with my feet. I'm not helpless, silly. Oh, we can now order clothes online, too. That's good timing. Sam's outgrown his first outfits. No one told me babies grow like weeds."

"With all the crime from South Chicago infiltrating everywhere else, I feel much better knowing you are snug in our apartment and don't have to go out," Tom said. "I had to shoot three more looters yesterday. Not safe to walk the streets of Chicago."

154

Chapter 21 Trials of Honey Bunny Mounds

Alerted to replacement bunnies, Miss Mounds kept a close watch on events in and around Governor-mayor Bebo Ritzker. Late summer, the first of her replacements appeared, a younger, prettier woman named Honey Bunny Mountains. Then came the shocker. His wife, Nancy, teetered into the Governor-mayor's office as Honey Bunny Ritzker. That surprised Bebo. He along with the other Honey Bunnies stared at her. Nicely done light brown hair, form-fitting red gown, matching six-inch stilettos and two-inch nails, and the same titanic bosom as the other Honey Bunnies.

Quietly, Honey Bunny Mounds slipped out of the office, packed her bag, and left the mansion. Familiar with the Med Center and Dr. Merryweather, she headed there. In the basement, she found an available temporary room and arranged for meals, trading cleaning duties for her stay, just as she'd done at the beginning of her Honey Bunny career.

The doctor had given her the name Honey Bunny Mounds when he'd recruited her and transformed her body to meet Bebo's requests. Sabrina Stanway would turn twenty-eight come Halloween. As a young girl, that had been her claim to fame—the Halloween child.

When President Snowden announced free college, she enrolled at the University of Chicago. With all the speculation of settling the two Earth-like planets, Brussels and Pylon, she chose to study astronomy on the chance she might be chosen to immigrate to one of them.

She finished her bachelors when the Dem Socialists' policies brought about the total economic collapse. With no job prospects, no food, no place to continue living, Sabrina found ways to survive.

For six months, she lived on the streets of South Chicago, turning tricks for food and a place to crash. Then El Gato convinced her to sign up to be a nurse-in-training at the Med Center. He introduced her to Dr. Merryweather. The doctor looked her over and gave her a physical exam before offering her the position.

"It comes with food, clothing, and living accommodations. I'll show you around."

The cozy rooms in the basement appealed to her. It beat the drafty, filthy places she'd been staying. Food shortages had become acute. Sabrina now thought being a qualified nurse would enhance her chances of immigration. She signed the contract with the doctor.

Then came the surprise body transformation period.

"We wish our nurses to have specific appearances. It's my job to make you look like the perfect nurse. You want to become a nurse, don't you?"

Sabrina knew she ought to have made more inquiries before agreeing to any of this, but desperation overruled common sense or even curiosity.

It began with hormone injections. At least that's what the doctor claimed. A day later, her breasts ached, and the doctor gave her something to ease the pain.

Sabrina never knew if it eased the pain, because she drifted into a deep sleep. Later she learned she'd been unconscious for about a week. When she woke, her breasts had more than doubled in size, and her feet throbbed. She looked down to see casts on both feet. Also, a nail technician had applied two-inch nail extensions and painted them bright red.

For the next couple weeks, she faded in and out of consciousness. She suspected that was unnatural and speculated they kept her drugged. During various lucid periods, she observed her bosom continuing to grow.

Later she learned her feet had healed in two-weeks, thanks to the recent invention of new healing drugs. She looked at her feet and saw her arches were steep. After a bit of testing, she realized her feet couldn't lie flat anymore. That's when they brought her clothes and her first pair of six-inch stilettos.

"For the next month, we'll be slowly inflating your breast forms until they reach the optimum specifications for all new nurses-in-training," the doctor explained. "These are only temporary tops. We'll see you have high quality tops and dresses once your breasts have reached their full potential. For now, you'll begin your training. Janice will show you what your duties will be, at least for the next month until you've reached perfection. You'll make a superb Honey Bunny Mounds nurse-in-training.

"You'll help important people with their difficulties and challenges. But more about your nursing duties when your body is fully transformed."

Sabrina thought her breasts would explode before he stopped inflating the implants.

"Doctor, these are way too big and heavy. Other nurses are not like this."

"They are the perfect size, fifteen inches bigger than your under bust measurement. Honey Bunny, you'll be assisting the most important man in Illinois and Chicago, the Governor-mayor. He has severe stress issues, which you'll be able to relieve. If you treat him right, he'll reward you with luxurious clothes and delicious food. The finest dining in Chicago will be yours, as long as you use your training to keep his stress levels down and keep him happy. Tomorrow, Janice will train you in just how to do that for him. He's the most important man in this state and city. Keep him happy and satisfied and you'll be on easy street."

So a dirty old man wants me to be a nutty porn star. If he wants a bimbo, then that's what he'll get. Thus, Sabrina began playing her new role of Honey Bunny.

Over the many months, she observed how men perceived her massive, non-natural bosom and striking heels. She realized how easily she could influence men. In the background, she did just that. After a year, she could come and go about the governor's mansion, the Med Center, and much of northern South Chicago as she pleased when she pleased.

"How's my little Pooche Dooche tonight?" she said to a night security guard, while batting her eyes and smiling.

Sporting a grin that threatened to break his jaw, he unlocked the doors to the mansion for her.

"Oh, honey, this bag is *so* heavy! Would you mind terribly carrying it for me?"

The hospital guard rushed to her aid, all smiles.

Honey Bunny Mounds made the most of her influence. She ate as though she was the governor. While clothing stores and shopping had vanished, men somehow found the means to find her nice pieces and were rewarded by her charms.

Her shock at discovering Dr. Merryweather's intention to turn Rae Lin into a replacement Honey Bunny jarred her into the present. She used her wiles to spy on the doctor and Rae.

Until then she hadn't realized the size and scope of the crimes originating out of or because of Bebo and associates. Now she did, and saw how Rae had secretly escaped from South Chicago and this crowd. That these new Galactic corporations were growing and offering a new stable kind of money convinced her she needed to follow Rae's example.

Rae had attached herself to one of their many victims, this Major Callahan, whose arms the doctor had amputated only because she was GD's Chief Intelligence Officer. From a concealed position, she watched as orderlies whisked Rae off with the victim, presumably to be the poor woman's assistant in all things.

She'd overheard rumors that Bebo wanted others to suffer the same fate, especially the one he called the Assassin. Trouble was, thugs brought no one to the doctor for days, which turned into weeks and months. The time delay forced Honey Bunny to explore other avenues that might make the corporations look favorably on her and allow her to immigrate to one of the new worlds.

Since she knew both Bebo and the doctor's computer passwords, having seen them enter it many times, she took advantage of opportunities when they left her alone. Bebo kept exact records of his criminal dealings, logging dates, times, and personnel involved in the action. The doctor's secret logs detailed who he'd been ordered to do what to, including Major Callahan.

After scrounging through junk in the hospital's basement storage, she found a flash drive. With a grin, she headed off to make copies of both men's secret files. She often secured it in her massive cleavage. Where she went, so went her proof, which she hoped might buy her passage to Brussels. If not that, then a pile of credits.

With the sudden appearance of Honey Bunny Ritzker, she knew her easy street had ended. Thus, she took up residence in the hospital's basement, spending off-hours plotting a way to escape South Chicago.

The January deep freeze and deep snow didn't mix with the heels she had to wear. Nor did she have warm clothing to brave a lengthy MTES travel to flee South Chicago. Escape had to wait for warmer weather in the spring of 2037.

Late April, the Med Center began carrying the new entertainment channel, GEnt. She found ways to watch, catching a peek here and there, as she went about her duties in the Med Center.

To her, it appeared the corporations had already taken over control of the city. Stores were opening again. She knew she had to get out soon. But how? Sabrina had patience, though it had begun to run out.

Chapter 22 Bebo's Revenge

Months of searching and spying paid off. At last Bebo knew the identity of the Assassin, the biggest threat to his rule. And he knew the man's habits. He and his friends often visited a tea garden run by handicapped women. He ordered the attack for the evening of May Day. In celebration, he ordered a May Day party for those who could attend, turning a park in South Chicago into a festival. Free food and booze flowed during the day. But with a smirk on his face, he waited for the evening.

At seven, the first text came.

"Got uniform."

Bebo knew that meant his gang had killed a GPan guard to get the uniform. He paced back and forth waiting for the next message, the one that ensured his revenge and ultimate victory over these interfering corporations. He imagined the Assassin receiving the message to step outside, that a GPan guard wanted a word with him. Most urgent. In his mind, he imagined the Assassin stepping out to meet with the GPan man. He imagined his other thug firing the tranq into his neck. He hoped the two men could carry him to their electric car with no one seeing them.

Honey Bunny Ritzker teetered up, slipping a steadying arm around him. "Oh, Pooche, dear, is it happening now? Your revenge? This nasty Assassin thing?"

"Yes, my Honey Bunny. Probably as we speak."

His pacing grew more frantic.

"Pooche Dooche, why don't we go to the Med Center? Meet them. I wanna see this evil man, too."

"Oh, you scrumptious Honey Bunny. Brilliant idea. Come on. Let's."

"Slow down. I can't keep up with you, Pooche Dooche."

"Sorry, my sweet Honey Bunny. I'm overly excited. I need you to calm me down."

Grinning, she pressed her massive bosom into his chest and massaged his neck.

"Heavenly, my perfect Honey Bunny Ritzker. Off we go to see my revenge. I'm a patient man. I've waited for this night for more than a year. No, two years, perhaps more. Who knows how many this Assassin has killed?"

"Oh, Pooche Dooche, your revenge will be sweet to me."

He puffed up even more as they rode the MTES to the hospital. They headed straight for the basement and private office of Dr. Merryweather.

"All set?" Bebo asked.

"Always," the doctor said. "My, how perfect you look, Honey Bunny Ritzker."

"I'm proud of my Pooche Dooche Bebo. How soon?"

"You two have a seat. I'll go up to the Emergency Room. Text you when we have him."

The doctor left.

***

Neither man noticed Sabrina listening in from dark shadows. Both are here; it must be tonight. I should get ready in case it is.

She tiptoed away, trying hard not to let her steel-tipped heels make a sound, an action made challenging because of the extreme heel height. Hastily, she packed a duffle bag and made sure she had her flash drive secured. Then she returned to her spy position to wait.

***

"Here he is, doc. Texting the boss now," one man said.

Two others carried the unconscious man inside, laying him on a Gurney.

"Strip him," Dr. Merryweather said. "Then dispose of

162

his clothes."

"I think we'll keep them, especially those shoes. Mine are full of holes."

"Whatever," the doctor said. "Did you dump his possessions when you grabbed him like Bebo asked?"

"Yeah. Don't git riled up. Dumped them right outside where we snatched him."

"You. Help me wheel him to the elevator. Bebo's waiting to check on him before I take him up to surgery."

Bebo looked down at the naked man and gleefully clapped his hands. "Oh, superb. Wonderful."

"Oh, Pooche, is this the mighty Assassin? He looks, well... Ordinary."

"Yes, Honey Bunny. This is him. Tonight, it's payback. He's killed many of my men. Even El Gato, though I didn't like that man. Get on with it, doc. Text me when it's done. I want to come and see. I need to send a shot of what he looks like afterwards to all these interfering Galactic corporations. Once they observe your handiwork, they'll do everything I ask. Fear is a splendid weapon. Now, go. Go."

Bebo watched them wheeling the Gurney back to the elevator. Once it vanished, he took Honey Bunny's arm.

"Now, let's go partying, my scrumptious Honey Bunny."

She giggled as appropriate. Her heels clicked on the concrete floor, shattering the ominous silence.

***

Sabrina exhaled, unaware she'd been holding it while the Ritzker's left. She left her bag in an out-of-the-way corner and took the janitor elevator up. This time of night, only Emergency Room personnel ought to be here. She stopped off there first. Instead of stepping out when the doors opened, she held the Open button and listened. The faint sounds of the new GEnt station echoed off the empty halls. Had an operation been in progress or scheduled, a hive of activity would be present.

That meant Dr. Merryweather intended to use his private staff for the operations. She pressed the top floor button. Besides patent recovery rooms and an ICU ward, this floor housed his special surgery room and equipment. Her janitor elevator lay between the doors to the ICU and the long hallway of recovery rooms. The dimmed hall lights suggested these rooms were empty. The wall clock showed 7:30.

She heard muffled talking coming from the operating room at the far end. Long ago, she found trying to tiptoe in six-inch steel-tipped stilettos impossible except for very short distances. She knew she'd never be able to make a stealthy approach. Sabrina changed tactics.

A janitor's cart stood near the elevator. She picked up the floor mop and began dry mopping the hallway. While her heel clicks echoed, anyone looking would see her doing her usual cleanup work and think nothing of it. Partway down the hall, a nurse came out of the ICU doors and nodded to her. She smiled back, thankful she'd chosen this approach.

From her explorations, she knew the room next to the surgery room had a one-way mirror. Dr. Merryweather often performed his surgical miracles while budding young doctors observed him. She mopped her way there and ducked inside.

She saw the naked man lying on the table, a mask over his face. A nurse had installed an IV line in his right leg. That four teams prepped up surprised her. What were they planning that needed four of them?

When they started, their bodies hid what they were doing from her. She sighed and headed back down the hall, pushing a small pile of dust before her. Whatever they're doing to him can't be good. I best get into position to spy on what they'll do with him next.

Soon she picked up her bag and opened the back door of the doctor's basement office just a crack. She pulled a portable privacy screen close, hiding her position in the corner and from where she could peek into the room. Now she waited. Standing still in tall heels caused her to wobble. Soon her feet ached. But Sabrina knew she had to find out. Everything depended on it. If Rae could do this, I can too.

***

Hours later, Bebo and Honey Bunny Ritzker arrived, joined soon after by Dr. Merryweather, carrying an organ bag.

"He or rather she is in recovery now. Took some photos. Sending them to your phone," the doctor said.

"Oh!" Bebo jumped about, unable to restrain his glee.

"Honey Bunny, just look at him now! Isn't revenge sweet?"

"Oh, Pooche, he's a she now, right? Are you making her into a Honey Bunny, too?"

"No, no. There's only you, my scrumptious Bunny. Well, and Miss Mountains. No, when these Galactic CEOs see what we've done to their super assassin man, they'll cringe in fear. Maybe terror. The long arm of Bebo Ritzker can get to any of them and turn them into a helpless she. This is enough to scare any man. After this, they'll do whatever I order them to do."

"But Pooche, Dooche, won't gay men want this to happen to them?"

"Silly Honey Bunny, none of them are in charge of these Galactic corporations. But she's not yet a finished product. Much more to go. At least another month."

She gave him a puzzled look.

"Oh, you'll see, Honey Bunny. But we have to go. I need to get this bag delivered to the GD CEO along with this video warning."

He picked up the organ bag while she put a steadying arm around his other arm. Together, they left.

***

Sabrina listened as Mrs. Ritzker's heel clicks faded. She peered into the room. Ah, she could see the doctor's monitor. He had an image of his new patient on the screen, entering treatment orders. Must be a lot of orders, she thought, since he typed for several minutes before saving it.

He rose, stretched, and muttered, "Some of my finest work. Okay, sleep time. I'll send this transfer order off after I make my morning rounds and make sure no complications have arisen with his, er, her surgeries."

He turned off his lights and left. Soon, she heard the elevator doors and the soft whine of the motors. Only now did she sneak out of her hiding place, feet throbbing. She plopped into his chair. She massaged her feet as best she could before turning on the computer and entering his password.

Sabrina opened up the transfer file and scanned it. Routine transfer to Uptown Med Center. The usual after surgery checks. She didn't read that lengthy list. Instead, she typed in an additional line, saved it, and shut down the computer. Grabbing her bag, she headed up to the top floor. Sure enough, the victim or patient rested in the recovery room closest to the surgery room. She slipped inside.

The woman wore a hospital gown, though many tubes protruded from it. Casts enclosed her feet, casts like those she'd once worn. She felt sick. This person's gonna be hobbled like I am. Oh, God. He's removed her arms, too. He's got to be stopped.

She found a chair, sat down, and tried to calm her emotions. Soon, sleep came.

Distance voices drawing nearer woke her. She and her bag slipped into the bathroom, partway closing the door.

The doctor and nurse entered. She watched him examine the many bandages while the nurse logged the patient's vitals.

"Go get the bag of items I'm sending along for her

cures. We'll leave them on the bed. Can't have the orderlies forgetting them," Dr. Merryweather said.

He left. The nurse returned with a bag, sitting it on the bed beside the unconscious woman before leaving. Sabrina stepped out and sat down. Her stomach growled, but she couldn't risk missing the transfer—her only chance of escaping South Chicago. If only Rae's trick would work a second time.

Two orderlies with a Gurney walked in. One looked at the orders.

"Ah, female patient. Check the tag. Tomi Durbin?"

"Yeah, right."

"Oh, you must be Honey Bunny Mounds. You're supposed to go with this patient. Personal assistant. Hell, this woman's gonna need you! Come along."

"Where are we going? No one's told me," she said, feigning ignorance. In reality, she wanted reassurance and no surprises.

"Says here she's being transported to Uptown Med Center."

"Oh, thanks, fellows."

She relaxed. An hour later she sat in a comfortable chair beside the victim in her private room in the Uptown Med Center. Sabrina felt free as a lark.

Chapter 23 Catastrophe

Tom and the gang had gone to the tea garden just as most nights. Jenna, Liz, and the other women appreciated the warming weather and the fresh air. Cooped up most of the winter, their enthusiasm for life returned.

Around seven, Irene walked over to their tables.

"Tom, a security man from GPan is outside and wants a quick word with you. I asked him to come inside, but he didn't want to. I think my hooks scared him."

"They'd scare anyone." Tom jested and brought a smile to her face.

He stepped outside.

After some time, Jenna became worried. "What's taking him so long?"

"I'll check," Dave said.

Jenna sensed something was terribly wrong when he walked towards them. His stark white face said much. His hands held Tom's fancy phone and watch, and smaller personal items, including his shoes.

"He's gone! Found these lying on the ground. With scuff marks. I think he was dragged and put into a car."

"Someone's abducted him!" Jenna wailed. "I just know it."

Liz said, "Dave, I'll get everyone home. Call Art now and stay here. Gang, let's get going before anyone else gets hurt or kidnapped. God, I feel so helpless like this."

"I got you," Rae said, slipping an arm around her. "And you, too, Jenna."

Irene said, "Let me push the baby stroller. I should have asked for some ID or something."

Liz said, "He wore the purple and gold uniform of Gpan. Who would doubt him? It's not your fault. But we could use a little help. I feel frustrated. Just when I was getting a little comfortable with being handicapped."

"That's always gonna happen," Jenna said. "I still have times like that."

Phillis pressed into Rae and shared a kiss, before saying, "Same here. I think we all get frustrated, Liz. It's natural. Accept it and move on."

Dave hugged Liz as she walked outside and said, "I'll call you when I know anything."

He watched the sober group make their way to the MTES and vanish into the night. One of the new EMACs landed and a team of GD security guards swarmed out. CEO Art Townsend joined them.

Dave handed him Tom's possessions and relayed the little he knew. With nothing to go on, they headed back to GD, only to receive word that a GPan security man was found murdered and stripped of his uniform. Art sent his investigation crew to follow that up, while he and Dave summoned the day crew back, asking them to search through all surveillance videos.

Dave found a camera on the opposite side of the street, pointed towards the abandoned church.

"Everyone, watch. Tom was definitely kidnapped. Just like Major Callahan."

Art said, "Well done, Dave. Okay, everyone. Let's follow that car."

Hours passed before Art called a halt and sent everyone home.

"We'll resume tomorrow. Er, later today," he said.

Dave's sad face spoke volumes when he walked inside Apartment #1. As he expected, Jenna, Liz, and Rae sat around the kitchen table waiting for him.

"Art called all the day crew in. I found a surveillance video. Showed he was abducted. Just like Liz was. Stuffed into a car. We tried to follow it."

Liz said, "There's almost no direct routes left. The MTES blocks most all streets. Could anyone check if the car ended up at that Med Center?"

"Couldn't tell. Cars came and went, but no way to tell. Don't worry, Jenna. Everyone will get back on it after a little sleep. We'll find him."

Jenna said, "I always worried something bad would happen to him. That's what I get for marrying a security guard. Lot 'o worry. But I love that man. I think I'd feel something if he was dead."

Dave said, "They drugged him. If they wanted him dead, they could have shot him right there. I don't think he's dead. Let's get some sleep."

When Dave arrived at work later that day, Art called him into his office.

"Dave, get Jenna and Liz down here now. I got a grizzly video and body parts delivered to me this morning. They need to see this. I've a med team working on DNA samples. Should get those results by the time they get here."

"Is he alive? Can I see it first?"

"No, best you go get them here, Dave. Trust me on this one. We're pretty sure he's alive. We might even get to visit him in the Med Center later today if the video is correct."

Rae agreed to watch Sam. Jenna and Liz headed down to the GD skyscraper. Dave walked between them, an arm around each. While Jenna didn't think she needed it, Liz still felt more comfortable with his support. Falls had become nasty for her.

Around eleven, they sat in Art's office; his face lacked all color.

"Bebo Ritzker sent this to me this morning along with

an organ box. My med people confirmed the arms were Tom's."

Liz cursed. Jenna gasped.

"There's more. But I'll let the video tell you the story."

The image of a gleeful Governor-mayor Bebo Ritzker appeared on the large monitor.

"Greetings GD CEO Art Townsend. I'm sending you my final message today. As you can see, we've captured your top Assassin. While I could have had him killed, I am not an evil man. Instead, he will serve as an example for all you corporate CEOs. I am the mayor and leader of this city and this state. Not you.

"Tom Durbin is your only warning. This is what will happen to your CEOs if you do not follow my orders. Here he or rather she is in recovery. Yes, like that Intelligence Officer, I had his arms removed. No more assassinations by him, er, her. I made use of our latest medical breakthrough, complete gender transformations. I sent you his arms and male parts. As you can see, his body is now female.

"In fact, all the new parts work, except no ovaries, so no breeding. If you and your fellow CEOs do not follow my orders, then this will happen to you and your people. I'll keep doing this until you CEOs agree to my demands.

"More details. Pay close attention to this. I'm not done with him. Rather, the doc has more work to do. This morning, she's being transferred to Uptown Med Center. She's under heavy sedation and will stay that way while the healing process works.

"The doctor's instructions that accompanied her transfer are to be followed precisely. Two weeks of healing are mandatory. By then the hormones will have enlarged her breasts to the same size we made for Major Callahan. Must have women looking their best, don't we?"

Liz cursed and would have thrown something if she

could have.

"Her feet have been modified. She must wear the tall heels that the doctor's nurses-in-training do. Like Rae Lin, who disappointed me by running away before her complete transformation into a perfect honey bunny was finished. Ah, well.

"At least Tami Durbin will become a perfect bunny. To that end, she's to stay in the Med Center for some time. After her bosom has filled out, the doctors will insert the implants as specified in the treatment plan. My doc tells me she'll need two weeks for that to heal. During the next month of hospitalization, once a week, she'll get them inflated. Doc tells me she needs a week between each round. After a month, her bosom will be complete, and she may leave the Med Center. She'll be a perfect Honey Bunny.

"Caution. You must follow the doctor's orders and mine precisely. To make sure this transformation is completed, I've arranged some encouragement for you. My personnel installed bombs in sixty locations around the city, such as museums and other places where people gather. A bomb will go off at one of these sixty random locations for each day that you remove Tami Durbin from the Med Center or if you fail to carry out my doctor's orders. One day too soon, one boom. Sixty days too soon, sixty booms.

"I'm told the doctor's orders accompanied the transfer. I want to make sure Tami ends up a perfect Honey Bunny, just like my perfect wife is. This is what she looks like, in case you haven't seen her recent transformation from boring wife to exciting Honey Bunny.

"I am in control of this city. You will follow my orders. If you and your CEOs don't, then one by one, you'll end up like Tami here. Remove her too soon, and booms. I look forward to hearing some explosions. I wonder which CEO will become the next Honey Bunny?"

His evil, sadistic laugh ended the video. The audience sat in stunned silence.

Dave said, "I don't know what to say. This fiend. Must. Be. Killed!"

Art said, "I've sent this to all the other CEOs worldwide. Already, I've sent crews to search for bombs. But I'm afraid even if we find and defuse them, nothing can prevent them from setting up more. Jenna, my hands are tied. I'd love to pull him or her out of that Med Center right now, but..."

"I, we don't want other innocent people to be injured or killed because we didn't follow his sadistic requests," Jenna said.

"How can you say that?" Liz wailed, "He'll be as helpless as I am and now he's a she? I say take an army and wipe him out today."

Art said, "Wang Chan and I considered that and bounced it off Boris Borodinsky, the Sol Empire GD CEO. We agree it's too risky to disobey Bebo until we get him, er her, back. Boris has given me the okay to act as I see fit after we have her back. Trust me, Jenna. He's signed his death warrant. But there's something else you must know. It's rather personal. We can talk in private."

"No, we're all very close. I need them to hear whatever it is too."

"We disposed of the arms after the DNA results came back. However, one of my brighter med people examined the male parts. He retrieved sperm that survived. We don't know how viable they will be, since they weren't properly handled. This could be your last chance for a child by Tom. I'm told they could extract an egg of yours and attempt to get the surviving sperm to fertilize it. It's an iffy proposition. If it takes, then we must place it in a womb. I checked with some doctors. It's too soon for it to be inserted in yours. You still need recovery time. But now there's a new womb available."

"You—you mean Tom's?" she said, flushing.

"Yes. It's still chancy. I'm told it's fifty-fifty the sperm will take. Then it's fifty-fifty it'll survive in stasis for several weeks until Tom's womb is healed and ready. Even then the chance it'll take is only fifty-fifty."

Jenna sighed, "One chance in eight Tom and I can have another baby. Not good odds."

Art said, "Also, medical advances suggest that two women's eggs can be merged into a viable embryo, but such only produces female offspring."

"But this doctor didn't give him an ovary. That's out," Jenna said. "If we want another child, which we do, this is our only way. Though the odds aren't good."

"It's a long shot, but we could find a surrogate mother."

Jenna signed. "That brings many other factors into play. What if she wants to keep it after the baby's born? No, let's not consider that. What do we need to do to try this?"

"Act fast. Today, even. The longer we wait, the less the chances of sperm survival. That's what they tell me."

"Okay. Let's give it a try. I know how much children mean to Tom and me."

Art notified his med people. Everyone piled into one of the new company EMACs and headed to Uptown Med Center.

Once there, the doctors rushed Jenna into a special room, while the others checked if a Tami Durbin had arrived. She had, but out of respect for Jenna, they waited until her procedure was completed. When she joined them, they headed up to the room.

When they entered, two doctors and three nurses hovered over her, adjusting tubes and checking vitals.

One doctor said, "These are incredibly specific orders. Oh, is one of you her spouse?"

"I'm GD CEO Art Townsend. Yes, this is Jenna Durbin, Tom's wife. They kidnapped him last night and did this to him.

How bad is it?"

"Oh, sorry. Now the orders make more sense. Did he have an accident that forced them to remove his arms?"

Art explained the situation.

"Do you think the Med Center is in danger? A bomb?" the doctor said.

"I'll get a bomb squad over here right away. For now, how's the patient?"

"He did an excellent job. Should be no scarring about her shoulders. Nicely done. We should leave the drain tubes in for several days. Bandages might come off in a week, two at the most. Breasts are growing just fine. According to the instructions, she'll need breast implants in about two weeks. We'll see. Her feet. Now that's something we're still analyzing. I've ordered a portable x-ray. I want to see what she's dealing with. We're to keep her doped up for one to two weeks. Do we need to follow these instructions to the letter?"

Art said, "Yes, for now. He's threatened to ignite sixty bombs if we don't. Say, who's this young woman?"

Until now, no one had noticed Sabrina sitting in the corner as unobtrusive as possible. With all eyes on her, she swallowed and took a deep breath.

The doctor spoke first. "The transfer orders said Miss Honey Bunny Mounds is to be her personal assistant. She will need one."

Dave said, "Wait. I've seen her before. With Bebo. His play-toy bimbo!"

"I'm Sabrina Stanway. Are you the leader of Galactic Defense?"

"Yes," Art said.

"Pleased to meet you. I have something for you."

Her long red nails snaked down her massive cleavage and pulled out a flash drive.

"I made copies of Bebo's files and those of Dr.

Merryweather. There are so many crimes documented that I lost count. I hope to trade this for my freedom. And yes, I'm what she'll look like when it's done, except no arms."

"Oh, dear God, Jenna," Liz gushed, showing more emotion than normal.

Jenna's eyes bulged.

Sabrina said, "Bebo means it. I overheard him talking to his bomb maker last night. Maybe the locations are on that drive. May be not. I had to make that copy in a hurry. Couldn't risk him seeing me. He's insane. They both are."

Dave said, "Boss, you can't trust her. When I saw her, she was just a dumb blond bimbo named Honey Bunny Mounds."

"People do what they have to do to survive," Sabrina said. "I received my degree in astronomy. But I know some nursing."

Art said, "For now, we'll take you at your word. Dave, take this to HQ and see what's on it."

Another doctor walked in. "Ah, here you are. Good news."

Jenna said, "He's the one who's helping us make a baby."

"Yes, about that. We beat the odds. The egg is fertilized. Amazing, all things considered. Next question. Do we gamble on keeping it in stasis for a while? If a womb was ready, that would increase the odds of success."

Art rounded up Tami's doctor and explained the situation.

"Highly unusual. It's been a successful transplant, but it needs two weeks to heal. Stasis is a better choice. In fact, I'd hold off until we verify all nerve connections have formed—perhaps a month."

Jenna sighed and gave her okay for that. She said, "At least he's alive. We'll adapt, somehow. We have too."

Liz leaned into her, using her neck to pull Jenna tight.

Jenna said, "Doctor, can I sit with him every day for a time?"

"Of course. From nine in the morning to nine at night. But the medication will keep her from knowing you're here. When we wean her off, she'll regain awareness. Then shock will set in. Best if you're here when that happens. She'll need— well, you know. She'll have an awful lot to deal with."

Chapter 24 Conclusions

The next morning Jenna visited Tom. Dave and Liz came with her, but Sabrina wasn't in the hospital room.

Dave put down his phone. "Art says Sabrina's brought us a wealth of information. He has half of GD and GPan working with Sabrina and the data to find the sixty bombs. Guess she was telling the truth."

Liz said, "I feel bad. I should be there helping, directing, doing something. Damn frustrating. Tom's going to experience twice the shock I had."

"He keeps mumbling equations," Jenna said. "I think he said hyperspace. He's into topology. We've often talked about its theoretical existence."

Dave said, "He must be delirious."

Jenna bit her lip. "Perhaps not. Tomorrow, I'm bringing my laptop and taking down what he's saying."

"Ah, Mrs. Durbin. Made the morning checks. She's healing well, considering."

"Thanks. Say, if we have the credits, can any of what they've done to Tom be undone?" That question had burned in her mind all night. If only she'd had the presence to ask it yesterday.

He pulled up a chair beside her and thought a moment before speaking.

"The loss of arms: no. Despite the major medical breakthroughs we've had this past decade, total loss of arms has no remedy. As you probably know, whole arm prostheses are just cosmetic."

Jenna nodded. "Assumed that, but the rest?"

"We now have the medical ability to safely alter

178

someone's gender. In either direction. Once. No one's tried reversing it once it's done. Those new female organs came from someone. An organ donor perhaps, a woman who wanted her gender changed—though that's unlikely since they returned his male organs—or a woman whose organs were harvested before the killed her."

Pulling out his phone, Dave said, "Dear God. I'm alerting GD. Have them be alert for mutilated female bodies."

The doctor continued, "If that happened, they probably cremated the body by now, Dave. There is a fourth possibility. Experiments have shown organs, like ears, can be grown on pigs and then transplanted to humans once they've matured. Considering the location and doctor who did this, my guess is they kidnapped a woman, harvested her organs, killed her, and cremated the remains.

"So, Jenna, assuming you want this done legally and safely, finding a donor will be challenging and takes time. Even if you find a proper donor, to my knowledge, the reversing operation has never been done. It's always been one way. Male to female. Female to male."

"Doubly challenging," Jenna said.

He nodded. "We might be able to restore his voice, make it deeper. But we aren't sure what they did to his voice. We can't restore his Adams apple. Nor can we replace the lower rib pair that the doctor removed. That's a necessity if she's to have children.

"The breast situation bothers me, especially after seeing Sabrina's. Expect major back pains from carrying such a weight around. I'm hoping they won't force me to insert and inflate the breast implants the doctor sent over with her.

"No offense, Major Callahan, but even yours are way above average size."

Liz offered a rare smile. "Damned too big. But I don't want to endure more surgery. Yet."

"Understandable. There are homeopathic remedies and physical therapies known to reduce breast size. Eat more tuna or salmon. Or take omega-3 fatty acids found in fish oil capsules. Use ginger as a frequent spice. Drink green tea. Low impact cardio workouts such as a treadmill or stationary bike burns off fatty tissues. Doing pushups and dumbbell bench presses tighten up chest muscles. Speed up your metabolism rate by climbing stairs and cycling. Brisk walking helps. If you have someone who could massage them, put warm coconut oil or olive oil on them and massage in circular motions. Also, beat up egg whites into a paste and coat the bottoms of your breasts with the paste. Let it stand for say a half hour before removing. I've heard some women found results via yoga exercises.

"None of these are fast. If you need speed, surgery is the only answer. I'll get these written for you both. Jenna, if she remains female, she'll want breasts, just not the grotesque ones on Sabrina. And if Miss Callahan can get hers reduced, she'll feel much better and be healthier."

"So would I," Jenna said, looking at the flush face of Liz.

"Continuing, the organ transplant is taking. We would have seen organ rejection by now. If that had happen, we'd need a suitable male organ donor right away. Don't worry. I see no signs or even hints of a rejection. As I understand it, ninety-nine percent of rejections occur within the first forty-eight hours. But I admit I've never performed gender transformation operations.

"Finally, her feet. I consulted a podiatrist on this one. He had us x-ray her feet last night. His opinion is that they used a specific shoe last."

"Huh?" Jenna said.

"A shoe last is the solid form, often wood or metal, around which they form the shoe. They are specific to both foot size and heel height. In this case, the last is for a woman's

180

extreme heel. Since Sabrina was still here, he had me take measurements of her foot and the heels she must wear. After I sent them, he suggested how the foot surgery may have been done. They had a shoe last of the right size and shape for these six-inch heels. According to him, they broke her feet around the lasts, forcing her arches to fit the lasts. He thinks loud cracks accompanied the bone breaks. With the foot deformed, they bandaged it up in this new position and inserted the speed healing compounds."

Liz cringed. "That sounds awfully painful."

The doctor laughed. "Understatement. The podiatrist said the patient would have to be unconscious because the pain would have been excruciating. The question we face is: can it be undone? I explained the situation, that she's lost her arms and needs her feet as fingers. He got back to me early this morning.

"According to him, to undo it, we'll need shoe lasts that fits the shoes he wore. He's unsure how the re-breaking pressure could and should be applied. He ran several simulations late last night. Each test has resulted in the bones breaking in other places, yielding a foot that's more deformed than before, unacceptable for a person with no arms. He's trying other means and will get back to me. So, Jenna, we must wait to see if we can repair her feet.

"We want to be overly cautious with her feet. We can't afford to cripple her even more."

Jenna sighed. "Thanks. We appreciate all your help. For sure, when it's safe to do so, we'll want her breasts reduced. Even mine are too big. I'll give your suggestions a try. I don't want surgery either."

"I agree with both of you. I'd prefer not to do it, and I'm a doctor."

Jenna chuckled and relaxed.

Just then, the gynecologist walked in.

"Ah, everyone's here. I've news—both good and bad. Jenna, as I said yesterday, the fertilization succeeded. Today, my lab techs discovered the embryo cells have begun reproducing. It's growing. That's the good news. It's working like we hoped. The bad news is we risk killing it now by putting it into stasis. We should implant it in a proper womb. Today. Soon. If so, the chances of it producing a healthy baby are quite good, beating the one in eight chance we had before."

"Can I take it?" Jenna asked.

The gynecologist sighed. "I thought of that and checked with your physician before rushing up here. His answer is no. Your body is still recovering from your recent pregnancy. Another couple of months and it would be fine. According to her, if we did that, we risk both the baby's and your life. So, doctor, how's your patient's situation? We need to move on this soon."

"The transplant shows no signs of rejection. Like I told Jenna, there's only a one percent chance her body will reject the female organs at this point. It's too soon to use vibration therapy to help activate proper nerve channels. We'll start that at the two-week point. Will that interfere with embryo development?"

"Not likely at all. Women often continue to have intercourse until much later in their pregnancies, though I don't recommend it after the twelfth week."

"So, if Jenna takes the embryo, what are the odds? Best guess?"

"You're putting me on the spot. But if I had to guess, I'd say there's a twenty-five percent chance of losing both mother and child," the gynecologist said.

"One percent chance if Tomi takes it now before she's healed. Any chance of finding a willing surrogate?"

"Not in the needed time frame. Look, we don't have to save this embryo," the gynecologist said.

"Oh, yes, we do!" Jenna said. "Okay, I've got to decide for us. Put it into Tom's womb. Better odds. I'm sure he'll see it that way. Besides, this is the last child of our own we can ever have. We must try."

"Okay. They will perform the procedure now. By the way, it's going to be a girl."

Liz said, "How can you tell when she's a day old?"

"Using our extreme magnification scopes, my techs guided the surviving sperm to the egg. They confirmed the single cell embryo has two x chromosomes. Modern tech is astounding."

When he talked, a tech wearing total protective clothing entered and worked on the unconscious Tami. It took less than two minutes.

"Is that all?" Jenna asked when the man left.

The gynecologist laughed. "Yes. Ordinarily, I'd require the woman receiving the embryo to remain prone for as long as possible to give it the best chance for attaching itself. Won't need to in this case. Now the odds of having a healthy daughter just improved. I'll check tomorrow and see if all is well."

Liz said, "Congratulation, Jenna. Now you'll have a boy and a girl."

Jenna grinned. "But what's Tom going to say?"

Chapter 25 Dr. Chandra Hyber

The next morning Jenna, Dave, and Liz visited Tom again. The doctor dropped by.

"Good news. The embryo has attached, and everything looks perfect. I'm weaning her off the morphine today. I would recommend you visit her each day."

After he left, Jenna had Dave set up her laptop. With nothing they could do, Dave and Liz headed home, allowing Dave to get to work at GD.

When Tom began mumbling again, she touched the Record button with a toe.

"Hyper. Equations. Figures. Topology key. Saddles show," she mumbled. Bits of equations dribbled out, but Jemma recognized parts of her own ion engine equations. Has Tom figured out hyperspace?

The next day, Tom seemed more "present" when Jenna arrive. At least he spoke more.

"Jenna. I ache all over. Everywhere. Sound funny. What happened?"

She sighed and explained what had happened. Tom drifted off before she finished. When he became semi-alert again, he seemed to realize he'd lost his arms.

"I'm like you. Voice strange. Hospital?"

"Yes, Uptown Med Center." She told him about the gender change.

"But I want you still. You divorce me?"

"No, we can make it work. I love you."

"Love you, too."

When he came to, he said, "Hyperspace. Can see it. Figured out. Can't move. You take notes?"

"I have the laptop recording now. Go ahead. You figured out hyperspace?"

"Yeah. Can see it. Clearly. You were so close. Equations."

He began spitting out more pieces of equations, though Jenna didn't yet see how the pieces fit together into a completed whole. She continued making the recordings while Tom mumbled along.

After the drug effects wore off, he became far more lucid.

"It's all fresh. Vivid in my mind. I sound funny. I ache everywhere. It's like a saddle and ant. I figured out a way to tell others how to think of hyperspace."

"Go ahead. I'm recording it."

"You're an ant standing on the horn of a cowboy saddle. You see food on the back high rim. To get it, you walk down the horn, across where the cowboy sits, and up the backside. Long way. That's your reality, your space. Hyperspace is like us looking down at the ant's world on the saddle. We can see the shortest line from the pummel to the saddle back is straight across it, much shorter. But for the ant, it can't move through the air. It must travel along the saddle. Hyperspace is that direct, shorter route between two locations in our three-dimensional space. Topology. It's a topology problem."

The next day, he added to his story.

"Everything in our universe is moving. Our Earth, our sun. They are flying through space, always changing positions. If everything is in motion and thus positions are changing, how can we use hyperspace to shorten travel times?

"It becomes a close approximation. Hyperspace travel will pop you out in the vicinity of the destination. Key word: vicinity. No absolutes.

"Jenna, your ion engine is popping in and out of hyperspace about once each second. That's why it give the illusion of reducing ten years of travel at the speed of light down to one year. Stop pulsing, and you stay in hyperspace. Got the equations worked out."

The rest of the day until he fell asleep, he rattled off equations. Much later, they would have to translate that into written formulae to publish.

Another day, he explained, "We point the ship in the direction we want to travel. We need only one hyperspace coordinate, the distance to travel. No one can ever just sit on Earth, jump through hyperspace, and pop out sitting in a chair on Brussels. Everything is in motion. The best we can do is arrive in the vicinity with enough of a distance safety margin.

"My guess is we need at least a fifteen digit number for the distance, four of which lie to the right of the decimal point. Trouble is, we don't know where a 2.0000 jump will take us. Could land us in an asteroid belt. The middle of a sun, too close to a black hole, smashing into a dark dead star. List endless.

"I worked out a way to figure these jumps. To explore hyperspace. Take a fix on your position and verify nothing is in front of you. Make a one second jump. Note the new coordinates. Examine where you are—how far you've come in this direction. Then make another tiny jump. When you reach Brussels, you'll know the precise duration of the jump needed to get there.

"Using hyperspace and once the jump duration is known, a spaceship should be able to traverse ten light years in an hour or so, if my equations hold and using your ion engines."

The next day, Tom said, "Jenna, somehow I have to get all this written up in a paper. That way, others can follow it and make use of hyperspace."

"I know. I've been thinking about how we can do that. Look, I did this with my senior project, the ion engine. Let's do the same with your hyperspace theory. I have all your recordings. I can work on getting them into a paper and let you work out the details as we go along."

"That's wonderful. I have to do it now, because my insight might not last. I kept working on it while I was unconscious. How can I be unconscious and yet be conscious of working on hyperspace theory? Anyway, I was. I'm fearful it might fade away."

"It's top priority with me," Jenna said. "Let's get started."

"Okay, title it Hyperspace Theory and Application to Space Travel."

"By?" Jenna said.

"Oh, it can't be me. I'm a freak now. I best use a pseudonym like you did. How about by Doctor Chandra Hyber?"

Both laughed for minutes.

"Wonderful to hear you laugh again," Jenna said. "I feared I'd lost you."

"I'm worried I've lost you. That you won't want me now."

"Don't be silly."

"What are you two laughing about?" Major Callahan said, as she and Dave walked into the room.

"She still loves me," Tom said.

"You still working on that theory stuff?" Dave asked.

"Yeah. I'm stuck here totally immobile. What else can I do? Any word from GD on finding the bombs?"

Dave slumped. "Yeah, and we lost. GD has crews out searching for hidden bombs. They found one in the Nature Museum. The bomb crew arrived and began disarming it. But..."

Tom said, "There's always a but."

Dave grinned. "Yeah, well, the bomb had a surveillance

187

camera on it. As soon as they began working on dismantling it, a recording said, 'No fair disarming it.' Boom. They remotely exploded it. Massive damage to the museum. Several injuries in the bomb squad—none too serious."

Liz said, "That has ruled out searching for the fifty-nine other bombs and defusing them. You're stuck here until the body modifications are done."

The doctor walked in and overheard them.

"Yes, your CEO called me. She'll be here another month at least. But she should deal with the shock and trauma she's endured, her physical limitations, and gender change."

Tom said, "Have to get my theory paper done first before I lose it."

"I'm worried. You've not screamed or cried."

"Got to focus on this theory, first."

Jenna and Liz noticed Tom's taut facial muscles and gritted teeth.

When they headed home, Liz said, "Tom must be suppressing a wall of grief and terror."

"He is," Jenna said. "He's not confronting what's happened to his body. Somehow, his mind has worked out the monumental problem we've discussed for over a year. Came to him while he was doped up. He's convinced he has to get the details down on paper before he forgets it all."

Liz sighed. "Perhaps that's for the best. If GD can't prevent the bombings, he's stuck there for at least another month. Keep his mind off what's happened to him. But how about you? Are you okay with him being a woman now?"

"We love each other. That's what matters. No, I'm more worried about how he'll react to being like us. Handicapped. He's not shed one tear or let out one scream."

"You're the bravest woman I've ever known, Jenna Durbin. It's time I did something."

The next week, Jenna and Tom polished his paper.

Satisfied, Tom sighed.

"I'll send it to my GPan contact I used for Karl Oppenstein."

He said, "I can never thank you enough, Jenna. I couldn't have done it on my own. Not now."

"There. It's emailed. Now we wait to see what others think of it."

A blood-curdling scream caused Jenna to almost fall off the side of the hospital bed. Tom's suppressed shock burst, followed by uncontrolled sobbing.

The noise brought both the doctor and two nurses running into the room.

"What's happened to me? I can't do anything anymore. I don't even sound like me. I can't protect my family or anyone." She wailed and continued to bawl.

Over the sobs, the doctor and nurses check vitals.

"Jenna, all still looks very good. Casts come off in the morning, but I must install the breast implants or risk another bomb going off. Drop by say around ten."

After they left, the wailing died down to soft sobbing.

"Well, dear, we're stuck with your body being female. We can't keep on calling you Tom. Someone suggested Topsy, since your breasts will look like those of Sabrina. Monsters."

More sobs replaced a fleeting grin.

"What do you think of being called Tammy? It's close to Tommy, though I know you don't like the long form. We could call you Tam for short. That's close to Tom."

She nodded.

"Okay. I'll get the paperwork going for the name change, Tam. I love you. We'll make this work somehow."

"But I can't protect you or Sam."

When the next outburst of tears died down, Jenna continued.

"Your gynecologist—God, does that sound weird—says

we're having a daughter. Thank heavens they could salvage enough sperm to fertilize one last egg of mine. We'll have two children. If we want more, we can adopt, don't you think?"

"I'm pregnant?" Tam said, sniffling. "Guess if I'm to be a woman, might as well go all the way."

Jenna giggled. "At least this one last time. They didn't give you ovaries. No more kids for us. And it's awful having such large breasts."

"They're as big as Liz's."

"I know. But tomorrow, they'll install the implants. Bebo's orders say you can be released and go home in a month if the implants are inflated. After that and the bomb crisis has passed, we'll get the breast thing undone. Doctor said that's easily done. We're holding off on your feet. We dare not damage them further."

After Tam's sobbing died down again, she asked for a drink. Jenna used a foot to swing the cup over to her waiting mouth. Then she wiped Tam's face.

"Time to go home to Sam. Rae's been a godsend. She's changing his diapers and feeding him his bottle. We must thank her when you get home. Will you be okay until tomorrow?"

"I can cry myself to sleep. I sold my soul to GD. I've been expecting something bad to happen to me for a long time. I've killed too many people, even though they deserved it. I figured I'd be murdered, not maimed like this. Pay the piper time."

Tam broke into more tears, but Jenna had to return home. She leaned over, kissed her forehead, and left. She heard her soft sobbing drifted down the hallway. Her heart ached for Tam. I have to stay strong for our family.

190

Chapter 26 Major Callahan Takes Action

When sober-faced Dave dropped by, Liz knew GD had gotten no closer to handling the bomb threat. Jenna already told her about Tam's sudden explosion of shock and grief.

"Dave, I feel awful sitting here doing nothing. Tom went out, searched for me, and killed El Gato who did this to me."

Dave sighed. "We sorely miss your skills, Liz. The other Intelligence Officers are disorganized. Muddling along, I'd say."

"If I could do anything to help…"

"I modified an AI program you can use to control your surveillance systems. Got your office voice activated, including the lights. Still haven't figured out what to do with your drones."

Liz allowed a slight smile. "Voice activated?"

"Yeah. Called him Boris. Didn't want to use any name you're likely to find around GD. I've made a cheat-sheet of commands. Pasted on your wall. Oh, and made a low-to-the-floor keyboard. You can sit and type."

"You think I'll be able to return to work. Like this?" She shrugged her shoulders.

"When you're ready. Gotta have hope. I've faith in you."

"Hope it's not misplaced."

Dave grinned. "Hardly. Just need time. Learn how to do stuff."

"I can't tell you how bad I feel not being able to help Tom, er Tam. She's stuck there another month. I don't see how she'll be able to do anything wearing heels like Rae's and with breasts like Sabrina. Hell, mine are a huge annoyance."

"So Tom's gonna be called Tam now?"

"Yeah, Jenna said so. Apparently. He, or rather she, has been suppressing it these past couple weeks. Late this afternoon, Jenna said it burst out. Exploded, as she put it. Screams and sobbing. That's a damn good sign."

"I'm heading home. Anything you need done before I go?"

"No. Thanks. You've always been here for me."

Dave smiled. "Always."

The next morning, Liz had Rae help her into her altered GD uniform. The pants fit well, and she slipped into and out of the soft-soled shoes easily. Art had long ago sent over several new blouses that handled her enlarged bosom.

Rae said, "I've no idea how to tie your tie. You want your hair up in a bun? Dave said you used to wear it that way."

"Yes, but I can't do that anymore."

"Let me try."

Later, Liz looked in the mirror. Except for the dangling tie, she looked proper, except for how curvaceous her body was.

Liz sighed. "Another thing I can't do. Can't get dressed, put my hair up, or knot the tie. Pathetic."

Dave entered. "Wow! Liz, Major! Look at you."

Liz pivoted. "A helpless Major. Can't even tie it."

"Let me to it."

Rae headed off to help Jenna in the kitchen.

"Dave, walk me to GD today."

"Love to. Are you returning? To work, I mean."

"I can't live with myself if I keep on sitting here with Tam facing a hideous life. I must try. But..."

Emotions swept over her. She tried hard to suppress it, but failed. Tears trickled down her cheeks.

"I mustn't show emotions, but I can't help myself. God, my leg hurts, Dave. Have to sit."

She plopped into the nearest chair, while Dave

massaged her leg.

Liz opened her eyes wide.

"Dave, my Dad told me that. When I broke my leg. About ten-years-old. Fell out of a tree. It hurt like the devil. I cried and sobbed until Dad came. He told me, 'Liz, a good soldier doesn't show emotions. There, that's it. Stone face.' I tried hard to not show any reaction, but I had a broken leg. It hurt like hell. I kept a stone face at the doctors. Dad said he was proud of me. That's a silly reason to suppress my feelings, but I've done that my entire career.

"Weird. That pain is gone. I feel lighter somehow. You've been supporting me all these years, haven't you?"

Her eyes met his. She leaned over and kissed him. His arms encircled her waist, pulling her close.

When their lips parted, he said, "I've been dreaming about that for years. I love you, Liz Callahan. Ever since I met you."

She chuckled. "Dave, I love you, too. Only now I can say that. Couldn't show it before. How dumb is that?"

Dave slipped down on one knee. "Liz Callahan, will you marry me?"

"Get up, silly. Yes. Yes, only if we can do it soon! Jenna be my maid of honor."

"I want Tam to be my best man. We'll do it in her Med Center room."

"Make it happen today."

"Yahoo. Jenna, Rae."

He dashed off to tell them the news. Then he called Art.

When Liz joined them, Rae and Jenna hugged her and congratulated her.

"Let us know your date," Jenna said. "They're doing stuff to Tam this morning. I'm supposed to wait until ten to go to see her."

Rae said, "Think Phillis and I could get married with

you two? I don't have anyone to be my best man. She'll have someone be maid of honor."

Liz said, "I don't mind sharing our special days, Rae. Let's do it, but we'll must hold it in Tam's Med Center room. Who would you like to stand up with you?"

Rae said, "You, Liz. Getting you out of those monsters' hands rescued me. But if you're getting married too, I'll see if one of others at the tea garden will do it. Shame jewelry stores haven't reopened yet."

"I know. Dave and I'll get married first. Then I'll stand up with you. We'll hold a joint reception after that."

"Would you? I'd love that. Outside of Phillis, you're the closest person to me," Rae said. "I'll check with her tonight, unless Jenna gets back early. I'm on Sam duty."

Dave said, "We best head to work. Don't want the Major to be late on her first day back."

After well-wishes, the two left, taking the MTES. As Major Callahan activated the automatic doors and walked into the GD lobby, hundreds of GD personnel clapped and cheered, led by CEO Art Townsend.

Major Callahan didn't know how to react. Instead, she allowed her tears of joy to speak for her.

Art said, "On behalf of every GD employee, welcome back Major Callahan!"

This time the noise was deafening, before Art suggested everyone get to work. He followed Dave and Liz up to her office.

"Major, if there's anything you need, ask. We're desperate for your investigative skills."

With that, he left. Dave pointed to the chart of commands.

Liz said, "Boris, turn on my monitors. Show me the reports of what they have done to locate the sixty bombs."

As the monitors powered up, Dave smiled and left her

to do her work, returning to his IT post, presumably to pursue other ideas.

A few minutes later, she verified her fellow Intelligence Officers had done everything she would have. That realization produced a smile. This situation required a fresh approach.

"Boris, show me the info Sabrina brought us."

The rest of the morning, she studied the documents. Bebo had documented his every move. Dave dropped by at lunchtime.

"Is it noon already?" she said.

Dave grinned.

She sighed. "I guess it's time to show up in the lunch room and let them stare at me while I try to eat. You must carry the tray for us, lover boy."

"Wow. I never thought I'd hear you calling me that. Like Phillis said, everyone is curious about how you manage. A week from now, no one'll pay the slightest attention to you. Come on. Any ideas about how we can help Tam?"

Liz found everyone in the cafeteria either staring at her or sneaking frequent glances. Dave kept her calmer than she expected, chatting about Sabrina's assistance to the cause.

The embarrassing lunch done, Major Callahan called her top staff to her office for a meeting.

"Okay, I've been going over what Sabrina brought us. Bebo's guilty of so many crimes that I lost count. Most of his gang of thugs live south of old I55, nestled between the old I90 and Western. He operates out of a former Chase Bank in Bridgeport. He and his wife are often seen at the art museum a few blocks away.

"You've already done everything I would have ordered. Your list of potential targets, some six hundred of them, are all likely ones. Assuming his targets are on your list, we've only a one in ten chance of picking the right one. We already know he's got spy cams on them and detonates them via remote control the moment we attempt to disarm them.

"We need a new approach. Let's focus on what we can learn from the bomb that went off. Let's see if we can locate other bombs. Go undercover. Leave your uniforms at home while you search. My current thinking is the bombs are similarly constructed. See if anyone has recently activated sixty of those antiquated cell phones. We need clues."

When they dispersed to carry out her requests, she headed down to the IT department to find Dave. His door didn't open automatically. She bit her lip and struggled to open it with a foot.

"Major!" Dave said, dropping papers onto the floor as he rose.

"Surprised you, eh? Good. A question. The trigger for that first bomb—"

"One of the obsolete cell phones," Dave finished her sentence.

"Right. Our new phones—do they use the same cell phone towers?"

"No. They use comm sats that give far better coverage. Why?"

"How many of those old cell towers are there around Chicago?"

"I've no idea, but likely many hundreds. Why?"

"If we can locate a bomb and if we disable the cell towers, they can't activate the bombs."

"Hey, good idea. Never thought of that. But there are many of them. Plus, most of Chicago still depends on them. We don't dare destroy them. I've no idea where we might get parts to repair them."

"What about turning off their power?"

"That could work. But if they get wise, while we're disabling one bomb, they could trigger another one."

"Good point. Still, it's workable. Best if we located all

sixty bombs and disabled them at the same time," she said.

"Tall order. I think Art said they located five bombs before one exploded and he halted the search."

"Didn't know that. Any pictures of the bombs? Cell phone triggers?"

"Let me pull them up. I can get access to anything from down here."

His fingers flew over the keyboard, reminding Liz of what she could no longer do. She let that emotion sweep over her and didn't suppress it. That feeling vanished.

Five images tiled across his wide monitor. He used his fingers to zoom in on each.

Again, Liz stifled pangs of emotion. I can do that with my toes.

One by one, the ancient phones appeared embedded deep within the device. A spy camera lens couldn't be avoided if one wished to extract the phone.

"Looks like you're on to something, Liz. I told you we needed you back here. Well done. I'll relay this to Art while you head back up to your office."

Late afternoon, CEO Art Townsend summoned Major Callahan, Dave, and all other department heads to the auditorium. As they walked in, three chairs sat on the stage. Art sat in one. To his right, Liz recognized GPan CEO Wang Chan. The third chair was empty. When Art spotted Major Callahan entering, he signaled to her.

"Yes, I want you on stage with us. You deserve the credit you've earned."

After the last stragglers entered, Art rose and began the meeting.

"Today, Major Liz Callahan returned to work here as our Chief Intelligence Officer. In one day, she's shown us how much we've missed her. She's developed a way to prevent Bebo's people from detonating the bombs. I'll let her explain."

Liz's face felt hot. She rose. Her legs felt weak. "I think he's exaggerating. One of those ancient cell phones triggered the bomb. My assumption is that with sixty plus bombs to make, he's likely to have make them the same way. Thus, their triggers will be the old cell phones. On a small scale, if we locate one bomb, we could temporarily power down all nearby old cell towers. Then they can't detonate it while our people disarm it."

A distinct buzz filled the room as she sat down. Art took over.

"One possibility we've been looking into is locating all sixty bombs. Dave assures me we could shut down all cell towers in Chicago via IT methods. I took this to Wang Chan for his analysis. Wang," he said.

The immaculately dressed man rose and nodded to Major Callahan and Art.

"We most fortunate have Major back. Art and I discuss this in detail. We've decided to keep this plan as a last resort. Why? Assume we disarm all sixty. Bebo likely make more. Put them in other places and detonate them. All in revenge. We know he values revenge.

"We know location of five more. Fifty-five locations unknown. You identified six hundred likely targets. One in ten chance finding the bombs. Take many days to find them. Only reason for speed be your man in the Med Center. I told he be there maybe thirty days. May take that long to find other bombs.

"New plan is use plain-clothes guards find sixty bombs. Then see how long that takes. If done tomorrow, maybe we try plan. If take longer and Med Center releases your person, we still need to handle situation with Bebo. GPan's position is terminate Bebo and majority of his people at one time. Need plan to do that. Art and I work on that. You focus on finding bombs.

198

"Also, have other news for you. Dr. Chandra Hyber, an Indian mathematician, has sent GPan his paper outlining theory and application of hyperspace. My people have read it and believe this work. If so, we can adapt Karl Oppenstein ion engines. Travel time to Brussels might be an hour, not a year. If works, revolutionize space travel. Best news since ion engine. Have hope. That is all. Time go home."

As people filed out, several came up to the Major to welcome her back. She and Dave ended up being the last to exit the auditorium.

"What a first day," Liz said.

"Damn, lady, you're the hottest!"

Dave grinned, causing Liz to give him a big smile.

"It feels good not to suppress my emotions and how I feel."

Chapter 27 Tam's Progress

After feeding and changing Sam, Jenna put him down for a nap. Rae took over. Jenna headed to the Med Center hoping to hear good news. When she entered Tam's room, they had rearranged things a little. It surprised her to see Sabrina sitting in one corner.

Tam sat up on her bed. Staff had removed the many tubes, but she still wore the loose hospital gown. Jenna noticed her feet. The casts were gone. The doctor stopped rubbing Tam's feet and turned to her.

"Ah, Jenna. Right on time. Excellent news. First, as I told Tam, her shoulders are healed with almost no visible scarring. Magnificent surgery job. Her voice box, Adam's apple, and rib removal locations: healed. Undetectable scarring there. I've inserted the large breast implant forms per Bebo's orders. In two weeks, we'll begin the month-long process of inflating them.

"Her new female organs are healed. No tissue rejection has or will happen. The embryo continues to grow with no signs of future problems. Today, we'll start the last part of the transformation process.

"I've inserted a vibrator. Its purpose is to stimulate and help the new organs establish nerve pathways so they work as they should. Once the device brings on the waves of stimulation, the process is finished."

Tam said, "He means I'm supposed to have orgasms. IIope I know when it happens."

Jenna and Sabrina giggled.

The doctor, clearly feeling embarrassed talking about such things, continued.

"Tam's feet are healed from having been broken and reformed into steep arches. I asked Sabrina to assist Tam as she learns to walk. During the past two weeks, I've had people searching for proper heels for Tam. Finding shoes with such heels has been challenging. Most fetish stores haven't reopened.

"Since Tam must be able to slip a shoe off and on, this limits shoe styles. All the types I would prefer she wear, she wouldn't be able to. Sabrina's been a big help.

"We've settled on straight pumps and mules. If these work, we have boots lined up for winter wear. Sabrina's feet are malformed like Tam's are. Also, I've taken photos and videos of her feet and sent them to the podiatrist for analysis.

"Here, inspect for yourself. This is Tam's natural at-rest foot position. Have a seat by Tam and take off your shoe. We can do a side-by-side comparison. That will explain a lot."

"What a difference," Jenna said. "Can she even walk without wearing heels?"

"We don't yet know. Sabrina says that's painful, and she only does it at night if she needs to go to the bathroom. Otherwise, she wears hers all the time. But she's wearing the style I would recommend. It's an Oxford and gives her foot and ankle substantial support. But you can't slip them off. You untie them.

"Okay, Sabrina, you take that side and I'll take this side. Tam, see if you can stand up on your feet. We won't let you fall."

Jenna watched Tam's legs and torso. She knew what to look for. Could Tam keep her balance?

"Well, I'm up. God, this is freaky. Feet hurt. In the arches."

"Makes sense. That's where the stress is being applied. Now see if you can walk on them."

Jenna watched the wild wobbling, and suspected Tam

would have fallen without their help.

"Maybe I can get the hang of it," Tam said.

After sitting back down, the doctor put the tall pumps on Tam's feet. They had her stand. Again, Jenna saw wobbling.

Tam smiled. "Arch pain is gone. Can I walk in these?"

Sabrina said, "Oh, yes. But you must practice a lot since you've never worn heels."

For the next half hour, the doctor had Tam practice taking heels off and putting them on. Satisfied Tam could do it on her own, he gave Tam her assignment.

"I want you to practice walking around the room until you feel comfortable you can do it on your own. Sabrina will assist you but work on not having to depend on her help. If you're successful today, tomorrow, you two can walk the halls. Once I'm satisfied you're able to get home on your own, I'll release you. Return for checkups and further breast form inflations. I checked with the original surgeon who checked with Bebo, who agreed, as long as Tam shows up for each appointment. I will live stream them so they can verify breast size."

With that, he left.

Sabrina said, "They have assigned me to help Tam. I guess I'll be coming home with you tonight. I don't want to intrude, but you can't help Tam keep her balance."

Tam said, "Jenna, I'm scared. Really scared. What if I can't do this?"

"I could tell. Remember, Liz felt terrified at first, too. We will manage somehow. Sabrina, I don't know how to thank you."

"I can't imagine how you two do everything."

"Oh, Tam, Dave and Liz are getting married. He's made you his best man. We will hold the ceremony here."

"Now that's good news. Dave's been mad about her as long as I've known him. I don't know how I can be a best

202

man."

"And Rae wants to marry Phillis at the same time. She wants me to be her maid of honor. Phillis will ask Irene to be her maid of honor. Tomorrow we will hold two weddings in here. Better practice walking, dear. I want you home. Sam, too."

"He's too little to know," Tam glared.

Sabrina said, "Tam, heels like these are sexy. They give our legs a terrific shape and make men pay attention to us. Walking isn't hard, just takes practice to get comfortable in them. Going down stairs gets tricky. Think 'I'm looking sexy,' and you'll grow to love them. I sure do. Rae does too. Did you know Phillis loved them and wore them before she lost her arms?"

Thus, the practice sessions began.

The next day, everyone assembled in Tam's room. She felt self-conscious wearing nothing but the flimsy hospital gown. First up, Dave and Liz's marriage ceremony.

"Don't let go of me," Tam whispered to Sabrina as they walked to Dave's side.

Both wore their GD uniforms. Jenna stood beside Major Callahan who grinned.

Jenna whispered, "I've never been a maid of honor before. We'll hold a fancy party soon."

Art kept it simple. Besides, no jewelry stores had resumed operations. No rings. Wedding dresses likewise weren't available.

Next, Art married Rae and Phillis, while Jenna stood beside Rae. Irene, with her dual hooks, stood beside Phillis. The four looked radiant.

When the ceremony finished, Irene said, "You are all invited to the tea garden tonight to celebrate. Sorry you can't come, Tam. We will miss you, and Phillis, too, but she and Rae just rented apartment #2 across the hall from you and Tam,

Jenna."

After many hugs, kisses, and words, most left. Sabrina had Tam sit down to rest her feet.

A messenger knocked. "Jenna, CEO Wang Chan wants to see you in his office right away. Can you come with me now?"

"Yes. Rae is watching Sam. Did he say what he wants?"

The messenger said, "When the Sol Empire-wide GPan CEO calls, you don't question. Something big's come up. All hush. Hush. You must be very important for him to request your presence. You don't have arms."

Jenna chuckled. "Is it that obvious? I thought I'd hide them today."

The messenger flushed.

"Bye, love." She kissed Tam and left.

"Well, now it's just us," Sabrina said. "Up and at it. You need to learn to walk in these heels, swinging your butt. You'll drive Jenna nuts."

"You're kidding?" Tam said, obviously unable to tell if she was joking. "I guess if you and Rae can do it, then I should be able, too."

"That's the ticket," Sabrina said.

She has no idea how terrifying this is!

***

"Ah, Mrs. Durbin, come it. Come in."

Jenna took the nearest chair in this opulent office. That new carpet smell permeated the room while sunlight filtered in from windows that surrounded three of the four walls. The immaculately dressed man, who was standing behind his giant desk, rose but then moved around and pulled up a chair close to her.

"I asked you here as Karl Oppenstein. We need your expert opinion. Life and death matter. Critical situation. One of the engineering design staff be here soon with problem. He not know you are Karl. Let's keep it that way. He bring problem must be solved."

"Don't your engineers know how to solve this problem?" Jenna asked.

"With life-death matter I must decide, pays to get outside answer. Then I make better decision. Ah, here he comes."

A young man in casual clothes, but with the pink-gold GPan ID card, walked in. The most notable feature was his pocket protector jammed full of pens and pencils, Jenna couldn't have inserted another if she tried. He seemed flustered.

"Engineer Rook, this is Mrs. Jenna Durbin. She long-time GPan employee. Good physicist and mathematician. Show her problem and get her answer, please."

"But it's top secret classified," the man said, trembling. His nose twitched, and he stared at Jenna.

Wang pulled a lanyard with Jenna's ID card attached from his pocket and hung it around her neck.

"I summoned her from Med Center. She no have time to get her usual ID. Here's a copy card."

He flipped it up so the engineer could see its front.

"She long-time employee with highest clearance. No problem there. But no need for her to know all details of project or project purpose. She here to independently solve last problem: height."

"But we've already solved it," he protested.

"Most true. Good leader seek independent answer with life-death decision make."

"Very well. Follow me, Mrs. Durbin."

She followed the man out of the CEO's office.

Once in the elevator, Jenna said, "Just call me Jenna."

"Bill, here. How can you solve a very complex design problem when you don't even have hands to do it?"

"I use my feet and mind."

"How did you get the highest clearance? Even I don't rate that. And who are you exactly?"

"Sorry, I can't tell you that. I'm just Jenna Durbin. But he's right. I didn't know I'd be summoned here today. My ID is back home. I don't go around broadcasting I'm a key GPan employee. What is this life-death problem?"

"I can't tell you that. Here."

They entered a small conference room with a blackboard filled with equations and numbers. A long table and chairs filled the middle of the room, but it had no widows.

"I've laid out the basic equations."

While he went to the blackboard, Jenna pushed a chair out and sat.

"We have this energy source, S, with a specific output and dispersal pattern given by these equations. We've added a side panel six feet tall. The problem is find H, the height the source must be at such that the energy levels at ground level do not exceed this level here."

"Oh, I get it. Microwave radiation. Containment baffle. Wait, that's one enormous energy output. I don't see how your microwave oven can create that, unless you put a nuclear power plant in there."

His face flushed, and he mumbled.

"Find H. Okay. I need paper and pencil. On the floor, please, unless you want me sitting on the table. What you're missing is the equation for the height H. We get that by combining several of these and integrating, like so. Give me a couple minutes here."

Bill just stared at her, mouth half open, while her foot wrote out lines of equations.

"Now this is a cool max-min problem. With this combined equation, we get its derivative. Now force the minimum energy level as the boundary condition."

A minute later, she said, "And out comes H. Looks to me like a hundred-two feet up. We could program this into the computer and have it print out the ground level radiation level versus height. That might be even more useful."

"I can do that. Thanks. Amazing, Jenna. At first I thought CEO Chan had flipped out. Guess you know your stuff. I'll show you out. Please, don't tell anyone about this. Top secret and all that."

Jenna smiled. "I won't because I'm not sure what this is all about. No one has nuclear powered microwave ovens."

She knew she must be close to the target from his even redder face. Since lunchtime beckoned, she headed home to check on Sam.

Chapter 28 Disruptors' Fate

July 15, 2037

CEO Art Townsend again summoned the many department heads to the auditorium in the GD skyscraper. Dave and Liz sat in the back.

"Glad I'm not on that stage like last time," she whispered.

"I thought you looked fabulous up there."

She butted him with her head.

"Everyone, I've called you here to show you what we just received. Today should have been freedom day for our employee Tom Durbin, now Tam Durbin. She's endured all that Governor-mayor Bebo Ritzker demanded. He's kept his word and hasn't detonated more of the bombs, though as of today, we know the location of fifty-one of them. Teams are still searching. I'll play you the video I received early this morning."

The giant wall monitor showed the man's image. He wore a brown suit that looked expensive and sat behind an enormous desk. His wife, Honey Bunny Ritzker , wearing a red gown, sat beside him, her monstrous bosom dominating her image.

"Today is a remarkable day. You have proven that I, Governor-mayor Bebo Ritzker , am the actual ruler of our city and state. I kept my word. I didn't activate more bombs because you followed my orders to the letter. Well, after that one slip. Children must be taught lessons.

"I've done GD a great service by providing you with a superb example of what a glamorous woman can be, Honey

Bunny Durbin. I can't tell you the pleasure I get from my Honey Bunny wife here. Isn't she just perfection?

"Now that you recognize my supreme authority, I want every corporate CEO to have their own perfect Honey Bunny wife or spouse. To that end, I order you to send your wives or spouses to my Med Center this week. They'll be transformed into perfect Honey Bunnies. I do have a list of CEOs. Don't try to fool me. Again, for each CEO who hasn't complied by next week, boom! Another one goes off.

"Next, GD must deliver one of those devices that handled the Galactic credits to me, with ten million credits in my account. By Monday. Or Boom. Boom.

"Soon I will have more requests. In a few months, we will fill the city with gorgeous, perfect Honey Bunnies."

The video ended to a hushed audience.

A voice called out, "You can't go along with that!"

A chorus of "Yeah's" followed.

Art raised his hand, silencing them.

"I've been in touch with the many other CEOs. None of us are going along with him. Sol Empire-wide GPan CEO Wang Chan called us after we received the video demands. He said, and I quote, 'Leave him to my people.' Said he'll be coordinating with us. He wants our people to defuse the bombs we know about when he gives the signal.

"I tried to get him to tell me what he had planned, but he said, 'Top secret.' I couldn't get more out of him, except to be ready. But he asked that I send Major Callahan, our drone expert, and Dave from IT over to the GPan skyscraper. While I organize bomb disposal crews, you two scamper next door to GPan. Report to our local GPan CEO Eric Paddock. Wang Chan is letting our local group handle it. More when I know more. Let's move, everyone."

Minutes later, Dave and Liz entered the neighboring skyscraper. Two men in purple and gold uniforms met them, ushering each in different directions. They said nothing until they took their GD people into secure rooms.

"Wow! You've more monitors than I do," Major Callahan said.

A tech smiled. "Aye, special setup for this operation. GD claimed you're their best drone pilot."

"Was. That's before I lost my arms. What's this about?"

"I'm told you could fly them with your feet. I've set up a special program of linked drones. I'd like you to try flying them in this pattern. Up, then turnaround while offsetting a small horizontal distance, and then back down. The program simulator has wired the set of drone controls into one unit. You use this drone control. Should fly like a single drone. We'd like your opinion on how well my simulator works, compared to what you've experienced flying the real things. I saw the video of your drones shooting the Antifa rioters. 30-30 was it?"

Major Callahan smiled. "Yes. Only could carry thirty-six rounds, though. I've not tried to fly them with my feet yet. This might not go well."

"Take your time. Experiment with hit. It should be a valid simulation. I hope."

She sat on the floor, and he slid the controller to her.

"Press the Fire button to activate the simulation."

"I'll try the controls first. See how well I can manipulate them. Just remember, I've never tried this with my feet."

"We know that. We're after your experience behind the controls."

Liz activated the simulation and watched her screens. Instead of trying to watch six at once, she picked out one drone and followed it, presuming the others would mimic what it did.

"Hey, bit sluggish. I should have crashed it. Not good with my toes yet."

"That's all right. I expected the controls would be sluggish. A safety factor. The actual test is can you follow the pattern."

After playing with it for a half hour, Liz gave her conclusions.

"It flies like an overloaded drone. Responses are very sluggish. I have to plan my turns about a minute ahead. Not like real drones, which respond almost at once."

"Your last pass was perfect. I can see why they wanted you to test this. I think they expected the response would be sluggish. But that's one great clue you gave me. Plan turns a minute ahead. That's going to be the key to its success."

"What's it going to do?"

"Classified."

Lis chuckled. "Isn't everything? Thanks for letting me play with it."

He took her to reception where Dave waiting.

"How'd it go?" he asked as they walked back to their building a block away.

She told him what she'd done.

"They had me going over the IT connections that harness a bunch of drones, making them act as one unit. I found one glitch that might have caused a crack up. No one will tell me what's going on, though."

Art met them in GD reception. "Guys, go home, get some sleep. I want you both back here at three this morning. I think it goes down then. Liz, coordinate the bomb disposal groups. Dave, keep our field comm systems up. Now scram."

The pair returned in the wee hours, filing into GD along with hundreds of others. Most were security guards, but Dave recognized several bomb disposal experts.

At three, Art ordered everyone into action. He sat next to Major Callahan, watching monitors and directing his crews.

"It would have helped if we could launch out spy

211

drones," she said.

"Ordered not to do that. Is this line live to Bomb Disposal Unit One?"

She nodded.

"Okay, you are cleared to disarm."

She and Art watched via the security cameras in the area along with the live stream from the group.

Liz held her breath, expecting to see the bomb go off as threatened, to watch body parts flying. When she gasped for air, they saw a thumbs up sign, indicative of bomb deactivation.

"All Bomb Disposal Units, it's a go," Art ordered.

"Is that a good idea? To risk everything at one time?" she asked.

"I don't think they are that organized."

A tense hour passed before fifty more "bombs disarmed" messages came in. That meant nine hadn't yet been found. Still, catastrophe diverted. After thanking everyone, Art sent his people home. Later, they learned even Art hadn't known what else was to happen at three that morning.

**

"Guys, turn to Galactic Entertainment on Channel Nine," Rae said across the hall to Jenna's apartment.

She and sleepy-eyed Phillis joined them.

The image of Wang Chan appeared on their screen.

"... last night, I ordered end to continuous treachery of evil self-proclaimed Governor-mayor Bebo Ritzker and his extensive gang of thugs. His continued disruption of Chicago and extortion schemes died with him last night. We not stand for thugs, mobsters, crime bosses in Chicago or anywhere. If you need a job, contact your nearest Galactic corporation."

The report then panned to a section of South Chicago. A reporter interviewed bystanders.

"We didn't hear nothin."

"I hear popping and tiny explosions. Like miniature lightning."

"I thought I heard a scream, may not, though."

"I thought I smelled hot dogs roasting. Ya, know, like we used to have on the outdoors grills years back."

In the background, men in white protective apparel carried bodies out on stretchers, dumping them into waiting EMACs. Various logos suggested they belonged to every Galactic corporation in Chicago.

Liz said, "Well, something major happened last night. There's gotta be hundreds of dead bodies."

Her phone rang.

"I'm supposed to report to Uptown Med Center this morning. What's going on?"

Rae's phone rang. "Hey, I'm supposed to report there too."

Sabrina entered the room, having gotten dressed. "Say, I've got a message to report to the Med Center. What's going on? I'm going there anyway to help Tam."

"I'd like to go see Tam," Jenna said, "but no one's left to watch Sam. Guess I can take him with me if we pack up stuff."

"I'll watch him," Phillis said. "I know I haven't done it yet, but I need to learn. Rae and I want children, too. If I can't manage, I'll call Patsy."

"Are you sure?" Jenna said.

"I've been watching how you do it. I have to try."

"Well, call if you have any trouble with him," Jenna said. "I can get back in a few minutes."

The small group headed to the Med Center, speculating about the sudden messages and what had happened in South Chicago.

Dave said, "I bet they've unleashed a new super weapon. But that doesn't explain why they want you at the Med Center. Keep me posted."

He peeled off to go to GD. The others continued on the MTES.

Lacking more info, they visited Tam's room. She sat on her bed, still wearing the hospital gown. But she had gotten her mules on and used the toilet on her own.

While they all chatted about the latest news, Sabrina turned on the comm system, but kept the volume down, as she'd already seen this part.

The doctor walked in, a big smile on his face.

"Well, I see you are all here. Okay, then. Here's the situation. CEO Art has informed me that Bebo and his organization has been terminated. It's on the news, though I suspect you've seen it. They're repeating everything.

"So, I have the okay to undo as many of your body modifications as we can and as you wish. Today, I'd like to work on breast reductions. I've brought in several plastic surgeons skilled in this operation. I'm not.

"I've already scheduled Tam here. GD is paying for your procedures, if you wish this done. If so, you must let the surgeons know the final size you wish them to be."

Tam and Jenna chatted, and Tam said, "I told them I want to be your size. Then we'll be a matched pair."

"Still big, but I like it. Thanks," Jenna said.

Sabrina said, "I want them back to what they used to be. C."

Liz said, "I don't want to miss any work. Things are happening."

The doctor said, "You'll only be unavailable for perhaps an hour."

"Well, okay then. Back to what they used to be. B."

Rae called Phillis to ask her mate's opinion. After a giggle, she said, "F here, too."

A few minutes later, four nurses entered carrying charts. They whisked the women off, though Tam's nurse used

214

a wheel chair for her patient.

With only Jenna still in the room, the doctor said, "Tam and Sabrina will take about two hours, but the others will be back much sooner."

Jenna headed home and relieved Phillis, guessing that caring for Sam overwhelmed her.

When they later met, Sabrina's comment echoed the women's sentiments. "I feel a thousand pounds lighter. What an enormous relief. My back loves it."

Jenna stuck around with Tam after the others headed home or to work.

"They want me here one more night. Just in case," Tam said. "Then I get to go home. And pick up beans."

"Yeah, we'll work on getting your toe strength stronger. And more flexible, too."

"I don't know how I will be able to do much. I have to be sitting on the bed to get my shoes on. Or lean against the wall. But even that's tricky."

"We will work it out. I promise you, dear."

Just Then the doctor rushed in, x-rays in hand.

"Oh, good. You're both still here. I have good news, I think. Remember that podiatrist who's been looking at your feet? Well, he's just sent me his latest findings. He's been going over all the x-rays and observations for weeks. He believes he's found a fatal flaw in the foot modification procedure they used on you. Best if I show you on the x-ray."

He clipped it to the light box on the wall and used a pen to point to a tiny white line at the heel end of the arch.

"At first, we believed they broke your feet and forced them to heal in this giant arch. But this white line suggests something else. He believes the process didn't break your foot, but forced the heels to rotate. Hence, the white lines. If so, standing with feet flat on the floor for some time may well force it to rotate back to where the heel belongs. Of course, that's painful. We'll numb them. He says we should hear a loud pop when they move back into position."

Tam gushed. "Do it! Now!"

Thirty minutes later and surrounded by two nurses, the doctor injected each foot. Soon Tam couldn't feel him sticking a needle in her toe. The nurses got her up, holding her securely. The doctor examined each foot to make sure they were lying as flat as possible.

"Now we wait," he said.

"How long?" Tam asked.

The doctor laughed. "Who knows? We're in uncharted waters. A loud pop if the podiatrist is right."

Time passed, and the nurses traded arms holding Tam. About an hour later, Tam's body jerked a little lower when two loud popping sounds broke the silence.

The doctor got down and inspected her feet.

"Get her up on the bed. Amazing. Jenna, come look. They look like a pair of normal feet to me."

"Yahoo!" Tam cried.

"A billion thank you's," Jenna added.

"Okay. I still want Tam in overnight. We'll re-examine them in the morning. If she has no pain when she stands or walks, then home you go. And I don't want to see you in here again."

"I don't want to be," Tam said.

"I best head home. I'll let Rae and Sabrina know about this good news," Jenna said.

The next morning, both women showed up with Jenna. They found Tam fully dressed and wearing soft slip-on loafers. While Jenna and Tam headed home, the other two had their feet repaired. By nightfall, they returned home.

Chapter 29 Aftermath

Morose, that's how Jenna described Tam's attitude. True, Tam worked hard picking up pinto beans and putting them into a bowl, just as Liz had done. And Tam tried to feed herself, feeble as her attempts were. It's just that her attitude seemed stuck. Or was it her emotions that seemed stuck on something which Jenna suggested might be no sympathy.

Based on Rae's advice, which accurately pegged Liz's recovery, Jenna had expected Tam's terror to shift to despair and fear and later slide into resentment, hate, and anger, as Tam pulled out of the horrible trauma. Yes, Tam showed terror and then despair. But as Rae had said, next in the recovery would be fear. Tam displayed that. Even the mention of going down stairs caused her legs to quake. But the everyday fear faded after the first week home. Now Tam displayed no sympathy for anyone, anything, or any action or minor success.

Phillis's remark, "Tam's like a dead head," stung Jenna.

Still, Jenna could not complain about Tam's progress in learning how to do the actions of life with her feet. From all the data Jenna had gathers, getting dressed always proved frustrating to those without arms and was voted the hardest thing to do, though carrying things proved a close second. Having Sabrina living with them and Rae in the adjacent apartment proved critical, since Dave had his hands full with Liz.

A week had passed since the mysterious deaths in South Chicago. The new comm center channel, Galactic Entertainment or GEnt, continued to report on the destruction. Rampant speculation filled the airwaves, since the cameras showed countless bodies being removed from the disaster zone. On Saturday, GPan, had to respond.

The announcer said, "Today, we have the Sol Empire-wide GPan CEO Wang Chan with us. He's promised to provide more information about last week's attack on South Chicago that killed Bebo Ritzker and many of his criminal mobsters."

The camera zoomed in on the immaculately dressed, thin man.

"Good day. Since the global total economic collapse and subsequent depression worse than Great Depression of last century, evil men, mobsters, thugs, criminals, and other selfish people sought power. Here in Chicago, Ritzker and his associated committed sixteen thousand five hundred four crimes."

He waved a large stack of computer printout. "Here documentation, often in his own words. I consider stealing someone's food rations tantamount to a death sentence by starvation. Murders, robberies, mutilations, extortions. Extensive list All here.

"During big depression, no one step forward to lead us back. Galactic corporations have. Kept food supplies, though meager, coming to city. With no gas, no cars. MTES vital be done. Corporations continue to pay for its construction. Your Galactic corporations lead world back to prosperity.

"Decades ago, scientists, engineers from US, Russia, EU, and China work together to build space station, then Moon Base #1, Mars Colony, and the Federations. Prove we all work together for mankind's benefit. Today, Galactic corporations only ones preventing world collapse into Dark Ages of abject poverty and suffering.

"Last week, Galactic corporations decided Ritzker and his mob go too far, disrupt and harm people of Chicago too much. Time to end his tyranny. Galactic engineers design new stealth machine. Used it on South Chicago where Ritzker and his mobsters live. Can report he dead now. Total dead: ten thousand six hundred fifty-five. Chicago now safe from Ritzker and his followers.

"New O'Hare Spaceport must expand. Soon much more traffic. People living south of old I90 and east and north of old I290 must move. Can have homes vacated in South Chicago. New O'Hare Spaceport be five times bigger. Includes Elk Grove, Wood Dale, Bensenville, Franklin Park, and North Lake.

"Why need bigger spaceport? Wonderful news. Hyperspace exists. Dr. Chandra Hyber's recent paper provides both its theory and how to use it. Our first test ship proves it works. Soon, can travel to Brussels not in one year, but in one day! Must now build new colonizing ships using hyperspace travel. Immigration to Brussels moved up to perhaps December this year.

"Conclusion. If you wish immigrate to Brussels or Pylon, contact your local GPan office. Not all accepted, though. Your Galactic corporations bring all newfound prosperity and security. That is all."

"About time! Yeah!" Rae said, punching her arm in the air.

"Yes!" Liz said, showing her emotions.

"Wow, a new death machine," Dave said.

"All those people have to move," Jenna said. "Glad we don't have to. Can you imagine living your entire life there and being ordered to move out while they bulldoze your house?"

Tam replied in a monotone, "Has to be built. Have to move them. Tough."

"I'll make us something special for lunch," Rae said. "Best news ever. Right, Phillis?"

"It's true," she said, "only the scientists used to work together. Like on the Moon Base making."

Just Then Sabrina's phone announced an incoming text

message. The flashing red light told all it had top priority.

"This is weird. I have to report to GPan at once. On Saturday?"

Jenna asked, "Did it say why?"

"Nope. Whatever Rae makes, save some for me."

Jenna found it curious that both Rae and Sabrina continued to wear their tall heels, even though their feet had been repaired. Rae said they were fetish, whatever that meant, and Sabrina said they made her look good. She watched Sabrina's tiny steps as she left the apartment. Meanwhile, everyone discussed the CEOs speech, speculating on what this new weapon was. Jenna suspected its nature, but wasn't allowed to discuss it.

***

Sabrina entered the tall GPan skyscraper. She'd only seen the local GPan CEO on the news, but Eric Paddock met her himself.

"Ah, Miss Stanway, thank you for coming. This way."

She took a seat across from him in his office. Unlike Wang Chan, his small desk suited him. A folder with her name on it lay on top.

"As you've likely heard, a Dr. Chandra Hyber has worked out hyperspace and how we can use it for fast interstellar travel. One day to reach Brussels, ten light years away. If this works out, a whole new avenue of stellar exploration awaits us."

"Yes, we heard that news. It's true. But why am I here?"

"Because no hyperspace coordinates are known, Dr. Hyber outlined how we can proceed. Jump into hyperspace for one second and drop out. Work out the ship's new location, scan ahead for black holes, dead stars, and such, then jump back for one second. Dr. Hyber believes the ship won't get lost or collide with other objects.

"We're about to send the first exploration ship out

220

utilizing this approach. We need someone who can look at the stars and tell where they are at, compared to where they were.

"I've searched many university records. Yours stands out in an unusual way. You used to spend many hours at the planetarium using the galaxy display."

"Yeah. Hours of fun. I'd use the travel through the galaxy simulator. Punch in some duration. When the new star field appeared, identify where I theoretically was. Talk about fun. The best."

"This is why we need you on this trip. Once they make the jump, you'll be in a new place in the galaxy. The ship must know where it now it located and if there are barriers ahead to avoid on the next jump. Are you ready to put your unique skills to work?"

"You want me to go on this first exploration ship?" Sabrina said.

"Exactly. You'll be a valuable crew member and receive top pay, plus insurance in case a catastrophe happens. If you agree, GD will reassign your corporate sponsorship to GPan."

"Yahoo. When do we leave? Where do I sign?"

***

Sabrina walked into the apartment, though she thought she floated in, her new lanyard displaying her GPan ID card.

"Well, what happened to you?" Liz said. "You're shining."

She waved her GPan ID. "Yahooie, I'm heading into outer space on the Explorer I. I'm their astronomer. We're testing Dr. Hyber's hyperspace theories and mapping the coordinates to Brussels. Incredible. Little o' me! The pay'll make me a millionaire in no time. Oh, Jenna, in case I don't come back, you're my insurance beneficiary."

Tam took the news stone-faced and said nothing.

"But why you? I'm envious," Liz said. "That was my dream. To go to Brussels."

221

"When I was in college, I spent hours and hours using the planetarium's simulator. I'd simulate traveling light years in one direction. When the new star field appeared, I'd see how long it took me to ID where I was at. Id the stars. I loved doing that. I had them program random jumps. I got very good at figuring out the new locations. That's what I'll be doing on each hyperspace jump. Isn't this just fantastic?"

"Wow. You bet it is!" Rae said.

"You're a GPan employee like Tam and me. Coolest," Jenna said.

"Congratulations. We should celebrate," Dave said. "Astronaut Sabrina Stanway!"

"Space Explorer Stanway," she giggled, correcting him.

Chapter 30 Alexa Adriana Soros

August 15, 2037
Los Angeles Area

Alexa Adriana Soros came from money, lots of it. But at a price she'd already paid. Today, nothing, especially men, was going to interfere or stop her from her goal. Her six-inch heels clicked in rhythm on the tarmac at her private airport near LAX. Behind her, a porter struggled with her six bags.

She heard no planes, unlike just a few years back. Even the smog that made LA famous had cleared up. No one could afford gas. Except Miss Soros. At long last, Alexa knew where she had to go. Chicago.

As she walked, words her father ingrained in her from childhood echoed in time to her clicking. "Alexa Adriana, we live in a vicious, dog-eat-dog world. Men grab attention by physical force. Yet, I want you to be the best. As a woman, you must be stunningly beautiful to grab attention. Do that, and you are in charge. Fail, and men win."

How many times had she heard that Alexa Adriana could not say. She had lost track of how many cosmetic surgeries she'd had, all to make her stunningly beautiful. Small adjustment to her nose, lower cheekbones—on it went during high school. Entering Berkeley, her father praised her appearance. Only the finest. Her long, wavy, platinum blond tresses shown and bounced as she walked. Her piercing sky-blue eyes drilled into others, who could not fail to miss her luscious thick lips and perfectly shaped facial features.

Mom would be proud of me, she thought as she walked to her private plane. Her father met the super model Aria in

Milan. He knew perfection when he saw it. And he spared no expense on Alexa Adriana's physical appearance, including designer dresses.

In college, a new top fashion style burst forth on the LA scene: the Honey Bunny appearance. At once, many top fashion models adopted the style. Although Alexa Adriana had her head in her books, her father continued to look for ways to help his only daughter become the most powerful woman in the States. Since movie stars made the leap into this look, he insisted she do it too.

"Look, Alexa Adriana, if you don't, when one of these women walks into the room, all eyes will leave you for her. You'll be giving her your power. We cannot have that."

She always wore tall heels to aid in making her impression. Higher heels wouldn't be a problem. She kept her nails long. What did another inch matter? Thus, in her Freshman year, she had the surgery done. After that, she tossed all her old gowns and dresses. None fit her now much larger bosom. She discovered finding elegant bras and tops that took a J cup were hard to find. But soon, such appeared in the most expensive boutiques in the LA area.

Thus, when she teetered into a classroom, all eyes focused on her, including the professors. That's the way it should be. Now, she resumed her studies. However, she soon discovered most students' interests focused on taking selfies, booze, coke, and hash. Partying superseded studying for many, but not the focused Alexa Adriana., who continued to pound the books, as others complained.

Students and men often vied for her attention, but she refused all offers of dates. Once, a "fan" tired to insist she go out with him. He latched onto her arm and dragging her along. "We're gonna have fun. You'll see."

Alexa Adriana reached into her purse, pulled out her snub-nose .357 Magnum and fired once. He never bothered another woman again, or anyone else. Again, during her high school years, her father's insistence on being a crack shot paid off.

She graduated with honors from their engineering program, a woman with money, beauty, and brains—a combination hard to beat. She loved to help others, especially women who asked. Her friends told her she had a caustic attitude toward men. That she wanted nothing to do with men might have affected how she treated them.

Then the global economic collapse brought on a depression so dark that most believed the entire world would enter a new Dark Age. Dollars became worthless, unless you didn't mind paying a thousand of them for a loaf of bread. Alexa Adriana listened to her father and invested her fortune in these new Galactic corporations just making their appearance worldwide. Of course, she invested in the corporation that rested atop their hierarchy, Galactic Expansion.

Via their new phone devices, she had all the gold backed Galactic credits she desired at the moment. While others in LA struggled day to day just to stay alive, she helped her girlfriends survive quite well. Meanwhile, she spent these past few years working on her passion. Last month, she'd finished her design. Now the time was right to implement it.

EMACs became available. She bought her own and studied its technology, incorporating it in her design. But the key to her invention lay just beyond her reach. Well, not exactly. She could have stolen Dr. Karl Oppenstein's plans, but that went against her sense of justice. He'd revolutionized space travel.

During her junior year, space junkies talked of sending space arcs to Brussels and Pylon in which several generations passed before the ship arrived. Thanks to this man—for the life of her, she couldn't figure out why a woman hadn't invented it—a spaceship could reach it in a year. She waited for that ship's return and recorded the news conference from GPan when it arrived home.

Trouble was she couldn't locate Dr. Karl Oppenstein. She tried all search engines, including a Dark Web one. The man didn't exist. And yet he did. She had his paper in her hands, having printed it off from the Internet. The man existed. Alexa Adriana even admitted this *man* might even be smarter than herself, something she never did. Only her father carried that notation.

Undaunted, Alexa Adriana took this as a personal challenge. She would find this Dr. Karl Oppenstein. She was unused to being frustrated this much. Many curses filled the past month, along with trips to the firing range and the expenditure of boxes of ammo. Last week, she took a different approach. She logged the dates of the appearance of comments and discussions about the man's ion engine. After days of checking, she discovered the first mention of his paper came from GPan in Chicago.

Chicago was her destination on this fine July day.

"Put my bags inside. Here's a twenty for your aid. Yes, it's the real gold back credit."

She ignored the man's prodigious thank you's and boarded her plane, a six-passenger Lear jet. After going through the pre-flight checks, she called the tower for clearance.

"It's not like any other planes are taking off, if ever," she said to the instruments before her. "Hope I'm not too rusty. Here I go."

Once in the air and the autopilot set, she headed to the galley to make a cup of tea and try the bag of scones imported from Scotland she'd just bought.

When she contacted the tower at New O'Hare, she gasped. She had to circle the air-space port twice before enough traffic died down to allow her jet to land. She took her annoyance out on the man in the control tower and later the porter who carried her stuffed bags to the rented EMAC.

Alexa Adriana studied the map of Chicago and entered her destination. For once, automation proved useful. The new style transport took her there. Landing became problematical. The MTES occupied the nearby streets. Annoyed, she set it down, squeezing in between the sidewalk and the edge of the mass transport. After securing it, she marched into the lobby of the GPan skyscraper.

Her clicking heels and swaying bosom got everyone's attention, as she intended.

The receptionist said, "Wow. Movie star?"

"No, I'm here to see the CEO. I am Alexa Adriana Soros. Tell him I demand to see him immediately. Aren't there any Honey Bunnies in Chicago? All the finest women are in LA."

As she stood by the desk, she tapped her right toe on the floor, making an audible sound, noticed by those closest to her. She ran her claws through her hair as though adjusting it. Finally, a man wearing a somewhat nice black suit arrived.

She observed his eyes sweeping up her form from her heels, then meeting her piercing sky-blue eyes, which she riveted on his.

"I am CEO Eric Paddock. I run the local branch of GPan. What is it you wanted?"

"Alexa Adriana Soros. I demand to see Dr. Karl Oppenstein, if he works here. If not, his address will do. Today. I don't waste time."

The man flushed, just as she intended. Perhaps I am being too caustic to him.

"I'll take you to see the Sol Empire-wide GPan CEO, Wang Chan. I'm not privileged to have access to that information. This way."

As they walked to the elevator, he said, "Are you from

227

Chicago? I don't recall seeing you before. Are you an actress?"

"LA. First time in Chicago. No. An engineer, if you please. I can't believe Dr. Karl Oppenstein is this hard to find. Do you realize it took me a month to zero it down to Chicago? His place of origin. He's only revolutionized space travel."

"He has. And Dr. Chandra Hyber had just taken it one step further. Hyperspace theory and application. We just launched our first deep spaceship working out the coordinates of Brussels. Once they're back, travel to Brussels might only take one day."

"What? You're kidding."

"No, he just published his paper here at GPan Chicago." Eric chuckled. "And that man is as elusive as Oppenstein. Ah, here we are."

She noticed it said floor one hundred. That new carpet smell permeated the foyer, and they bypassed his receptionist.

"CEO Wang Chan, this is Miss Alexa Adriana Soros."

Now here's a man who knows his suits, she thought. He rose, offered her a seat, and dismissed Eric. His face seemed displeased that he couldn't stay. She saw Wang only gave her stunning body a cursory look. She found that annoying. But maybe he was gay.

"Now Then Eric said you want to see Dr. Karl Oppenstein."

"No, I *demand* to see him. I have important things to discuss with him."

"Karl insists on his privacy."

"Don't care about that. We need to discuss aspects of his ion engines. Today. Now. Chop. Chop."

Her insistence raised a smile on his face, not at all what she'd desired. Men. Then pondered what she should say that would produce compliance on his part.

"You not patient woman."

"I spent the last month figuring out where he must be."

"And you decided Chicago?"

"Yes. The first mention of ion engines came from a post on the Internet from Chicago. So, does he work for GPan? If not, give me his address, and I'll visit him."

"Clever. Had not thought of that angle. I do what I can to protect his privacy."

"That's not my concern. I must discuss engineering with him. Today. Now."

"He work for me. Yes. You clever detective. He live Chicago. Best I can do is ask him if he'll see you. Please wait with Su Lin."

He waved her out of his office and closed the door. That annoyed Alexa Adriana, who had hoped to record his phone conversation. She turned off her cell phone.

He opened the door and beckoned her inside.

"Do you understand meaning of Top Secret, Miss Soros? I know you've donated a substantial fortune to this corporation. That why I make this happen."

"Yes, of course."

"Identity Top Secret. I warn you, tell no one the identity or location. If you do, I must terminate you and all you told. Is this clear? I never warn twice."

"You're joking? Killing me if I tell anyone about Oppenstein?"

Her piercing eyes met his. For the first time in her life, Alexa Adriana flinched.

"Must have your signature on document so stating."

He slid a document over for her to sign. As always, she read every word. He wasn't kidding. If she told anyone, they and she would be hunted down and killed as traitors to the Sol Empire. She signed.

He slid a second paper over to her and said, "Go to address here. Knock three times. Then you see why secrecy when meet."

"Thank you. Can I use my rented EMAC to get there?"

"Yes. It north of here. Uptown area. Can land near apartments. Good day."

With that, Alexa Adriana marched out of his office, past the receptionist, and entered the elevators. When the doors closed, she punched a fist into the air.

Her head held high and heels clicking, she marched out of the ground floor, aware of many eyes watching her movement. What puzzled her was Wang Chan hadn't been impressed like he should have.

When she landed her EMAC, she declared, "I have to add this auto pilot to my design. It's too darn convenient. Well, here goes."

She checked her appearance in a mirror. Satisfied she looked stunning, she walked up to the door of Apartment #1, prepared to make the desired impression on Karl Oppenstein so she could get what she needed. She knocked as instructed.

A woman's voice said, "Come in. It's unlocked."

Perhaps he has a secretary. She opened the door and entered. Alexa Adriana stared at a young woman with gorgeous shiny hair that fell to her waist. She had a large bust for a normal female, but her arms weren't there. Her smile, contagious.

"I came to see Karl Oppenstein. The GPan CEO told me he was here."

Jenna laughed. "You're looking at him. That's my pseudonym. When I published my initial paper on the ion engine, I knew no one would take an armless woman seriously. I chose a name that sounded important. I was right, too. It's a secret. Only my husband or spouse knows I'm Karl. All the others who live here or drop by don't know. Please don't tell them. I'm Jenna Durbin. I sent the others out for ice cream."

"Alexa Adriana Soros."

"Relation to the left-wing radical family?"

"Yeah, but I don't associate with half of them. Dad's okay, though. What happened to you?"

"Born this way. Got trained as an engineer. The ion engine became my senior thesis. The others will be back soon. We can talk shop, though. They're used to such discussions. Just don't reveal my identity. My husband and many others here have had no end of troubles. Bad people kidnapped Major Liz and cut off her arms. They did that to my husband Tom and put him through gender altering surgery. Now he's Tami. So, it's vital we keep identities a secret. This way to my cluttered study. Our infant son keeps us hopping."

"You have a baby? How can you manage that?"

"I do most everything. Tam is just learning how to use her feet as fingers. Liz does pretty well now. Oh, good timing. They're back. I'll introduce you and then we can talk."

She watched as a horde entered, tossing bags of ice cream on tables. Three of the women had no arms, causing Alexa Adriana to stare at them.

Chapter 31 Alexa Adriana Fits In

"Guys, this is Alexa Adriana Soros. She's come to chat with me about ion engines, but after we eat our treat."

"Wow, another Honey Bunny," Phillis said. "Your appearance, incredible."

"That's my good friend—heck, we're all good friends here. Lives across the hall. Phillis. Newlywed to Rae Lin." She nodded to Rae, who raised her hand with the dipper in it.

"This is Major Liz Callahan and her husband Dave, the IT expert. Both work for GD. And my spouse, Tami, who's carrying our daughter and learning how to use her feet. Here in Chicago, terrible people used Honey Bunnies as a torture weapon. And this is Sabrina Stanway, who's leaving tomorrow on the space Explorer I to map the hyperspace route to Brussels. Heard about that?"

"Pleased to meet all of you. I can't believe so many of you. Wow. I'm from LA. Out there, Honey Bunnies are the epitome of high fashion. Elegance factorial, as I always say. And no, only a bit ago from CEO Chan. Hyperspace travel is a real thing?"

Almost bored, Tami said, "Oh, yes. The calculations suggest ten light years travel in one day. Sabrina's ship will prove it."

Dave laughed. "You must be another one of them engineers. Or maybe a math hotshot like Tami here."

Rae said, "Jenna's right. They turned me and Tami and Liz into Honey Bunnies to torture us, but now that those terrible people are dead, we had the operations undone. But Phillis and I kind of wanted me to keep the changes. We're both into wearing fetish outfits. Well, she was until she lost her arms. It's the hot style in LA?"

"Sure is. Sabrina, what's your position on the ship? Cook?"

"Hardly. I'm worse than Tami at that. No, I'm their astronomer. After we make a short hop through hyperspace, my job is to examine the new star field and determine our position and then check ahead for things to avoid, like dead stars and black holes. Man, is doing that ever fun. Tomorrow, it happens. Yippee."

Dave said, "Liz in GD's Chief Intelligence Officer. I head up our IT department. Tami and Jenna work for GPan. What they do is a secret, but it makes them lots of money. Sabrina now works for them too. And Rae is Jenna and Tami's GD personal assistant. Ah, ice cream's dished. Dig in everyone. Hope you don't mind seeing many feet in action."

Alexa Adriana stared at the women whose feet held spoons and scooped chocolate ice cream up to their mouths.

"Say, tonight if you're still around," Phillis said, "you're welcome to come to our tea garden. That's where I work. Order taker. This group goes there every evening for tea and muffins. The best muffins in Chicago."

"Thanks. I brought my bags in case I had to stay."

Jenna said, "Let's go into my study and talk. Otherwise, this group will keep you occupied for days."

Following Jenna into the small back room, she said, "Fascinating people. I'm a little shocked. Nothing like what I expected times two. I expected to have to fight tooth and claw with a man to hear me out, but then I see you and many others and my mind gets blown again."

"We're people too. Anyway, now you know why GPan keeps my secret. What's so urgent that you came from LA and forced Chan to give me up? Must be important or did you use your wiles on him?"

"Ha," she laughed. "I don't think he likes women. He's

the first man my appearance hasn't grabbed his full attention. Okay, I got my engineering degree from Berkeley. As I graduated, these EMACs came out. Incredible machines. I bought one. But they are large and clunky. How often is anyone going to carry a dozen people around? Then I read about your ion engine. I had this idea why not make a two-man shuttle that darts around the city? Perfect transportation to get from here to there. Yes, the MTES is fine, but travel is risky. People are always getting robbed.

"But if they had a tiny shuttle, they could fly to work. That would be fabulous. I designed one. I received permission from the EMAC company, Cartwright Enterprises, to modify their levitation magnet scheme."

Jenna grinned, "Now you need a thrust source."

"Precisely. These are small, lightweight ships. I can't use a full-sized ion engine. I wanted to ask you two questions. Can your engines be scaled down a hundred-fold to work in my shuttles? If so, can we work out some form of tech licensing arrangement so I could use them in the shuttles? On my way here, I observed how marvelous the auto-pilot guidance system in the EMACs is. I must design that into the shuttles.

"Imagine this. You need to go to work downtown. You step outside and into your shuttle. Press a button. Presto, the shuttle flies you to the skyscraper. They'll need to provide parking spaces for the shuttles. But my shuttles will be smaller than these useless electric cars. That is, if your ion engines will work and not add more weight than I've estimated."

"Oooh, a design challenge. Let's do it. See if it can be scaled down enough and still provide the thrust you're gonna need. I wish I'd thought of this. Great idea. If we can scale it down, did you want to start your own company and make them or do like I did? I let GPan make and use the engines. They pay me a royalty fee for each one. I like this approach."

"Intriguing. Why do you like it better? Mr. Cartwright owns the EMAC patents and makes them. He's on his way to becoming a millionaire."

"I don't want to be tied down running a factory or business. I want to be free to do what I like and when I wish. I want time to invent new things, though having Sam has put much of that on hold. I never expected to be married, let alone a mother. More challenges than I bargained for."

"I can't imagine how you manage any of this, let alone design the most revolutionary engine in our century. But I get what you mean. I presumed I had to use my beauty, charm, and brains to get my two-man shuttles built and used. You know men. I figured I'd have to control the process every step of the way.

"GPan took your ion engine and made it a reality? I've seen they're equipping all existing and future spaceships to use your engine. And you didn't battle them on any of this to get it done and done right? They don't cheat and cut corners, producing an inferior product? That's a way of life for men of LA."

Jenna replied. "GPan did. I haven't seen any inferior or wrong specs in the working engines. They can't afford anything going wrong when the ship is ten light years away from help. Dependable is their motto. When I was in college, women engineers weren't taken seriously. And an armless one—well, I couldn't even get lab partners. When I finished my paper, I sent a copy to the top dog. Mr. Chan runs everything. He's the Sol Empire-wide Galactic Expansion CEO. The many local GPan CEOs are subordinate to him."

Alexa Adriana chuckled. "A woman after my own heart. You bypassed the men and went straight to the top dog. Good move. It's what I would have done and have done on many occasions."

Jenna smiled. "I bet you are a powerhouse. Always get

your way. Well, I knew if I showed up, Chan wouldn't take me seriously. Probably wouldn't even see me. I pretended to be a man. After he pursued the ion engine, he insisted on meeting me. I've never seen a more shocked man than Chan was when I walked in."

The stunning woman laughed. "Oh, I'd *love* to have seen that. Jenna, you are a kindred spirit. That local GPan CEO, that Eric fellow, he met me when I walked into GPan. I thought he might drool all over me. But my looks and attitude didn't cause Chan to bat an eye. He only looked me over for a fleeting second."

"He's always treated me fairly. Wang Chan used to be Mission Control Director for the Space Station and then for Moon Base #1. He knows how to run organizations. As far as I can tell, he's responsible for pulling the world out of what was going to be a second Dark Age. Well, we're not clear of that just yet."

"That explains much. Why he's a cool cucumber as we say in LA."

"Can I peek at your plans? Have you got a place to stay?" Jenna asked.

"Sure. On a flash drive. No, I can rent a hotel."

"Please, you must stay with us. We've plenty of room, and to be honest, I could use another pair of hands. Tam is barely functioning, just learning how to do things. And Sabrina's leaving tomorrow. Rae can't handle Phillis, Liz, Tam, and me. Please stay and lend us a hand. Mornings are the worst. Takes me forever to get dressed. Tam just can't do it yet. Liz and Phillis more or less can, but they take twice as long as I do. And everyone wants breakfast."

"I'd love to help, but are you sure I'm not imposing?"

"Not in the least. Let's join the others. They're dying to tell you the latest news and find out about you."

They found the others sitting around the living room

filled with baby items and chatting about the stunning woman.

"So, Alexa Adriana," Phillis said, "are Honey Bunnies popular in LA? Like we said, they used them as weapons here in Chicago. They made Rae, Sabrina, and Tami into Honey Bunnies. Rae and Sabrina looked gorgeous, but had to escape from the gangsters."

"Yes, in LA, many women choose to become Honey Bunnies. Very popular among the elite and Hollywood. But then the west coast always has been avant garde. Not saying that's such a good thing. The Dem Socialists destroyed Frisco. It's a dung heap. No one goes there. Hear several big West Coast cities are. We're just waiting for one of the yearly big fires to wipe it out so people can start again. I looked into it. Forest mismanagement. Save the frogs, lose the forest and towns."

Rae said, "Sabrina and I had it done just to survive. We were alone and starving. They convinced me I needed it done so I could be a nurse-in-training. They gave me food and shelter. I didn't mind much, cause I used to wear such heels and latex gowns to fetish clubs. Before the big crash, that is."

Sabrina said, "And they used it as torture on Tam. This is what will happen to all you CEOs if you don't do what I say."

"Leave it to men to turn beauty into weapons!" Alexa Adriana said. "LA's become a battleground between illegal aliens and the Sons of Liberty. I've had to kill three men who tried to accost me in the streets. Trusty .357 Mag in my purse. LA GD is struggling to bring any kind of order. But I can't believe they'd turn the beauty enhancement of the century into a torture thing.

"For me, it's been a powerful tool, second only to my Ruger. When I walk into a room, men do one of two things. They gape like puppy dogs and do whatever I want or I've captured their attention that they listen to me and go way out of their way to assist me. Either way, I win. Except for CEO

Wang Chan. Can't read him."

"Yeah?" Tam said. "Well, I'm proof they did. Look at me. I'm still a man inside. You're the most beautiful woman I've ever seen. You can't imagine how frustrated I am. I can't even have a wet dream. They removed those parts. No way to satisfy my dearest Jenna. Not like I used to. I hate those bastards!"

Jenna's eyes opened, but Rae recognized Tam had just risen above her chronic no sympathy tone. Tam's resentment and hate had to come off as part of the grieving process.

While the others continued the silence, Rae said, "Yeah, Tam. You should hate those bastards for what they did to you. Here's the most gorgeous woman I've ever seen, and you can't even have a pleasant dream with her. It's awful what they did to you."

Tam's face tightened flush with red. "Damn right, Rae. Those men. That doctor should be tortured. Rip his arms off. Turn him into a freak like me. But no, they boiled him alive.

"Wait. They boiled him. New weapon thing. My god, I bet that hurt like hell. Well, serves him—all of them—right. Even those who just went along with their shitty deeds. Boiled like lobsters. Wish I could have seen that. Seen them writhing. Serves them right."

She stamped her foot on the floor and took a deep breath. Tam looked at Alexa Adriana.

"You sure are a knockout. Don't worry. I've only got eyes for my princess," he said, grinning at Jenna.

Rae said, "Well done, Tam. Your complexion looks much better now, don't you think, Jenna?"

She nodded.

Tam said, "Sorry for that outburst, but I feel lighter somehow. Have I been really morose around here? Well, I should've. After what they did to me. How can I ever satisfy my Jenna again?"

238

Rae said, "And how can you be satisfied? Don't forget yourself. I'm sure you had just as much enjoyment as Jenna had."

Tam flushed bright red.

"Don't worry," Rae added. "I'll show you what you both need now. Won't we, Phillis?"

Her spouse flushed and nodded.

Alexa Adriana had been silent, watching the drama unfold. At last, she grasped what Tam meant.

Since the tenseness vanished she asked, "What just happened?"

Rae replied. "Last stages of grief. I am or was a nurse-in-training and found a chart that shows the various emotions a person in grief goes through on their way to recover. Some never recover, and some, like Tam, got stuck on their way through them. She's been pinned in no sympathy for weeks. You caused her emotional dam to burst. Now Tam can heal from that awful trauma."

"Guys, I'm off to work. Are you coming to the tea garden?" Phillis said.

"Don't worry, love. I'll drag them there if I have to."

An hour later, Alexa Adriana's eyes continued to stare at the women running the shop.

"Amazing," she said.

"No, terrific courage and steely determination," Jenna said. "Yeah, since you've never been around a person who's physically challenged, I understand your amazement. But from ours—we who live it—it takes courage and determination."

Tam added, "One hell of a lot. Almost more than I could muster."

Chapter 32 Birth of the Two-man Shuttle

Alexa Adriana accepted Jenna's offer to stay with them. The group had watched Sabrina in her new purple and gold uniform depart from New O'Hare on her first exploration of hyperspace. She stayed in part because she wanted to fill in for Sabrina lending much needed hands and because she and Jenna spent many hours each day downsizing the ion engine for use in the two-person shuttle.

Each evening, they spend many hours at the tea garden. Alexa Adriana, Jenna, and Tam monopolized the conversations, sometimes lasting until closing.

As the Dog Days of summer yielded to September, the plans for the two-person shuttle neared completion. As the group crowded around the dinner table, feet and hands stuffing mouths, someone knocked on Jenna's door.

"Expecting anyone?" Liz said, since most had their mouths full.

Jenna shook her head.

"I'll get it," Alexa Adriana said. She'd seen them having to stop and wipe their feet before getting up and putting shoes on. A major production just to answer the door. Heels clicking, she walked to the door and opened it.

A young man wearing brown corduroy pants and matching jacket with a cowboy hat and boots stood, hand raised to knock a third time.

"Wow! Who are you? Doesn't Jenna Sweet Durbin live here? I must have the wrong apartment."

He saw a gorgeous woman in a cherry red satin gown and matching very tall heels and two-inch nails. His eyes lighted on her enormous bust. Her wavy platinum blond hair draped over her shoulders.

His mellow voice caught her attention.

"Yeah. We're just having supper."

Having wiped her feet, Jenna moved up behind Alexa Adriana. Besides, she recognized the voice of her younger brothers.

"Ace? What brings you all the way up here from Flagstaff? Come on in. We're just eating. Care to join us? Oh, this is my brother, Ace Sweet. This is our new friend from LA, Alexa Adriana Soros. Come in. Bring your bags too, unless you plan to sleep in the hallway."

"Hi, Big Sis. Didn't know you had bimbo friends now. Guess things change. Hug," he said, ignoring Alexa Adriana and giving Jenna a big hug, though careful not to push his hat off. "I ate already. I'll dump my bags here."

Still ignoring the platinum blond woman and with an arm around Jenna, he headed past the living room into the dining room.

"Hi, everyone. I'm Jenna's little brother. Ace. Where's my nephew, the next great baseball player? Ah, there you are."

He spotted Sam sitting in a walker beside the crowded table.

"Uncle Ace brought you your first baseball glove and ball. Course, you must grow some, but it'll be here for you when you're ready. Which one of you is Tom, er Tam? Sorry we couldn't get up here for your wedding. Planes were grounded since the econ crash."

He's eyes roamed from Liz, to Phillis, landing on Tam, who sat beside one empty seat.

Jenna nodded to Tam. "This is my hubby Tam. I'm not sure Sam is going to be a baseball player. Like I said in my message, Tam's carrying our daughter. We have been lucky to have one last chance for a child."

"Hi, Tam. I can't imagine what you've been through.

241

But I'll say this, you've made my big sister a happy woman. For that, you have my undying gratitude. You ever need something, just say so. And let's see, you must be the Intelligence Officer Major Callahan."

"Liz, please. Join us. Jenna never told us about you. Oh, my husband, Dave. He's GD's IT man."

"Hi. Yes, Jenna's told me about you two. And who are these charming women?"

Jenna said, "Rae and Phillis Lin. Newlyweds, too. They're in Apartment #2 across the hall."

Rae said, "Hiya. I'm Jenna and Tam's personal assistant. Phillis is a waitresses at the tea gardens. You must come and see it tonight. We always spend evenings there."

"Jenna's told me about it. Herd of horses can't keep me away. Who's this bimbo with you? I can't imagine what you're doing with someone like that. I heard I missed Sabrina. Glad she's landed a stellar astronomy job. Pun intended, guys. Is the bimbo her replacement? Lending helping hands around here?"

Alexa Adriana slipped into her seat next to Jenna, her jaw clenched, having moved about half their speed. She appeared ready to launch a fiery comeback, but Ace didn't give her a chance.

"So, Big Sis, GPan CEO summoned me here. On a corporate jet, no less. Some hush, hush project. Guess I'll be staying a while. You can let your hired helper here go while I'm here. I don't mind helping. Have to show me what Sam eats. Hope he's not breast feeding. Can't help with that. Oh, Mom and Dad said to say hi. I know they hated to miss your wedding. If they ever get planes flying again, I know they'll be up to visit you and Tom, er Tam. Sorry. Takes some getting used to. Must be awful for you. I doubt I could adjust if they'd done that to me. Course, I grew up around Miss Hot Shot here. Have I ever got the stories I can tell you, Tam! The inside scoop. Has she told you how she moved the giant monitor when she moved back home? All by herself. Couldn't wait for Dad or me."

"Don't you dare tell, Ace. You'll get a resounding kick if you do," Jenna said, causing everyone to laugh.

"But inquiring minds want to know all," Ace teased.

"Don't you dare, Ace Sweet, or you'll be soured," she replied.

After the laughter died down, she said, "Ace is a professor at the university in Flagstaff, Arizona. Teaches electronic engineering. He's received five national teacher of the year awards."

"Ah, ha. That accounts for his over-sized ego," Alexa Adriana said. "Just like a man. Don't know how you put up with him. Guess you didn't since you're here in Chicago, a very long way from Flagstaff."

Liz said, "Ouch! The war begins. Bet you didn't know she's a billionaire, Ace. The name Soros should have been a clue."

"Oh, I got that bit. No respect for those who helped destroy our country," Ace said. "Guess the econ collapse wiped out her wealth. So she's working as a personal assistant now, though given her looks, other lines of work would seem more appropriate."

"Ace, you're putting your foot in your mouth," Jenna said. "She's a GPan stockholder and has an engineering degree. She's anything but a bimbo. Alexa Adriana is from LA, and there this Honey Bunny look is the fashion statement among the wealthy and Hollywood. Not like it was around here. You owe her an apology, Little Brother."

"Oh, sorry. Deceiving looks. I admit I'm brash and sometimes jump to conclusions. Haven't seen my Big Sister for years. We're proud of her and what she's done up here in the Windy City. I wasn't expecting to see someone like you at her door. Let's start over. I'm Ace Sweet. I teach EE at Northern

Arizona University."

"I don't think we need to start over, Mr. Giant Head. You're here to visit Jenna?"

"Well, yes and no. I got an official GPan summons. Our local one connected me via vid call to the Sol Empire GPan. CEO Chan. Ordered me to come at once. Sent a jet to fetch me. Had to, Commercial jets still aren't flying. Doubt if they ever will. Hey, heard someone in England is adapting EMAC tech to airplanes. Anyway, got some big hush-hush meeting with him tomorrow. Haven't seen him since last year. Sorry, sis, I couldn't visit with you back then. No time. All rush-rush. You know what I mean. At least this time, I get to see you and Sam and Tam."

"And us," Liz said. "Jenna never talks about you, Ace, but then we never asked if she had siblings."

"Just Ace," Jenna said. "The four of us. Mom and Dad doing okay? Still on the dude ranch?"

"Yeah. Don't see them much since I started teaching in Flagstaff. I try to drop in on them once a month when I can scrounge up some gas for the truck. Electric cars can't go that far. Only two EMACs in the town. University's got one. Used it twice to visit our folks. Dad says I should get a horse. Dependable transportation. Duh.

"Crazy how things keep growing. There's talk of Prescott becoming a suburb of Flagstaff. This overpopulation's becoming an unsolvable problem."

"Hey, Ace, perhaps not. Dr. Chandra Hyber just published hyperspace theory and application. When Sabrina gets back with the coordinates for Brussels, a ship might get there in one day. Immigration is coming. Darn soon," Jenna said.

"Have you heard if they'll let you immigrate?" Ace said. "I know how much you had your heart set on moving to Brussels. A real pioneer, my sis is."

"Not a chance. With everything having to be built from scratch, they didn't think I could handle it. And they're right, Ace. There are some things I just can't do that are needed by the settlers."

"Like?"

"Carrying things."

"See what you mean. I'll tell Mom and Dad when I get back. Don't worry. I don't want to immigrate. I just wish you didn't live so far away," Ace said.

"Or that commercial transports resumed operations. Then I could visit more often."

"You haven't visited once yet," Ace said.

"No transport," Jenna said. "We best head to the tea gardens now. Just leave the dishes."

Ace yawned. "I'll do them and then crash on your couch, if that's okay with you. Dead tired."

***

Sipping tea, Alexa Adriana calmed down. "Boy, your brother sure is full of himself. Stuck up snob. Calling me a bimbo. Hardly."

"He's brash and opinionated. And you took him by surprise. He expected to see me," Jenna said.

"I can't imagine what GPan sees in him. Men like that give all men a bad name. I could have scratched his eyes out. What a pig."

The next morning, the smell of hot coffee and pancakes greeted those staying in Apartment #1. Rae and Phillis joined the sleepy-eyed bunch as they wandered into the kitchen. Ace left a note, which Jenna read.

"Mornings everyone. Sorry I had to leave early for the meeting. Back sometime. Have breakfast on me. Ace."

"Coffee and pancakes? Just like a man," Alexa Adriana said, though she sampled one. Then ate a plateful.

Just as Liz and Dave were heading off to GD, both

245

Jenna, Tam, and Alexa Adriana's phones buzzed with text messages.

Jenna called out, "Hey, wait up. We got summoned to GPan. We'll tag along."

Rae said, "Sam boy, looks like you and I get to spend the morning together."

When the trio walked into GPan, the receptionist for CEO Wang Chan led them to a private meeting room on the hundredth floor.

As they rode the elevator up, Jenna said, "Meeting in the bug-free room?"

The receptionist smiled. "Yes, you'll be inside a Faraday cage. And there's no windows. Yes, bug-free. You've been there before, Jenna."

"Impressive," Alexa Adriana said. "The room," she added. "Not that it isn't also impressive you've been here before."

When the trio walked into the room, Ace and Chan rose to welcome them.

"You?" Ace said.

"You?" Alexa Adriana said.

"Oh, you know each other. That simplifies things," Chan said. "Please sit."

Alexa Adriana's eyes bore into Ace's.

"No misunderstandings. What we say here top secret. Do not tell anyone about what's said. If you do, I must terminate them and you. Okay. Jenna invented ion engine, though world knows her as Karl Oppenstein. Tami Durbin invented hyperspace theory and application, which we test now. Ace Sweet invented and programmed the AI system and global satellite network that controls all EMAC flights. We here because GPan has accepted Alexa Adriana Soros' invention: two-man shuttle."

"Two-person," she corrected him.

246

"I show her presentation now."

CEO Wang Chan had recorded her official presentation. At one point, she'd said, "Yes, these two-person shuttles resemble that antique cartoon show the Jetsons whose reruns I saw as a child. Small, efficient, they dart about the skies."

When it finished, CEO Chan said, "Now that Jenna and Alexa Adriana have designed a micro ion engine to power them, a prototype is being made. She has requested that each two-man shuttle be controlled by the same system as the EMACs. That's why Ace Sweet be here. Same concept. User enters destination. GPS knows start location. AI flies ship there and lands it. No user controls in ship.

"Many questions. Alexa Adriana needs your help in designing needed controls into two-man ship. Will existing system handle much extra traffic? Or does new parallel system be built? We must answer these and more. Galactic Manufacturing notified to begin production soon. GPan wants one million produced first year."

"Damn, why didn't you tell me this when we met?" Ace said. "And Tam invented hyperspace? Wow."

"Double wow, Tam. I had no idea. You are Dr. Chandra Hyber," Alexa Adriana said. "Course, now I can see why you did that."

"Secrecy orders, Ace," Jenna said. "I'm glad he brought Tam into our confidence."

"Had too," CEO Chan said. "We might need hyperspace to make automatic control of two-man shuttles work. I leave you to work it out. If need something, contact my receptionist."

After he left, Alexa Adriana powered up her computer and displayed the engineering plans that she and Jenna had been working on, adapting the micro ion engine.

"What do we need to add to interface to your system?" Alexa Adriana asked.

The four dove into the project.

Ace said, "Yes, that's all that must onboard. It's a square box about four inches on a side. We can incorporate the antenna wire into your unbreakable glass canopy. I need to do some calculations. A million more plus all the EMACs will likely overload one system. Best we keep the control of the two-man shuttle—"

"Two-person shuttle," she corrected him, while drumming her nail tips on the table.

"In a separate system. But both systems must exchange data to avoid collisions."

"I envision the shuttles flying higher than say the EMACs, she said.

The discussion filled the morning. The receptionist brought in lunch for the group. When they finished up, Alexa Adriana had all she needed to finalize her design. CEO Chan approved them and sent them off to Galactic Manufacturing.

"Come spring," he said, "we'll have two-man shuttles flying skies of Chicago."

"Looks like I'll be in town a while, Jenna," Ace said. "Going to have to spec out this second system and the cross interface."

"You can stay with us, Little Brother. We can use more hands, if you hadn't noticed."

Chapter 33 Contempt to Respect

Both Alexa Adriana and Ace accompanied everyone to the tea garden that night.

As they entered, Ace said, "Ah, you must be Irene. Jenna's told me all about you. I'm her little brother. One of the most admirable traits anyone can have is to look out for the well-being others. And you've done that so well you can hang your hooks on that."

Alexa Adriana watched Irene's eyes sparkle and her smile forming.

"Ah, that's a good one. Better be careful. I might just put my hooks into you."

Ace grinned. "And you must be Patsy Wells. Jenna never told me what happened to you. I'd say you've adapted well. Never give up, right?"

She sighed. "Yes, I can't. Just can't. Industrial accident. A guy high on weed knocked over a crane. Severed my left arm and the lower part of my right leg. That was around the time the dollar crashed. Like Phillis, Jenna, Tam, and Liz, a whole arm prosthesis is unbelievably expensive and almost non-functional. With the runaway inflation, insurance couldn't cover a working leg, so they gave me this peg leg. It allows me to work. Yeah, I can't give up."

"Is it harder to get around in the winter?" Alexa Adriana butted in, apparently unwilling to let Ace charm these women.

"I need help to walk through the snow. If I fall, it's hard to get up on my own. I can still serve everyone here. What choices do I have? Have you seen what Snowden's free food welfare was? Slow starvation diet. I've got Irene and these ladies here to thank. They took me in and gave me this job when no one else would. Her Galactic credits are worth tens of thousands of paper dollars. But you wealthy LA people, you probably ate well these past few years."

"Well, that is true, Patsy. You have me on that one."

Once seated, Jenna, Tam, Ace, and Alexa Adriana chatted.

Ace said, "Alexa Adriana, I had no idea you were such a talented engineer. I saw your appearance, damned sexy too, and jumped to a horribly wrong conclusion. This Honey Bunny modification is wildly popular in LA?"

"Likewise. I had no idea you are the brains behind the autopiloting of the EMACs. And yes, exceedingly popular. It's shocking that men here used it as a weapon."

"It's obvious you've had work done on your body to make it stunningly perfect. Mind if I ask why you did that?" Ace said.

"It's a man's world. Brute strength gets most men what they desire. Men are physically stronger than women. Just look at the fiasco when they let gender-switching men compete in women's sports. But you mention the precise reason I've had all this work done."

"Er, stunningly perfect?"

"Exactly. Like I told Jenna. When I walk into a room with men, they respond in two ways. Some act like lap dogs and do whatever I ask. Some stare at me but do listen to what I have to say and then do it to please me. Either way, I win."

Jenna said, "Except it didn't work with Chan."

She laughed. "Right. My charms failed utterly on that CEO. Still not sure why, though."

Ace said, "Something I've come to realize. A person is more than their body and mind. There's a presence there, like a being or personality. Chan has a personal presence that's commanding, perhaps dominating. He hardly says much, but I always end up doing what he suggests. Furthermore, he's always been right. I've not met many people who have that kind of presence. Well, maybe with my sister here. Jenna's presence can be dominating."

"Am not, Little Brother," she retorted. "Well, maybe a little."

Ace grinned. "That's why I love you Big Sister. Tam, you captured the heart of the finest person I know."

"It'd be incest otherwise," Jenna teased him.

Tam said, "I knew it when I proposed, but now that they did this to my body, I know it even more. She's a gem among gems."

"Is your wife back in Flagstaff?" Alexa Adriana asked.

Ace laughed. "Hardly. Never married."

Jenna said, "Barely even dated is more like it."

Ace grinned. "Never found a woman I could admire and respect. In my opinion, admiration and respect is what love is all about. I kept comparing them to you, Big Sis. None even came slightly close. *Questa è la vita.*"

The others gave him a quizzical look. "That is life. Mom's Italian. She was Miss Universe in 2024. She and Dad run a dude ranch outside Flagstaff, but they have a winter house near Phoenix where it's warm in the winters."

Ace changed topics. "Alexa Adriana, has being a Honey Bunny been valuable for you? Gotten you things you needed? I'd have thought with all your money, you could have everything you desire."

She chuckled. "Well, money has bought me designer clothes, sexy heels, and my own Lear jet and EMAC. It got me into Berkeley, too. But that first year, I found money couldn't buy me the respect of male students. None wanted to be my lab partners, even though my grades often topped theirs. Dad was right. To compete, I needed more than my brains. I never was any good with sports. Stunningly beautiful rescued me that second year.

"Now, I had the fellows fawning all over me, doing whatever I asked of them. At last, I had control in the men's world. Then the Honey Bunny craze hit. My junior year became a smashing success. Men did what I wanted, not the other way around. So, Ace, yeah, it's helped me make my two-person shuttle a reality, though I can't seem to get them to stop calling it a two-man shuttle."

"Man's world," Ace teased, causing the four to chuckle.

She added, "And I can see why they needed to publish their works under male names. Unless you're drop-dead gorgeous, getting men to take you seriously is nearly impossible. But handicapped? Well, forget it, and we've never have the ion engines or hyperspace travel."

Patsy brought more tea and muffins. And again. And once more.

Finally, she said, "Guys, it's midnight. We're going to close now."

"No way!" Ace said.

"Absolutely," Alexa Adriana said. Then checked her phone. "What happened to the evening? Six hours gone?"

That story continued the ensuing weeks. During the day, Ace and Alexa Adriana worked in different areas overseen by GPan. He worked on expansion of the autopilot system for the new two-man shuttles, while she monitored (GMan) Galactic Manufacturing's construction of the shuttles. Jenna worked with Tam and cared for Sam, though she pushed Tam to begin assisting, because come April Tam would have to care for their daughter.

As always, they looked forward to their nightly time at the tea garden, where the four engaged in lengthy conversations while time flew by.

One day in late September as the large group ate supper, Ace said, "Rae, you wanted to be a nurse, right?"

"Well, yes, I always have."

252

"Good. Tomorrow, you should report to Galactic Medicine (GMed) representative Gladys Shone at the Uptown Med Center. I've pulled some strings and got you the interview. I told them you were being the personal assistant for these people. She agreed with me. Your study hours will be flexible, something like ten in the morning until four. Unless you completely blow your interview, GMed will take over your sponsorship. They will train you to be a general practice nurse specializing in the care of handicapped people, assigned permanently to Phillis and Jenna's group."

Rae's mouth opened, but only a squeal emitted.

Phillis responded with, "Yahoo! I knew she could do it. This is the greatest news ever. You're going to be a nurse like you've dreamed of."

"Thank you! How can I ever thank you?" Rae managed to say. She hugged him.

"Just be a good nurse. That's the best thanks I could have."

Alexa Adriana's mouth gaped. Finally, she replied.

"That's—that's incredibly sweet, Ace. Didn't know you had such contacts."

"I look out for my friends. Yes, as a top professor, I've fingers in a lot of pies. I've met many other teachers—excellent teachers—through the teaching awards I've earned."

The following week, when Patsy served them their first order of tea and muffins, Ace stopped her.

"Patsy, how would you like a quality leg prosthesis?"

She smiled. "Who wouldn't? But I might be able to afford one in maybe ten more years."

"How about tomorrow? I reached out to a contact of mine. It seems GMed is looking for some partial leg amputees to test out their newest ones. No charge. But you'll need to provide them with valuable feedback on how it works. Stuff like that. To help make them better for others who've lost part

253

of a leg."

"You're teasing me?" Patsy said. "No one's ever done that for me. If it wasn't for Irene…"

"I told them you worked as a waitress at night and have afternoons free. Drop by Uptown Med Center tomorrow. Ask for Dr. Blake. He's expecting you and Stumpy, too. She'll get a pair. Best go tell Irene; she can let her know. We don't see her unless we stay past closing."

Patsy wiped tears with her right hand. Jenna leaned into Ace.

"Way to go, Little Brother," she said, her attempt to hug him.

When Ace returned, Alexa Adriana said, "That's amazing. What a wonderful thing to do."

"I wanted more, but they didn't have new arm-hand versions ready. Besides, whole arm prosthesis are cosmetic and functionally worthless. We tried them on Jenna when she was young."

Jenna laughed. "No kidding. My feet work just fine. Thank you very much."

Phillis giggled, but Tam and Liz frowned.

"I told Irene I'd let her know if such an opportunity for her appeared."

"You are quite amazing," Alexa Adriana said with a huge smile.

"So, Alexa Adriana, what is it that you really want from life?" Ace said.

She shrugged, saying nothing. Later durning their long talk, she answered his question.

"I'd love to be in a position to encourage and help young girls to become engineers and scientists. But without having to get the many body modifications that I did. Luckily, I had a dad who could afford it. Most girls can't. Girls can be as inventive, as creative as men. Just look at what Jenna and I've

254

done. But back at Berkeley, few women enrolled in these programs."

Jenna said, "I think you need to reach them when they are young—high school age. Freshman year. That's when I really got interested in physics and math. I should say applied math. Tam's the pure math genius. Me, I needed to put it to use in the real world. Of course, I make extensive use of mechanics. Levers, fulcrums—stuff like that. Had to in order to figure out how I could do things."

Ace laughed. "No kidding. For Christmas, Jenna wanted Lego and Erector construction kits. Never dolls."

Jenna flushed. "What would I want with a doll when I could build skyscrapers from Lego blocks?"

"Yeah, but I had to pick up the thousand pieces when you were done," Ace said with a grin.

"Well, you try picking up beans with your toes sometime," Jenna retorted. "Just ask Tam or Liz how easy that is."

"It's a bitch!" Liz said, jumping into the conversation. "Me, I just wanted spy toys for presents. Magnifying glasses, do-all tools. I even had a Sherlock Homes hat when I was a teen."

Dave said, "Oh, I wish I could have seen that!"

Liz gave him a hip bump. Everyone laughed.

That night after most everyone had gone to bed, Alexa Adriana joined Ace, as he prepared to sleep on the couch again. She slipped her arms around him, pulled him close, and kissed him. Ace returned her affections.

That evening at the tea garden, everyone saw the budding relationship between the two.

Over tea a week later, Ace said, "Alexa Adriana, I did some checking. The university in Flagstaff is looking for someone to teach engineering to incoming freshmen, with a primary focus on drawing more women into the field. I took the liberty of recommending you for that position. When I told them of your credentials, they begged me to beg you to consider this teaching position. Here's a golden opportunity for you to reach out to many young women, showing them the vast potential they have. What do think?"

Alexa Adriana said nothing. Instead, she gave him a very passionate kiss.

"I take it that's a yes. Starts in January. Don't worry. I can help get you grooved into teaching."

The next night, Phillis spoke up.

"I've decided I'm going to write a history of these times. Tell what's happened. The book's title is 'Economic Collapse, Fall of Earth's Governments, and the Rise of the Galactic Corporations'. I'm putting in chapters on many different angles of the mess."

"Great idea!" Rae said.

"Really good one," Jenna said.

All backed her.

"You know what I've just found out? There's almost no one in the populated sections of Earth that is older than about sixty-five. It seems there is a pandemic of dementia-like illnesses affecting older people. No one's noticed it or investigated it before I did. GMed is insisting anyone reaching sixty start taking their new dementia prevention drug. But the drug isn't having any effect as far as I can tell."

"Incredible, Phillis. I didn't know that," Ace said. "Jenna, Mom and Dad are approaching their sixties. We'll have to pay close attention to them. This is awful. A pandemic for sure."

"GMed told me they are testing several new drugs, hoping one will be effective," Phillis said. "Still, this epidemic hasn't made the news. I think it's being suppressed."

"By whom?" Jenna asked.

"Can't say yet. Still digging."

256

"Great work. I can't wait to read it. Maybe I can be a beta reader," Jenna said.

"I'd love that. I'm taking a clue from you and Tam. I'm using a pseudonym. By Professor Hector Black. Sounds professional, doesn't it?"

Everyone laughed, none harder than Ace.

The next Saturday night, Rae dolled Phillis up in her old fetish outfit before donning her own. With her arm around her spouse, Rae brought Phillis over to see the others before leaving for the Cat's Night Out Club, where they both once went.

"Wow! You look incredible, Phillis. Both of you," Ace said.

His eyes roamed their exotic latex skintight outfits, each a different shade of blue glistening from the light coating of oil. Each gown had only the tiniest of walking slit, hobbling them.

"Found her old boots," Rae said. "Smashing, don't you think?"

Phillis wore black boots whose tops reached about halfway up her calves. A pair of tiny padlocks ensured the six-inch heels couldn't be removed without the key. Rae's black oxfords sported identical spikes.

Phillis said, "This is my old outfit before the accident. I used to dress up in this and go to the fetish clubs." She giggled. "Now I'm totally dependent on Rae. Don't let go of me."

"I can't keep my arms off you, silly."

The group watched as the pair took their tiny steps out into the night.

Alexa Adriana said, "Those two have incredibly good taste. Smashing outfits."

Chapter 34 Longstanding Problems

In October, Sabrina returned with the final coordinates for Brussels.

She reported, "Yeah, Tam, we determined the coordinates for Brussels. Heading in the opposite direction brought us home. Well just outside the Oort Cloud. Then we entered the new coordinates. Presto, twenty-three hours later, we popped out of hyperspace in Brussels' Oort Cloud. Now we get R&R for a week before doing the same for Pylon. Your theory works, Tam. Perfectly."

"Thanks. It's a piece of good news for a change," Tam said.

Later that same day, Major Callahan called him.

"Hey, Tam. I need you here as soon as you can get here. Something's come up. I must have your opinion. Art wants you here for this."

An hour later, Tam entered the familiar GD building. Her shoulders twitched as she took the MTES. This is scary. I should have asked Rae to come with me. Jenna, I never realized how awful this is for you. And now, I can't do a damned thing to help her. I'm mostly a burden. I feel helpless. But I did sell my soul to GD. Now I pay for it.

Tam took a deep breath and moved close to the automatic front doors. Thank god for small things. She went inside.

"Oh, Tami," The receptionist said. "I'll let them know you're here."

"Can't tell me what's going on? Why I'm here?"

I know better than to ask. She never knows critical information.

258

The woman shook her head.

I hope I don't get too embarrassed. Ah, Liz is coming.

"Hi, Major," Tam said.

"Tam, this way. We're in the auditorium. I asked you here because I need your opinion."

She couldn't say more out in the open. The two armless women entered the elevators, Liz pressing the buttons with her nose.

Tam recognized CEO Art Townsend and one security guard whom Liz said had replaced Tom. The other man she'd never met.

"Tam Durbin, thank you for coming on such short notice," Art said. "This is an engineer from Moscow GD, Ilya Petrov. Ilya, this used to be our ace sharpshooter before the mobsters kidnapped him and did this to him."

In a thick accent, Ilya said, "Ah, not what I expected times two." He glanced at Major Callahan as well. "I invent new type gun. A blaster. Uses waves in microwave zone. Best show him video."

Art wisely activated closed captions.

"Moscow, like most big cities, has experienced many rioters and looters. Rubber bullets proved useless. Real bullets have become hard to come by. Enter Ilya Petrov and his new weapon called a blaster. Here you see it in use."

Several men wore bulky backpacks with thick cables leading to the strange looking gun in their hands. It fired in short pulses. Rioters dropped when hit.

Ilya explained over the sound, "Shorter range weapon. Here, is long range. One hundred yards."

Again, other looters appeared before the small squad of GD men. This time when the soundless pulses activated, the line of thugs dropped to the ground, writhing about like a fish in a net. Eventually, the downed men struggled to their feet as other GD security men arrested them.

"Twenty-five yards and closer," Ilya said, "results death. Stunned out to a hundred yards. Watch autopsy. Gross."

True, the bodies of those shot at close range lay in lines in the morgue. The doctor proceeded to cut open the chest cavity. Instead of organs, the shocked look told Tam much.

Ilya said, "Liquefies organs less than twenty-five yards. Instant death."

Tam said, "Ilya, this is an impressive weapon. What does it do to objects? Looks like the victim's clothes sustained no damage."

"*Da*, no damage. Only to living tissues. Up close. Can heat metal things if blasted much times."

Art said, "So, Tam, what do you think? If we have to fight a battle on a spaceship, we can't use bullets. Heck, we can't use bullets on Moon Base #1, Mars Colony, or Ceres Federation, for example."

"A bullet hitting a dome or someone's space suit spells death," Tam said. "This blaster doesn't harm non-living materials?"

Art said, "Apparently not. We're testing one in our basement lab, but Ilya says it only breaks weaker forms of glass at close range."

"I'd say it's what you need, Art. Perfect. Amazing weapon. But what's with the backpacks?"

Ilya said, "Battery packs. Provide ten minutes continuous pulses before must charge. Working on more compact power supply."

"Wish we would have had these during last year's Antifa riots. Wouldn't have needed the Sons of Liberty's help," Liz said.

"Should help at close range," Tam said.

Ilya added, "Created fear. Few dare riot in Moscow now. Looters afraid. Works good, eh?"

"Very good," Tam said, "but is it always deadly at close

range? Is there a lower setting or something? Do we really want to kill all looters?"

"Only on-off."

Art said, "Looting is becoming a major problem in most cities, Tam. We need some deterrent that works. In Moscow, the blaster has. GD is going to adopt it empire-wide. Thanks for coming in."

Tam recognized that tone. He was being dismissed. But Ilya spoke up as she turned to leave.

"Sad you life so ruined. Major's too."

Tam nodded and left. That's not what I wanted to hear. But isn't it the truth? Oh, God. I've got to deal with the MTES by myself again! Funny how I never worried about falling down. Now I'm terrified of that.

***

Early November, CEO Art Townsend again summoned Tam to GD. Once again, Major Liz Callahan took him to the auditorium where Art and another man waited to show him another video.

"This is Dr. Anton Frist. He's invented another weapon that our small space fleet needs. He calls it a disintegrator. Watch," Art said.

In a lab, a man fired what resembled an Uzi at a block of steel perhaps twenty feet away. Smoke curled up, blocking the small beam as it drilled into the metal. When the smoke cleared, Tam saw the disintegrator had pored a quarter-inch hole straight through the six-inch block of steel.

Next, the same man fired it at a rabbit about a hundred yards away. Once the smoke cleared, the rabbit lay dead. A closeup shot showed a cauterized hole straight through its body.

Anton said, "You see all material is disintegrated until it's total energy is utilized, whether that is short range with the steel bar or long range with the rabbit. Tests show the beam travels in a straight line, disintegrating everything in its path until the beam's total energy is exhausted. If nothing is hit, but air of course, the beam travels about a mile at sea level. Even farther at higher elevations or in space. Haven't been able to determine max distance in space yet."

"What happens to the material in its path?" Tam asked. "This intrigues me. Matter can't be destroyed. Is it converted into energy?"

"No. It breaks all molecular bonds within the beam's path. Everything becomes isolated atoms. Even breaks up O_2. That's why it looks like a hole. You're actually seeing a transparent gas form composed of individual atoms. Ions in many cases," Anton said.

Tam laughed. "Good thing I'm not your long range sharpshooter any longer, Art. This device would put me out of business. Anyone can shoot out to fantastic distances."

Art grinned. "True, but the downside is anything that gets in the way of the beam gets disintegrated. Collateral damage is likely going to be a major problem. Except in space. Now our fleet can defend itself."

"Does the Sol Empire have enemy aliens I've not heard about?" Tam said. "Don't answer that. Destruction of all molecular bonds. That intrigues me. I need to work out the math behind that."

Anton smiled. "If you do that, please let me know. I invented it, but can't explain how it does what it does."

That evening over tea and muffins, Tam told them of the new disintegrator. That started the four off in and all-night discussion, ended only by closing time.

Chapter 35 The Good and the Bad

Middle November, Ace Durbin and Alexa Adriana Soros married in a simple ceremony conducted by CEO Eric Paddock of the local GPan corporation. Marissa Larson, CEO of Galactic University, also attended, interviewing Alexa Adriana for her new teaching position at the Northern Arizona University.

Marissa said, "I can't recall when we ever had such a qualified woman engineer. You bring the highest credentials to the Galactic University Corporation. Of course, you'll be monitored to make sure you are able to teach others. There's no question you'll influence countless women into pursuing vital careers in science and engineering. But not to worry. You are marrying one of the best teachers we have in the US."

Alexa Adriana didn't tell her father about the wedding, since he was in Rome at the time. Because commercial travel still hadn't resumed anything that resembled normal operations, Ace and Jenna's parents weren't told either. They'd find out soon enough when Ace returned around Christmas.

At their usual meeting at the tea gardens, Patsy walked up carrying a wedding muffin for the pair.

"Wow, you're walking like a normal person," Ace said.

She beamed. "Yes, still getting used to it. Much easier navigating in the snow. And you should see how excited Stumpy is. She stands as tall as the rest of us now. Incredibly wonderful gift, Ace. Thank you and congratulations you two."

"Snow. Ugh," Tam said. "Jenna, I'm sorry I never truly grasped just how hard it was for you to deal with the cold and snow."

Liz said, "Duh. Now that, Tam, is a gross understatement! I don't think I could manage if I didn't have Dave hanging on to me."

Jenna said, "I've dealt with it all my life. Mom and Dad's dude ranch is south of Flagstaff where it snows a lot. But yeah, I understand what you both and Phillis mean. Winters are hard for us. Cloaks don't keep us very warm, but we can put them on easier than parkas, whose arms continually get in our way. At least I've gotten you each a pair of the fleece lined pull-on moccasin-like boots. They keep our feet somewhat warm. Wearing socks makes using our toes next to impossible."

"I'm terrified of slipping and falling," Liz said. "I still keep trying to use my arms to catch myself or break a fall."

"Ditto, here," Tam said. "It's scary. I still feel terrified when I have to go out on my own. I feel helpless."

"Don't worry, Tam," Liz said. "That feeling doesn't go away. At least not anytime soon. Maybe in years..."

After the solemn silence, Liz said, "On the brighter side, GPan and GD are preparing to colonize Brussels. We've sent out the orders for the initial one thousand settlers to report here on New Year's Day. They've converted one of our largest ships into a shuttle settlers ship."

"A colonizer," Tam said, correcting her. "Scuttlebutt says they plan to send a million people there next year. Plans call for sending a billion people before the immigration is done."

Liz said, "Next year, they're refitting a second ship and sending a similar amount to Pylon. Of course, our outer colonies are complaining they want more people."

"I hope they get them," Tam said. "Let people immigrate where they want to. A round trip to Brussels takes two days using hyperspace. They could get one hundred eighty trips per year. That's a very long way from moving a billion

264

people."

Dave laughed. "Bet they have to build lots more big ships."

"Mark my words," Liz said, "big troubles are brewing around the world. Even in Chicago. Not everyone is being employed by a Galactic corporation. In this world, if you can't get a corporate sponsorship, you can't get Galactic credits. And those are the only means of exchange worldwide. I think many are bartered out. Many believed they'd be accepted as immigrants, but those without corporate sponsorship are not even considered. When that info gets out, well..."

"Big trouble," Ace finished her thought.

***

Late November trouble broke out on several fronts, precipitate by GPan's latest picks for immigrants. They lined up a dozen groups of a thousand each, flying each thousand to Brussels every couple days. By Thanksgiving, the general population launched protests against GPan's criteria being used to decide who can immigrate. It didn't help matters when CEO Wang Chan took to Galactic Entertainment [GEnt] airwaves to explain the criteria. Rather it fueled the conflict.

"Many ask what criteria use to choose who can immigrate to Brussels. We want best people with pioneering attitudes. Those who backed policies of free food, free education, free living wages even if person not work, free health care, no country borders—these people be undesirable and never be chosen to immigrate. Neither will sickly or weak people or the handicapped or mentally deficient. Brussels is virgin world. No infrastructure. No housing. No agriculture. Everything must be built from scratch. Only hardy pioneers unafraid of hard work be needed. Also, no one over child-bearing age accepted. Must be equal number of men and women. Goal be one billion people for Brussels and for Pylon. That help solve Earth overpopulation."

The Chicago rioting began the next day. Once more, CEO Wang Chan appeared on GEnt's channel.

"Rioting must stop. We not tolerate lawlessness. Instructed GD offices worldwide use lethal force. This, only warning."

The next day, hundreds more joined the protesters. GEnt crews televised the riotous crowd as they marched down streets, masks hiding their identities, while tossing bricks and firebombs at buildings and chasing people off the MTES.

Major Callahan coordinated the operations via her drones and told the others about the actions that night at the tea gardens.

"Chan meant what he said," she said. "Art ordered us to fire on these animals. After we killed one hundred six of them, the others fled. But they managed to cause significant damage to six buildings and injured a dozen innocent pedestrians, mostly women."

"What's the odds that'll convince them to stop?" Ace asked.

Tam said, "Zero. It's only going to get worse. These are Antifa-like mobsters. Freeloaders."

"I think she's right," Liz said. "Deadbeats who expect the world owes them everything. That's what the screwed up education system has taught them. A whole generation believes such drivel. I heard protests and riots have broken out in London, LA, Paris, Moscow, and Berlin. I've lost track to be honest. It's all I can manage to fly the surveillance drones."

"She's getting better at it," Dave said, giving her a kiss.

For the next three weeks, the rioting and looting occupied the GEnt channels in all major cities around the world. Liz reported that Chan ordered all GD offices to relay the names of those they killed and the body count to Sol Empire-wide GD CEO Boris Borosinsky. Since he recently moved his offices to the hundredth floor of the Chicago GD skyscraper, Major Callahan found her duties now included combining the daily reports into one spreadsheet, forwarding it to Boris. Thus, she had a unique view of the carnage.

When the riots died down in mid-December, nearly twenty million people had been terminated. With the holidays coming, everyone hoped this marked the end of it.

***

At Tam's next checkup, the images showed her growing daughter.

The nurse said, "You're doing just perfect, Tam. Your daughter, likewise. She's quite healthy, but..."

"But what? What's wrong?"

"She isn't developing arms."

"What?" Tam stared at the image and sighed.

"I'm sorry, Tam, Jenna."

"Well, so what?" Tam said. "As long as she's healthy otherwise. Tia Kate Louise, you'll have to work harder than most, but I'll bet you're going to be a knockout like your mother, Jenna."

Jenna said, "Must be my fault. I was born this way. Maybe my genes are messed up."

"I doubt that," Tam said. "Sam is perfectly normal." She thought Jenna looked relieved. "Anyway, we'll love Tia just as much as Sam."

Then on Christmas Eve as the group partied in Jenna's apartment, Phillis said, "Hey, everyone. Rae and I have an announcement. We're both pregnant!"

After the congratulations died down, Dave asked, "I'm kind of ignorant about such things. But how can you both be pregnant?"

"We're having each others," Rae said. "I learned about this in nursing class. They take an egg from both women and under a microscope, merge them into one fertilized egg. They did it twice to make sure it took. Both did. Now we each carry

267

one of our babies. Isn't this just amazingly cool? We're going to have our own family."

Dave said, "Darn cool. So you can only have girl babies?"

Rae giggled. "Of course, silly. Though we could have made use of the official sperm bank."

Dave's face flushed. Liz took this chance to make her own announcement.

"You took my thunder. I'm pregnant too. Dave and I are starting our own family."

Liz basked in the good wishes from everyone.

"We're going to be mothers at the same time," Liz said. "It couldn't be more wonderful."

The three women hugged, sharing a new bond.

***

January brought Alexa Adriana's two-man shuttles into the skies of Chicago. By the end of the month, hundreds of these darted about the downtown area. Further, she gave a shuttle to Ace, to Jenna and Tam, to Liz and Dave, to Rae and Phillis, and even one to Irene and her crew.

Now Liz understood why Boris had moved his offices from Moscow to Chicago. He received the second one off the Galactic Manufacturing assembly line. Chan received the first, while Alexa Adriana got the third one. The factory turned out hundreds each month and couldn't keep up with the demand.

Tam and Jenna climbed into theirs. When the glass dome closed, a main menu appeared on the center screen. They could control the shuttle either by voice or by using their nose or feet to select from the localized menu of destinations. Alexa Adriana explained each shuttle carried menu destinations unique to that location.

"To Museum of Science and Industry," Jenna said. "Activate."

"This is cool!" Tam said. "Everything is automated.

268

There's nothing we have to do."

Jenna chuckled. "There's no controls to manipulate, silly. She said it's speed varies, based on the distance to be traveled. The range is three hundred miles, max. But if you need to go more than thirty miles, the system flies you to several thousand feet and goes at its top speed of a mile a minute. Damn impressive."

"Yeah, Ace's nav system is wonderful. Bet it's impossible to have an accident in these."

Jenna laughed. "Especially since there's no controls for us to use. For once, something is made especially for us, Tam."

After landing at the museum, Jenna said, "Home. Activate." The shuttle made the return trip.

"I wonder how we can just fly around sightseeing?" Tam asked.

Jenna scrolled down the extensive menu. "Hum, have to ask Ace when we get back. I don't see such an option."

"Figures. He's all about business, not sightseeing. Boy, do I ever hate winters now. Didn't used to, but like we are winters are torture."

"Liz and Phillis agree with you. I got used to cold feet. But it's a challenge dealing with deep snow. Without the MTES, I'd likely be housebound all winter," Jenna admitted.

"Being a blimp doesn't help," Tam said. "I think she's kicking again."

The next day, Ace and Alexa Adriana packed up and returned to Flagstaff. She still had ten days to prepare for teaching her first engineering class.

"I'll miss you all," she said. "Come and visit often. Or move, too."

After the two departed, Rae had to wipe many eyes.

***

A new problem surfaced in early February. Religion. On Sunday morning, the group watched GEnt on Channel Nine

News.

"It's criminal. How dare the Galactic corporations refuse to sponsor priests and churches around the world?" one pastor in his collar said.

The camera panned the collection of men and women. From their apparel, Ace guessed a representative from all religions attended. Each took a turn protesting the fact that no Galactic corporation would sponsor them as religious leaders or even their churches or houses of worship.

Phillis said, "I saw this one coming gang. They are correct. Not one corporation will sponsor them directly. The only ones who've gotten corporate sponsorship have gotten it because of their secondary skills, such as an electrician. Not one are being paid to perform their religious duties. It's like the Galactic corporations want to kill off all religions."

Dave said, "If they don't get a Galactic sponsor, they can't survive very long on parishioner donations."

"Precisely," Phillis said. "The average person's wages are enough for housing and food, but little more. None of these people look particularly healthy. Kind of skinny, if you ask me. I'm predicting the end of organized religions."

"What about some of the spectacular cathedrals around the world?" he asked.

"Oh, I've discovered Galactic Housing is preserving them as museums," she said. "I'm uncovering all kinds of interesting facts the public doesn't know. Only we're just now finding out about this one. Let's listen."

Another priest said, "What about the spiritual beings? The actual person. Man is not just a fleshly body with a mind. Who will assist the beings? Comfort those in need? Galactic corporations care only for their profitable bottom line."

The leader of the discussion group said, "There you have it. We pastors and religious leaders will take our protests to GPan tomorrow. This persecution against religion must end."

This situation became the focus of the group's discussion that night at the tea garden.

CEO Wang Chan did issue a response the next day.

"Galactic corporations do not care what an individual person's faith or religious beliefs might be. We cannot support churches and priests, as they do not provide any tangible final product. We will consider preserving representative houses of worship and historical cathedrals."

Phillis said, "Told ya so."

Chapter 36 Jihad

Late February, religious leaders struck back. Using a hijacked GEnt studio in Cairo, bearded men wearing ski masks broadcast their message to the world.

"Now is time to strike. All Muslims and Christians alike. Jihad now. Destroy the infidel Galactic corporations that promised to destroy you. Strike today. Show them no place on Earth is safe. Strike now or die the slow death promised by CEO Chan."

"Have you seen the news?" Jenna called Liz at GD. "Is anything going on?"

"Hey, Jenna. Yeah, something is happening. I'm flying surveillance drones over Chicago. We're on high alert. You guys watch out. Gotta run. Probably on Channel Nine."

Jenna switched the comm channel. GEnt cameras focused on three protest groups marching north up several main avenues.

"Those are Muslims." She pointed to one group in the scene.

Another group carried a giant cross. Some wore loose robes. The third group, a mixture of Jews, Christians, and others. All carried signs or banners.

Religious freedom. Support your local church. Condemn GPan, not Christ. Salvation is at hand. Many others, too.

"Looks peaceful," Rae said. "I've never been to a church. Couldn't see any point, really. God—Devil—angels—demons? Never seen one. If you can't see it or touch it, it's not real. That's what I've lived by."

Phillis said, "Religion is a touchy subject. Entirely too

personal to discuss with others. Some still cling to their bibles and beliefs. The modern generation have abandoned organized religions. Notice those marching are all older people. Don't see a younger person among them."

"Might be because many priests molested children and got caught," Rae said. "When bad things happen, people must have someone to blame or some higher power to pray to. Always been that way."

Phillis said, "I've included a chapter in my history on organized religion. Guess I'm going to have to revise it. Still, you're right. The statistics I found show a dramatic drop in parishioners among all major religions over the last three decades. I included that graph in the book. Ace is right. Stats show most under thirty have never been in a church or never attend one. Chan is right. Why support churches when they are dying out? In another couple decades, the churches will be empty. At least in our country. Can we call it a country anymore?"

Jenna said, "I heard that they're still calling them countries, but the word means something different now. It's a geographical area often with the same boundaries as before, but all borders are open. The economic crash ended illegal immigration and drug trafficking. Drug cartels lost their means of exchange and stopped shipments. I bet a lot of users had horrid withdrawals right after the crash."

"I'm putting in a chapter on this," Phillis said. "If you remember, everything sort of blacked out right after the collapse. I had to communicate to hundreds of shelters around the country to find out anything. Most had a huge increase in drug addicts begging for shelter. But six months later, they claimed most of them had perished. Vague on the causes of death, though."

"You're becoming a gold mine of information," Jenna said. "Way to go!"

"Hope it stays peaceful," Rae said. "Wait. What's this?"

The coverage switched to an overseas GEnt outlet. Gunfire echoed in the background of the reporter who spoke Arabic. The voice of a translator broke in.

"This just in. Firebombs and explosions shook Cairo this evening. Reports are coming in from Jerusalem of a mass attack on the Jewish state. Hundreds of videos swamped GEnt studios. This just in from GD Cairo.

"The Mideast once thought to be no longer habitable because of the radiation has erupted in massive violence. Some describe the jihad movement as a wave of locusts destroying everything in their path.

"GD Cairo has asked GD Moscow for assistance. They want more nuclear strikes, but Moscow claims they used their stockpile to stop the earlier war. Eastern Iran has fully mobilized. Word has it they want revenge and have joined the jihad.

"This just in. Lybia has joined the jihad, sending their forces eastward into Egypt. The numerous terrorist organizations of Africa are rising up against the corporation offices there. It remains to be seen if Israel and Egypt can withstand the massive onslaught. Also, we've heard that Somalia and Pakistan have sided with the jihadists. Their forces are on the move as well. Turning it over to Z-TV."

Coverage shifted to a battle scene.

"I'm standing behind the Israeli line of tanks behind the perimeter fencing. Hundreds, thousands of screaming jihadists are rushing the tanks. Machine guns. Mowing them down. Unbelievable. They just keep coming. Zulu wars. Reminds me of the British defenders. They're climbing over their own dead still charging into instant death.

"Wait. That tank's guns ceased firing. Are they out of ammunition? Others seemed to have, too. The men continue to swarm the tanks. I can see very few have guns. A few rifles here and there. They can't stop—no, wait. Dozens swarm the lead tank. Firebombs. They're tossing homemade firebombs into the tank. Grizzly. The crew bailed out, but their clothes are flaming. The other tanks are backing up. Air cover. I see a squadron of planes. Swooping down, strafing. They're falling back. But for how long

"My god! I've never seen anything like this slaughter. Here comes a second group of jets. They seem to be dropping a liquid on the waves of jihadists. No, could it be? My god! Gas. They've ignited the fuel, burning retreating men and dead bodies alike."

GEnt apologized for showing such graphic images. Coverage resumed from within a studio.

Phillis said, "I wonder if they'll use that new super microwave weapon they used on the Ritzker mob in South Chicago."

"Do we even know what it was?" Jenna asked.

"Yes, I've put a chapter in my book on it. I'll show you. Er, can you fetch my laptop, Rae?"

Her mate rush back to their adjoining apartment.

"Here's some photos taken by some witnesses. Middle of night. Not clear what they are. Looks kind of like a drone with a giant box. Anyway," Phillis said, "I gathered some eyewitness accounts of those who helped clear out the dead. The bodies looked boiled. Plastics melted or deformed. Here's some inside pics."

"It must have been a very powerful microwave beam," Jenna said, deep in thought.

"Yeah. I bet they take that weapon over there," Phillis said.

"You're doing a fabulous job with your book," Jenna said. "More like amazing."

Phillis smiled.

Just Then the Sol Empire-wide GPan CEO Wang Chan

appeared on the comm set. The Chinese man spoke slowly and clearly.

"The rioting and firebombing occurring 'round world particularly in Mideast not tolerated. Must stop now. I not allow rest of world be victimized by radical jihad people, who contribute nothing to well-being of Earth. No more warnings. Stop insanity today. Final warning. That is all."

"A man of few words," Phillis said. "Bet he takes action."

They continued to watch the news.

When Liz and Dave came home for supper, they had news.

"Something big is happening," Dave said. "Half of the entire GD security force has departed New O'Hare along with many very large transport cargo planes. Not sure where they found all that jet fuel."

"Are they going to war?" Phillis asked.

"They took only small arms," Liz said. "Not the fancy new blasters or disintegrators. Maybe not."

"I bet I know," Phillis said.

"Are we going to have to tickle it out of you?" Rae said.

Giggling, she said, "I bet they are transporting their super microwave weapon to the Mideast."

Liz said, "They better do something fast. Israel has already lost half of its land. They didn't have all that much to begin with."

After dinner, Liz and Dave looked over the images and stories in Phillis's new book.

The next day after Liz and Dave headed to work and Rae headed off for her nurse training, the three watched the news while Jenna fed Sam.

"Yes, something definitely happened here last night," a reporter said. "Pan over there."

The camera swept over a section of Israel that the

jihadists had taken yesterday. Dead bodies littered the ground.

"Look, they look like partially cooked hotdogs," Phillis said the obvious.

"That new super weapon," Tam said.

"Yep, just like the South Chicago photos I got."

"Thousands dead. Like this all the way back to Sinai and the Canal. Reports are coming in. Large sections of Jordan and Lebanon that abut Israel are massive graveyards. We've tested for radioactive fallout. As you can see, my dial isn't registering anything. Not like it did in central Iraq after the Russians dropped all those nukes on the Iranian Red Guards. Something has killed thousands here. A new super weapon.

"Satellite surveillance shows the vast Muslim combined jihad army marching across the desert of southern Iraq, avoiding the radioactive central highlands around Baghdad. Images show a million-man Pakistani army driving across Southern Iran to join in the attack. New reports show a massive confrontation along the border with India. Will these two nuclear powers launch nuclear strikes?

"Other reports suggest Turkey has invaded northern Iraq, attacking their age-old enemy the Kurds. On the western front, GD Cairo forces are battling the jihad sweeping out of the western desert regions. Just like in World War II, the Qattara Depression has bottled up the Muslim radical army, making it easier for GD Cairo to defend. But the sheer number of attackers threaten GD Cairo's vastly smaller forces.

"This entire area of the world is now up for grabs. Hatreds fomented across centuries have boiled over. Wait, African Muslim terrorists are now striking at the lower Nile valley. Are we involved in World War III?"

While they continued to watch, Tam said, "You wait and see. When this is done, the Mideast won't exist. I should know. I sold my soul to GD."

The next morning news showed total devastation of all

living things across the Egyptian desert, through Lybia, up to Tunis. The following morning, nothing lived across northern Sudan, Ethiopia, and Somalia. A month later, nothing lived west of India across the Middle East until the border of Israel. Even the southern portions of Turkey held no life. Few made any note of the deceased Congo rebels or other smaller terrorist fractions of Africa.

With uncounted millions dead, vocal and visible protests against the Galactic corporations vanished.

Tam said, "See, I told you I sold my soul to GD. I wish our daughter would hurry up and come. I thought it was hard to do things before, but now I'm a fat pig."

Jenna and Phillis giggled.

Chapter 37 Baby Time

The world situation and that of Chicago settled down. Early April, Rae received her nurse's diploma.

"I'm officially a home-care nurse. I'd have to have a lot more training to work in a Med Center or even a surgical nurse. But I don't want to do that. Besides, soon we're all gonna need me around here. Tam's due soon. Then the rest of us. This fall's gonna be big baby month around here!"

Tam said, "I can't wait for Tia Kate Louise to come. I must weigh a hundred pounds more. I almost can't feed myself, let alone brush my teeth. I guess I'll just sit on the toilet."

"Don't you dare," Jenna said. "I've only got one bathroom."

Everyone laughed.

April 15th, Tam's water burst.

"I think Tia-Kate is about to join us," Tam said. "I'll be glad when I cradle her against. Ouch. Something's happening."

Rae got Jenna and Tia into the EMAC while Phillis promised she'd take care of Sam.

"Bottle's in the fridge," Jenna said. "Diapers—oh, you know the drill. Call if you need me."

"Send me a pic of Tia-Kate," Phillis said.

Once at Uptown Med Center, the doctors whisked Tam into a birthing room. After giving the nurses check in data, Jenna and Rae joined Tam.

"This isn't fun, but should be over soon," Tam said. "I can hardly wait to welcome Tia-Kate to our family! Ouch. It's hurting some. Doc said they'll do Cesarian cause my pelvis is too small. Hope soon, real soon. I forgot the new baby bag."

Rae said, "Got it." She waved the bag.

For the next half hour, the room bustled with activity as the doctor and nurses prepared for the birth.

Just as they were about to begin the process, a shocked look swept over Tam's face. "Something...Is...Wrong..."

Rae and Jenna stared at Tam before they realized she'd just died. Once nurse cried, "BP dropping fast. Pulse is—gone! We're losing her."

"Quick, scalpel," the doctor said. "Signal code blue. Get cardiologist now. Oh, no!"

He'd begun the incision to get to the baby, but the second he made the incision, blood poured out. A crimson tidal wave flowed over the doctor, Tam, and the operation table.

Jenna screamed. Rae's hand covered her own mouth; she stared in disbelief.

Later, Jenna thanked the doctor and staff for their very fast extraction of Tia-Kate from Tam's dead body.

While the nurses washed the blood off the baby girl, the doctor and cardiologist opened Tam up, looking for the damage.

"Aorta rupture. Nothing we could have done to prevent it," the cardiologist said. "Look. Someone's partially cut the artery. Probably during the gender surgery. Nicked it and didn't repair. That aorta could have ruptured at any time. Best call for an autopsy."

While he took care of the details, the doctor told the sobbing Jenna and shocked Rae what had happened.

"Tam's aorta could have ruptured at any time since she had the gender surgery. There's no way we could have known about it. The positive thing is it happened here. I was able to save your baby daughter. That's her squealing now. I'll bring her out to you soon. Got all her toes. Looks like a very healthy baby.

***

Tam or Tom had never been religious. Unless you can see God, he doesn't exist. Lying on the table, she felt a popping sensation. That's when she uttered her last three words, though pausing between each as she fought to retain consciousness.

She blinked and found herself looking down on the body and the frantic medical staff. Tam heard their words and Jenna's screams. This can't be happening to me. I want Tia-Kate to live. No one can hear me. God, that's a lot of blood. I'm dead!

Wait, if I'm dead, how can I be aware of these things? Tia-Kate! Yes, that's her. She's got to live. Just got too! Come on, breathe. Breathe.

Tam found herself floating over the tiny baby body, willing it to live. A crack on Tia-Kate's butt did two things. First, the little body gasped for air and then cried. Second, Tam found herself being pulled into the tiny head, as it gasped.

I'm freezing! Blankets! I hate being upside down. God, that's cold. I'm starving. Help me. Jenna, help me.

All that the others heard was a newborn crying or screaming.

Warm water and towels. That's better. Best stop crying.

"What name do you want on the birth certificate?"

That jarred the baby alert again. She heard Jenna's weeping voice.

"Tia-Kate Louise Durbin. That's with a dash."

Rae's voice said, "Her lower aorta ruptured where it had been partially cut?"

"Yes, but the autopsy will confirm it. We were lucky it burst here so we were able to save her baby."

"I'll take them home, doctor. Thank you for saving her. Come on, Jenna. I've got Tia-Kate. Let's get you home."

I tried to talk to Jenna or Rae, but all the body only

gurgled. Oh, how I longed to comfort my Jenna, but could not figure out how. I drifted into slumber land. When I was awake, I understood what everyone said, but beyond crying and gurgling, I couldn't communicate with them. A month later, I forgot about my past. I was a baby girl now named Tia-Kate, the name I chose for my baby girl.

***

Rae helped get the grieving Jenna and the baby home. Dave and Liz took off work and met them. Together with Phillis, the five shared their grief. Rae ordered baby formula for Tia-Kate, and Dave made last minute preparations for the baby in Jenna's room.

When Jenna calmed, she began making the worst calls of her life. With Tia-Kate cradled in a leg, her phone sent video of the pair.

"Ace, horrible news. Tam's dead, but Tia-Kate survived." Her eyes watered so much that Phillis dabbed them while she blurted out the details.

After condolences, he said, "You want us to come up? Lend you a hand?"

"No. You have to teach your classes. We'll get by. More later. I have to call Mom and Dad."

"Why don't you let me do that, sis? I'll break it to them gently."

Later, Rae asked, "Anyone else you need to call? We got GPan and GD covered."

"I better call his older brother."

Using her free foot, she scrolled to John Durbin's number. When she connected to him, Jenna told him the terrible news. He, too, had a phone that sent video. She could see how much the news affected him.

"Here's your new niece, Tia-Kate."

"She's got Tom's nose. Anyway, if there's anything you need... I can come up for a few days, if I can get a substitute

282

teacher. Or maybe Janine can come for a while," John said. "If we can figure out how to get up there. Still no planes are flying. No jet fuel."

"Thanks, John. I think we can manage. You're still in Flagstaff?"

***

Mid-June, the home situation stabilized but with some new developments. First, the autopsy proved conclusively the mob-doctor who performed the gender surgery was responsible for Tam's death. GPan and GD settled over his/her death. Since the death came as a result of his official duties, they deposited ten million credits into Jenna's account. That was in addition to the ongoing sums from their ion engines and hyperspace applications. Also, Major Callahan received five million credits compensation. Plus, since the world situation had settled down, GD opted to release Major Liz Callahan from active duty. GD CEO Art Townsend allowed Dave Shirts to go on inactive duty so he could help the others, though his salary was lowered.

Thus, the five began thinking about possibly moving south to warmer winters.

"We should see if Irene might want to move south with us," Jenna said. "I'll pay for their move and everything."

Jenna answered her phone. "Hi, Ace. What's up?"

"It's Mom and Dad," Ace said. "We just had to move them into an assisted living home. It's a new one on the south side of Flagstaff. Doctors said onset dementia."

"How awful! Do you think I should come down? Maybe I should move back home?" Jenna said.

"I'd love to have you here. But don't move on my and Alexa Adriana's account. We have to figure out what to do with the dude ranch. Last weekend, I went over all Dad's records. They had zero customers since the econ crash. But the ranch is paid for. Then again, mortgages got cancelled after the econ

283

crash."

They chatted, but the idea of moving took hold.

The next day, Phillis brought a bag over to share. She danced from foot to foot, while Rae dug out the contents.

"My book! It's here. Got copies for each of you," Phillis said, her eyes aglow.

Economic Collapse, Fall of Earth's Governments, and the Rise of the Galactic Corporations by Professor Hector Black.

The four congratulated her. That afternoon, they spent reading her history book.

"I didn't know that!" became the most frequently heard comment from Jenna, Liz, Rae, and Dave. Phillis scored a hit.

The final factor happened July fourth. John Durbin called Jenna. She knew something was wrong from his bloodshot eyes and wavering voice.

"Horrid. Jenna, terrible news. Janine is dead. Car crash. On Lookout Road. She and Ali had gone to visit Sunset Crater. On the way back, a stoned driver hit her electric car and shoved it over the cliff. They said she died instantly. Head crushed. But Ali."

He broke down and sobbed. A minute passed before he could speak again.

"She survived. In intensive care. They say her child seat saved her life, but..."

Again, John broke down. Jenna knew enough to maintain silence for now. Besides, what could she say to make anything better?

"But the flimsy car's metal sliced or crushed her arms as they rolled down the cliff. She's in surgery but with no hope of saving her arms. Jenna, I don't know what to do? She'll be helpless. Her life's ruined. And Janine..."

He broke down again. "Maybe it would have been better if Ali died too."

284

"John, I'm sorry. I'll be down soon and help Ali adjust. You be there for Ali until I can get there. She's going to need you to be strong for her, especially since she's lost her mother. Can you do that? Be strong for my niece?"

A sobbing John agreed. "Tom always said you were an angel."

When Jenna ended the call, Liz said, "When do we move? We're not letting you go by yourself. Besides, Phillis and I are still learning how-to from you. Can't lose our mentor, right Phillis?"

"Absolutely. We're moving too. But where?"

"Mom and Dad's Dude Ranch. It's just north of Kachina Village, about five miles south of Flagstaff. We'll move into the main quarters," Jenna said. "There's four separate suites that connect to the main lobby, dining hall, and living room. We'll each have our own suite. Maybe John can bring Ali and stay in the fourth suite so we can help Ali learn. Best call Ace. He'll be happy. Well, Tia-Kate, you're going to get to meet your two uncles soon."

"Hey, and cousin," Rae added.

Chapter 38 A New Location and Life

"Wow! This is cool," Rae said, as they walked into the foyer and lobby of the Dude Ranch main section. "Like the Old West must have been. Wagon wheel chandeliers and all."

"I had Ace hire a man from Galactic Housing to change all the door knobs to levers," Jenna said. "That way, we can't get stuck in some room. Here's where guests would first enter this complex. Here's our communal areas. I don't think we'll be hosting a large dinner party anytime soon."

"Gosh, Jenna, it's huge. Fifty people?" Liz said, gazing at the long, pine log tables.

"Probably, should be a giant comm center. Ah, yep, still here. This is our communal gathering area. Living room. This hall leads to Suites A and B, while Suites C and D are the other direction. I'll be in A. Rae and Phillis gets B. Liz and Dave gets C. I'm hoping John and Alison will stay in D. Let's get the workers to move our stuff now. Ace and Alexa Adriana will be here after their classes are done."

Chaos reigned for the next hour. With all the boxes delivered into the right rooms, Jenna sighed and began the arduous task of getting things operational. With two infants, she cursed several times and would have thrown things if she could have. But she knew Phillis needed Rae to help her get settled in. She and Liz were in their eighth month and had much reduced mobility.

"I got Phillis and me unpacked. Can I lend you a hand?" Rae said.

Jenna exhaled sharply. "Absolutely! It's taken me all this time to get this far. Had to get the changing pads out. Sam and Tia-Kate needed a change. Then they both got hungry and wouldn't wait. I've not gotten very far."

While Jenna cradled Tia-Kate in a leg and held her bottle up with the other, Rae set about stowing kitchen wares.

"This place is fabulous," Rae said. "Phillis loves it already. And the views out our windows—spectacular. And she can easily do laundry. Front loaders. Even dishwashers. That's going to spoil her."

Dave popped in. "Jenna, Liz says this place is wonderful. Absolutely perfect. She even thinks she'll be able to learn to cook now. Oh, they've delivered our three EMACs and two-person shuttles. I'll reprogram them for the Flagstaff area. Okay?"

"Thanks, Dave. Then we can zip around and see the sights," Jenna said. "Ace said the folks sold off most of the acreage and our horses during the econ collapse. Guess we can't go horseback riding."

"You can ride a horse?" Dave asked, his brows rising sharply.

"Yes, when I was younger. If you want, I can check around and see who bought the range land and horses. Maybe we can get them back."

Dave laughed. "If man would have wanted me to ride horses, he'd never given me an EMAC or MTES or shuttles."

Jenna replied, "Ace said they've almost got the MTES running from here up to Flagstaff. By next year, it may extend all the way down to Phoenix. That'll make it easier to visit my folks."

"Well, I still wish Irene would have taken your offer to move her, the tea garden, and her employees down here. I'm going to miss going there each night."

"I am too, Dave. We all are. But Irene has her own life to live."

Liz joined them and asked, "When do we get to meet Tom's brother and Ali?"

"Last I heard, John said they'd release Ali from the Med Center tomorrow. He'll bring her down then. We'll have our hands full with her."

Liz glanced around the room. "Jenna, I seem to have misplaced mine. Will that be a problem?"

Dave roared. Jenna hip-butted Liz.

"Yeah, good one, Liz. Still, she's only five and just lost her mother and her arms. She's had several operations."

"And must be terrified. I know I was when I first awoke," Liz said. "I will never get over feeling like the space I controlled shrunk from about three feet all around me down to my face. Collapsed space. That's how it feels to me every damned day. I keep hoping my space will open up, but it doesn't. Lifting up my foot isn't the same thing. Besides, it's awkward."

Phillis wandered in and overheard Liz. "Yeah, Liz, that's a good way to put it. To me, it felt like someone put me in a straightjacket, one that's never coming off. It feels like that every time I wake up in the morning."

Jenna said, "How curious. I never felt that way, but then I've never known anything different. Ali's young. I think she'll do well, if we can get her over her losses. Don't you think?"

***

That was my last memory of my Tom Durbin lifetime. My God! I'm free. I'd sold my soul to GD, committed countless murders, but now I was free of GD. I drifted into sleep. A dark curtain slipped down, obscuring my past. I'm in the present. I'm Tia-Kate now.

Chapter 39 Validation of My Past Lives

July 2376
Domes

"Celeste, these memories are incredible. So vivid, so real. Like I'm watching a 3d movie," I said.

We sat in my bedroom in my new home on Domes where she'd been running me through my more recent traumas. Considering how many times I've lost my arms only to eventually have Eve regrow them, it's fantastic I had missed this time.

"Perhaps, this life was more deeply buried," she suggested.

"Well, now I know Holly Ann Durbin's great grandparents or her lineage more accurately."

Eve, my geneticist sister who'd heard much of my sessions, said, "Your wife, Jenna Sweet, must have had that defective gene. A recessive one most likely. Passed down the lineage here and there. That's some remarkable information for me. Have to ponder that one."

My friend, Ambassador Katya Binsk, had also listened in to some of these events. Of course, Celeste had run her therapy sessions on Katya, erasing her similar massive traumas.

Katya said, "Well, yes, I, too, came across what you're calling past lives. How do we know they are real? I mean how do we know they actually happened? Maybe those trauma memories are figments of our imagination. Except when we re-experience the pain and unconsciousness, it does seem to erase the real trauma."

"That's the whole point," Celeste said. "By re-experiencing these previously hidden but similar traumas, the current trauma is erased. There's no doubt that these past lives memories must be thoroughly viewed in order to erase the recent incidents of trauma. If I don't push a patient to look for, find, and re-experience them, their current upsets and traumas don't erase. Occasionally, they might get some relief if they don't find these past life similar incidents."

Katya said, "Because we look at them, the recent ones erase. That's the whole rationale for saying these past life things actually happened to us? That we've lived before?"

"Yep," Celeste said, clapping her hands together. "I've run many thousands of people from all walks of life through past life incidents. When these similar and painful incidents are re-experienced, the patient gets well. When they are not, the patient doesn't. Heuristic, yes, but I believe they must have actually happened. These past lives."

I said, "If only we had a way to prove they happened. Anyone have a time machine?"

We laughed.

"You know, I have such vivid memories of this Tom Durbin lifetime. I remember the apartment where Jenna and Tom lived. I bet we could find it again and see if it matches my memories of the place in Chicago. The Dude Ranch near Flagstaff is too hazy for me to get much. I was only months old when we moved there. Sure is funny how that black curtain just shut off all memories of Tom Durbin when I finally relaxed into being Tia-Kate."

Celeste said, "I think that's more a question of having lost all possessions you had as Tom. Plus new body. New geographical location. New everything. Out of sight—out of mind."

"Good point," I said. "Assuming these past lives existed, then every time I died, I not only lost the body, but I lost all my possessions, where I lived, who I knew, everything—gone! Yeah. Out of sight—out of mind. I buy that."

"Some of the times I've run," Katya said, "I died on some planet that I don't know what it was called or its location. Kind of hard to go back and check if such things happened like I recalled."

Celeste sighed. "Yes, that's usually the case I've found. People re-experience the trauma but don't often recall the precise locations well enough that we could identify them and perhaps visit them to check on their recalls."

"Hey, I do. My Tom Durbin Chicago life. We could take a quick trip to Earth and see if the places I recalled exists or used to. What do you say? Give it a shot? I'm just as curious about these past lives are you all are."

"Are you sure you can recall enough details so we could track things down?" Celeste asked.

"But that was nearly three hundred fifty years ago," Katya said.

"We should try it now while these memories are fresh and vivid. What have we got to lose?" I said. "Let the guys look after all the kids. Girls' get away weekend. Ashley also wants to come."

We four chuckled.

"Let's do it. Count me in," Eve said.

"We'll take my private transport. It's fueled and ready," I said. "Tomorrow?"

We met at my ship in the early morning, when I went down my pre-flight takeoff checklist. Once we slipped into hyperspace and on autopilot, we headed to the galley for tea and chat.

"Hyperspace. I wrote that original paper explaining what it was and how we could use it. Sure dense math. Amazing how I've had to struggle with math at Soros University on Cass-C."

"Well, you were under the effects of a lot of drugs," Katya said. "Trauma and the drugs could have played a role. I've heard of such things."

Celeste bit her lip. "Possibly, Katya. Perhaps I should look into that phenomenon. I've ignored it until now."

"I tried to read that original paper by Dr. Chandra Hyber. Back at Soros U. About all I understood was his simple analogy using the horse saddle. The rest of the math eluded me. Okay. I kept falling asleep while reading it."

"Maybe that was because reading it re-stimulated this whole lifetime and the drugged trauma you had when you invented it," Katya said.

"She's got a great point," Celeste said. "When these major incidents of pain and unconsciousness are not visible, anything that remotely resembles what happened may re-stimulate it bringing that unconsciousness into the present. We fog out. Fall asleep. Dope off."

I laughed. "I sure did that a lot when I was at Soros U."

Katya giggled. "I think we all did that at one time or another."

"I know all this happened three hundred plus years ago," I said, "but the one thing that is on our side is that Galactic Housing has always preserved homes and businesses that are unoccupied or unowned. If we're in luck, that apartment complex is still there. If it is, I want to get inside and have a look around. I can describe it to you first. Then we go in and see if my memory is any good."

I spent much of the travel hours to Earth describing Apartment #1 in Uptown and the Montrose Beach area. Celeste made a crude sketch of the room layout. Of course we didn't know if the building still stood.

We landed at New O'Hare, and I rented an EMAC. A half hour later, we flew along the street Tom and Jenna Durbin had lived on.

292

"There it is," Celeste called out.

I landed the EMAC. The four of us walked up to the apartment building.

"Well, it's still here. Looks like Galactic Housing is keeping it well maintained," I said.

"There's a sticker on the door," Celeste said. "Ah, it's a contact notice for anyone interested in buying or renting. We should maybe rent it so we can legally go inside."

That took nearly two hours. Much red tape. Once we had the key, hunger struck. I treated us to dinner at Bernardo's. He's my adopted twin son along with Isabella, who is back on Domes.

"Mom! Don't you ever look older?" Bernardo said, throwing is arms around me in a bear hug. "Why didn't you call? How long are you back for? How's everyone? Isabella? Got time to visit the wife and kids? Put that away; your credits aren't any good here, silly. Lunch is on me. Wait. Is she a—"

"Third Invader? Yes, Ambassador Katya Binsk. My eldest son, Bernardo, Isabella's twin brother."

Lunch, as fabulous as it was, blew another two hours. He allowed me to leave only after I promised to visit his family that night.

Finally, we walked up to the front door of the apartment complex. Celeste used the key to open it, pulled out the sketch, and led the way. Me? I brought up the rear. I didn't want to influence the verification process. After all, the entire purpose of this trip was to verify what I'd recalled of my life as Tom Durbin—to prove the validity of past lives.

"Well, the layout agrees with what Molly told us," Celeste said.

"But that's not definitive proof," Katya said. "There's any number of ways she could have known or predicted the room layout."

Eve said, "Guys, look what I found. It somehow fell

behind the kitchen stove. Awfully dirty, but look. It's Phillis's book: *Economic Collapse, Fall of Earth's Governments, and the Rise of the Galactic Corporations* by Professor Hector Black."

"We definitely have the right apartment," Celeste said. "Still..."

"Guys, in here, bedroom," I said. When they ambled into the room, I explained, "Tom walled off the back section of this room, making a place to hide his guns and keep them secure. There should be a pressure switch on the right side near the wall, shoulder height."

Celeste and Eve went a tapping on the wall. Suddenly, a door swung open.

"Whoa! She's right," Eve said.

"Wait. Before you go in there, you should find the pair of pearl-handled .44 Rem Mag revolvers, the .300 PRC sniper rifle, and reloading supplies. Oh, and lots of ammo. There's a number of other guns in there too."

"This I gotta see," Katya said and pushed past Eve to look inside.

The room was barely three feet wide, just enough to allow entry, work, and store Tom's weapons. Eve and Celeste followed Katya into the tiny space. Someone turned on a light.

"Well," I said, growing impatient. The guns had to be there. I was sure Jenna forgot they were there when she moved out. I heard Katya cry out and stuck my head inside.

"Wow! What a find. The guns. Coolest," I said. I was more pleased with finding all these historical weapons than the fact I'd just proven past lives were true. "The pair of .44's in Western style holsters. Incredible. Look at all this stuff. A bonanza. Yahoo."

"Calm down, Molly," Celeste said, her face aglow. "Past lives actually are real. You've given me positive proof. Best present ever!"

She hugged me. Katya stared at the guns and ammo boxes and then back at me, her mouth open.

"Neat," Eve said. "I never doubted the validity of past lives. This really does make a compelling argument, Molly."

"We gotta haul all this stuff out to the EMAC. I don't want to leave anything behind. Now to find a place to try out these guns. Sure beats my puny Glock. Wait, there's a Glock like mine. 9mm. Cool."

"These incidents I've been running," Katya said to Celeste, "these actually happened to me. I've really had other bodies, other lives."

"This is enough proof for me," Celeste said. "I know Molly has never been to this section of northern Chicago in this lifetime. Her mansion is further south. We can drop by it on our way back if you like."

"This is monumental," Katya said. "I know I always feel fantastic when we finish erasing a trauma or unwanted feeling or emotion, but to know I experienced similar traumas in an earlier lifetime—that that really did happen to me—it's mind-blowing. Celeste, this therapy discovery of yours is one of the greatest discoveries ever. Right up there with spaceships, hyperspace travel, and ion engines."

Celeste laughed. "Katya, and I can't get more than a handful of people to want my therapy, let alone learn how to deliver it to others. Out of Earth's billions, I've only been able to reach maybe fifty thousand over all these years I've been at it. People seem to want to believe that man is little more than a frail body with a mind, that they only live once. And when they die, they're dead, dead, dead."

"Governments and rulers," Eve said, "prefer it that way. Man, the animal, is much more easily controlled."

Katya grimaced. "My people, over the millennia we've conducted many experiments on humans. What have we done?"

"Probably built up a hidden hatred for Third Invaders," Celeste said, "from traumas they've endured at your hands in the past. But the important thing, Katya, is your people have come clean about it. That's what counts. You are now the Third Invaders' Ambassador to the Sol Empire. A decade ago, that didn't exist."

"Achoo. Dusty," I said. "The leather holsters aren't rotten, but they need a good oiling. Come on. Let's cart this out to the EMAC. How do we undo that reloading machine?"

Later as we headed back to Domes, Celeste said, "I've always suspected these Galactic corporations were anything but democratic and had their own agendas. From Phillis's book, we know they were that from the very beginning."

I laughed. "I sold my soul to GD, but I refused to murder the general in charge of the clone project that made us. But this first time, I became one of there best enforcers and murderers. Amazing how that unconsciously influenced me all these years."

"True," Eve said, "but don't forget those original scientists and engineers that started these worldwide corporations saved the planet from entering a vicious dark age. Global economies had vanished with the fiat dollars. Except for those who worked together on the International Space Station and Moon Base #1, the world would have disintegrated into crude bartering and unknown cruelty. They did solve the over-population problem, climate change, and massive food shortages."

I laughed. "But behind them were the world's billionaires who watched the econ crash and dumped all their billions into these budding Galactic corporations. Billionaires always want more billions. They're loathed to lose their wealth. But what struck me the most was the level of confront that GPan CEO Wang Chan had. He reminds me of the Varouna Empire and their Empress Kalindi Amandani on

296

Indrani-C. Both she and Wang Chan have this enormous presence. People obey them without question. Even though she told me I should be the Sol Empire's empress and I tried, I simply didn't have their level of presence."

Celeste said, "Molly, while that was true back Then you've matured, especially since you erased this Tom Durbin lifetime. You might give it another try."

"An empress must have the authority and means to rule. Given the long history of these Galactic corporations, I can't imagine them ceding that to me or to any one person outside of GPan."

Celeste bit her lip and said, "But have you considered what the other empire members outside of Earth think? I've always had the notion they disliked Earth's domination of the empire affairs."

"That's true," I said, thinking back over the years of decisions I'd witnessed. "They certainly have been adamant about not allowing anyone on their worlds who's been genetically mutated. They wouldn't allow their own senators to return home after they were turned into Galactic Dolls, not even after Eve managed to restore them."

"And with the robot mess on Earth now," Eve said, "I bet they are even more against Earth's domination."

"The only way to find out," Katya said, "is to pay a visit to each member of the Sol Empire. Discuss how they feel about Earth's role. That way you would have certainty."

"Brilliant," I said. "You have a knack for this ambassador position."

She grinned and we chuckled.

"After we deal with the situation on Domes, looks like I get to do what I always wanted: visit the other empire member worlds and see the sights."

"Mind if I tag along?" Katya said. "As your ambassador, that is."

"Sure. I wonder if one could find out where and who the others are now. Like Major Liz Callahan, Phillis, Rae, and especially Jenna Durbin. I wonder how they fared. I bet anything those Durbins were the ancestors to Holly Ann Durbin."

Eve grinned. "That is a certainty. Genetics don't lie."

After a pause, she said, "Actually, there might be a way. Each person, each spirit or being, resonates at a specific frequency or wavelength. I think it's formed from a combination of their unique experiences in life. Anyway, I have been able to locate some who followed us to Earth from Ross248. These were people I knew my whole life back then. I could sense their unique wavelength and reach out to them via telepathy."

"Because I knew Jenna so well, I could find her by looking for her wavelength?"

Eve nodded.

"Ah, but how do I know her wavelength?"

"That's the hard part. Besides, just because you might be able to find them now doesn't mean they will remember you or anything about that lifetime," Celeste cautioned. "After all, they've had many lifetimes during the past three hundred fifty years and many traumatic events, at least births and deaths if nothing else. It's almost a certainty that lifetime is deeply buried in the depths of their minds. Just look at yourself, Molly.

"You've had at least fifteen hundred hours of therapy sessions. Only now have you finally been able to locate and re-experience your Tom Durbin lifetime."

"Point taken. I sold my soul had really buried it behind a solid black wall. Still, I'd love to know what happened to Jenna. After all, we owe space travel to her ion engine. All these two-person shuttles to Alexa Adriana. I wonder what happened to her."

Eve laughed. "And we owe you for hyperspace travel. A good thing I hope."

I laughed. "And today higher math challenges me."

"Good point," Celeste said. "You did space-breaking math back then and moved on to do other things. I think that's the way it is for everyone. I'd hate to be stuck lifetime after lifetime doing the same thing, over and over. I'd go nuts."

Katya, who had been listening to us, gasped. "Whoa! We ran into a civilization like that several millenia ago. Third Invaders did. My ancestors. That was the biggest slave society ever. The denizens were bored factorial! Our people barely got away from their enforcers who tried to force them into their society. Can you imagine doing the same menial task day after day, year after year, lifetime after lifetime for ten thousand years?"

"I'd kill myself," I said with a snicker.

"Wouldn't help," Katya said. "They'd suck you back into a new body, hand you the same broom, and order you to sweep this street again."

"Argh! I think I'll just go visit all the members of the Sol Empire instead. If I get their support, maybe I can force Earth's Galactic corporations to accept the authority of Empress Parkinson."

"Now you're talking. Let's do it," Katya said.

"Just as soon as we handle the situation on Domes," I said, as my deep space shuttle landed on Domes. Once again, we'd have to confront the mess here.

The End.

Vic Broquard
A Favor to Other Readers

How about helping other readers? Many readers rely on reviews to make the decision whether to buy a book. You can help them make their decision by leaving your opinions and viewpoint in a short review of the positive things of this book. Writing the review and expressing your opinion only takes a few minutes, and other readers will appreciate your efforts.

Find on amazon.com The Sol Empire Volume 8 Origins
https://www.amazon.com/dp/B097LZ1G1W
Then, scroll down to Customer Reviews; click on Write a Review, and enter your review. Thank you.

Author Information

Visit My Amazon.com Author Page
Vic Broquard Author Page

Follow My Blog
Vic Broquard's Blog

Follow Me on Social Media
Facebook
LinkedIn
YouTube

Other Books by Vic Broquard

Without Warning (fantasy)

The Trident Series: (fantasy)
Volume 1 The Trident and the Book
Volume 2 The Trident and the Scepter
Volume 3 The Trident and the Resurrection

The Adventures of Elizabeth Stanton Series: (science fiction)
Volume 1 The Evolution of the Path
Volume 2 The Great Messiah
Volume 3 Of Kings and Queens and Troubadours
Volume 4 Chaos in the Aftermath
Volume 5 Power Plays
Volume 6 Age of Exploration
Volume 7 Abducted
Volume 8 The Emperor and Empress
Volume 9 A Job Worth Doing
Volume 10 Degradation
Volume 11 The Second Crusade
Volume 12 When Worlds Collide
Volume 13 Dark Ages

The Lindsey Barron Series: (fantasy)
Volume 1 The Rod of the Apocalypse
Volume 2 The Board of Governors
Volume 3 The Crown of Moses
Volume 4 Dominus for President
Volume 5 The National Health Care Program
Volume 6 States Justice
Volume 7 Cross and Double-cross
Volume 8 Down the Dragon Hole

Vic Broquard

Zoran Chronicles Series: (fantasy)
Volume 1 A Dragon in Our Town
Volume 2 Dragons, Power, Courts, and War

Planet of the Orange-red Sun Series: (science fiction)
Volume 1 When Kingdoms Fall
Volume 2 Dark Ages
Volume 3 Age of the Towers
Volume 4 Difficillis Exitus
Volume 5 Age of the Lords
Volume 6 The Renegade Tower
Volume 7 Rebellions
Volume 8 The Aliens Return
Volume 9 Power Struggles
Volume 10 Guilds, Genetics, and Gods
Volume 11 Magi, Witches, Swords, and Superstitions
Volume 12 The Voyage of the Eagle's Seed
Volume 13 Eagle's Seed and Origins
Volume 14 Justifications
Volume 15 Responsibilities

The Return of the Wizards: Twelve Companions – The Making of Wizards (fantasy)

Slow Comes the Dark Series: (science fiction)
Volume 1 Creeping Darkness
Volume 2 Serendipity
Volume 3 Darkness Descends
Volume 4 Perversion Incarnate
Volume 5 Extermination Wars

The Sol Empire Volume 8 Origins

Reclamation Series: (science fiction)

Volume 1 For the Want of a Pill
Volume 2 Organ Donors

Dragons, Magic, and Me Series (fantasy)

Volume 1 The Box

The Sol Empire (science fiction)

Volume 1 For the Want of Humanity
Volume 2 Fear
Volume 3 Greed
Volume 4 Power Moves
Volume 5 Genetic Engineering
Volume 6 Religion and Robots
Volume 7 Telepath Nightmares
Volume 8 Origins___

www.ingramcontent.com/pod-product-compliance
Lightning Source LLC
Chambersburg PA
CBHW060851250626
47159CB00008B/2693